YAKSHINI

Neil D'Silva moved into full-time writing after giving up a lucrative coaching institute job that he had helmed for eighteen years. Influenced by his life's journey, which initiated him to the works of Poe, Stoker, Shelley and our very own Ramsay brothers, he developed a strong penchant for creating new worlds of horror. His debut novel, *Maya's New Husband,* is a bestseller and has been acquired for screen adaptation.

Neil conducts lectures and workshops on writing for aspiring authors. He is also the founder and creative director of an interschool litfest named Litventure. After winning accolades at the Delhi Literature Festival for a short story competition, the Indian Bloggers' Award, and giving a TEDx talk on the subject of 'The Art of Writing a Bestseller', Neil has stamped his presence in the Indian literary world.

He lives in Mumbai with his wife Anita and their two children, Gilmore and Felicia.

YAKSHINI

NEIL D'SILVA

RUPA

Published by
Rupa Publications India Pvt. Ltd 2019
7/16, Ansari Road, Daryaganj
New Delhi 110002

Sales centres:
Allahabad Bengaluru Chennai
Hyderabad Jaipur Kathmandu
Kolkata Mumbai

Illustrations by Palak Jain

ISBN: 978-93-5333-674-5

First impression 2019

10 9 8 7 6 5 4 3 2 1

The moral right of the author has been asserted.

*For my mother who created me, my wife who made me,
and my daughter who completed me.*

Contents

Part One: The Sapling

Part Two: The Blossom

Part Three: The Seed

Part Four: The Withering

Part One

The Sapling

Year 1996

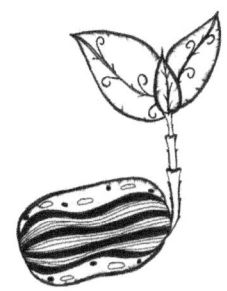

Little Bud in Full Bloom

The sal tree stood in the middle of the garden, proud and magnificent, once again abloom with its bright red and yellow flowers. The season had caused its flowers to attain their full bloom and their thick petals now resembled the hoods of many tiny cobras, raised to threaten anyone who might dare to witness their splendour without permission.

Nature thrived under the tree; the ground beneath was carpeted with its discarded foliage. Large yellowing leaves kept falling off the tree, adding to this carpet. Many had already turned brown and lay crumbling to dust. Ants and beetles marched on these leaves, busy with whatever held their tiny fancies. Knoblike heads of mushroom rose from under them, vying for their own little space, and sorely losing in that quest. And amidst all this nature-ordained chaos, a plump frog poked his head through the leaves, took a stance, and aroused by the early morning breeze, croaked a wild mating call.

Just then, a young girl's feet adorned with a pair of silver anklets came prancing into the garden, and the frog leaped away. Old leaves rustled and crackled under her feet, and the mushrooms were squished. Yet, nature bore no complaint, for this girl was one of them. A friend. In her presence, nature rejoiced.

Meenakshi—for that was the fifteen-year-old's name—came close to the sal and hugged its sturdy trunk. 'Companion,' she said in a voice that sounded like Mother Earth's own breath, 'how are you this morning?'

The sal did not respond. Only its leaves shook in the breeze. Meenakshi raised her dainty chin and peered at the far-reaching canopy of leaves that seemed to go as high as the mountains. She squinted and laughed.

Then, her brow creased. There was something under her bare right foot. She could feel its coldness, and yet, she did not take her foot away. Frowning, she stooped and shuffled through the foliage, and exclaimed, 'Aha!'

It was a gold coin.

'Thank you, Companion.' She hugged the tree again. 'You always make me smile.'

The hoods of the flowers nodded.

The next moment, this companionable silence was broken by a hoarse call that came from inside her house.

'Meenu, ae Meenu, where have you run away so early in the morning?'

'COMING, AAI!' Meenakshi shouted so loudly that her tonsils hurt. She ran into the house, hiding the coin in the folds of her skirt.

❧

Renuka was throwing spices into sizzling groundnut oil in her kitchen. Years of practice had turned such things into a learned reflex; in truth, her attention was focused on her youngest daughter, who had just walked into the house.

With some distaste, Renuka noticed the mud-marks her feet left on the floor as she scampered into the house, clutching her skirt as if it would fly away.

'Meenu, wait!'

Meenakshi stopped.

'Where had you gone so early in the morning?'

'Just out in the garden, Aai.'

Renuka kept her ladle aside with a pronounced clang and turned off the stove. Wiping her brow with the corner of her saree, she went to the girl.

'Meenu—'

She stopped. Her gaze fell on the front of her daughter's shirt, where the buttons were threatening to split.

'Meenu,' she said, 'how is this shirt so tight already? We bought it just last month.'

Meenakshi looked down. 'What's wrong with it?'

'You have another shirt, a looser one?'

'This is my newest.'

'Then wear one of Suparna's. It will fit you.'

Meenakshi began to run away.

Renuka grabbed her hand. 'Wait! Running, running, running. Like the wind. Look, Meenu...today you must behave.'

'Behave? Why?'

'Don't you remember? I told you last night.'

'Ho, that boy from Bombay is coming to see Manda Tai.'

'Yes,' Renuka said with a lingering smile. 'A proposal for your oldest sister. Can you see how wonderful that is?'

Meenakshi stared at her mother without comprehension.

'You won't understand.' But Renuka had to try and make her understand, and so she went on, 'You are seven sisters. If your eldest sister gets a nice groom, the line is clear for all of you. He is such a nice boy. Educated. Family business.'

Meenakshi blinked.

'Now don't you go about your usual shenanigans in front of them. He's a decent chap from the city. Not rustic buffoons like us.'

'I will behave, Aai.'

'And please wear decent clothes. God knows how you are growing so fast!' She looked at her daughter's bust with an uncomfortable feeling. 'You are already larger than three of your older sisters. You are eating the same food as them, aren't you?'

'You give us all the same food, Aai.'

'Go run away now, chatterbox!'

Meenakshi turned and ran away. Renuka's eyes followed her prancing form with a smile.

❧

Dressed in Suparna's finery (Suparna was four years elder to her), Meenakshi ran off to the garden again. There was an hour left for the guests to arrive, and her mother did not stop her. Maybe she was just glad to have her out of everyone's hair. She told her as much. 'Go, Meenu, go out and play. If you are in the house, you'll just be in the way. You won't even let your Manda Tai dress up properly.'

So, hitching up her skirt, Meenakshi played chhippi-langdi all by herself. She hopped on one leg over the squares drawn with chalk on the ground, picking up and throwing the little tile piece into the squares with dexterity and precision. Ten minutes into the game, she stood in the Home position, looking at the block numbered 8, the farthest. She stood, took a deep breath, closed one eye and spent a whole minute aiming the chhippi as accurately as she could. Then she muttered a prayer and threw it.

'Arrechya!' she exclaimed when the chhippi just missed the number 8 box and fell on the top line.

Sulking, she looked at the chhippi, which was mocking her defeat. No, this wouldn't do! She was winning; this was the last square!

A flicker of mischief arose in her eyes then, and she stood up. She cocked her head this way and that. None of her sisters were out; they were all getting dressed inside. Even Manjula, their cow, was not to be seen. She was probably sitting on the cool comfort of the straw in her shed and ruminating on her quota of the day's fodder.

Darting like the wind, Meenakshi went to the number 8 box. Making sure no one was looking, she bent to pick up the chhippi to place it in the coveted square.

But then, she stilled. Her hand stopped mid-air, hovering just inches above the chip.

A noisy rustling of leaves had stopped her, and she knew instinctively who it was.

She turned to look, and saw the sal tree, the hoods of its hundred blazing flowers looking down sternly at her.

'Sorry, sorry,' Meenakshi said and backed off, holding her

earlobes with her fingers. Then she ran up to the sal tree and hugged it. 'Sorry, Companion. I will never cheat again, even in a game. You aren't angry with me, are you?'

❦

She was still hugging the tree with her eyes shut when she heard a familiar call.

'Arre Meenu, why are you stuck to that tree?'

Meenakshi opened her eyes. At the gate was Tappu, the neighbours' boy. He was her age, and they went to the same class. Right now, he was in his Sunday finest, which was a pair of khaki shorts that came up to his knees and a loose shirt that was one of his brothers' hand-me-downs. Three of him could have fit into it.

Meenakshi went up, skipping, to him. 'Ae Tappya, you go away. I am busy today.'

Tappu jumped over the little iron gate and came into the garden. 'Finished Kulkarni Sir's homework?'

'Loooong back!' This was said in a singsong voice, pronounced with narrowed eyes and a pulling back of the hand to indicate the passage of time.

'Hey, new clothes?' Tappu asked, suddenly perking up.

The pucker on Meenakshi's face transformed into a blush. 'What's it to you?'

'Nothing...' said Tappu. 'You look...different.'

Meenakshi said nothing.

'Come, let's go to the well,' he suggested.

'No re,' Meenakshi waved him away. 'I told you na I am busy? We have guests coming today.'

'Who?'

'Aai said not to tell anyone.'

Tappu slapped his head. 'Ah, I know. The whole village knows. Someone's coming to see your sister, no?'

Meenakshi fretted. 'What's it to you? You go. They will come now and they don't want to see your torn chaddi.'

'Arre, wait!' Tappu protested. 'What else is there to do outside? Let them come; I'll dart away like a squirrel as soon as they turn into the gate.'

But that plan did not materialize. At that very moment, there was a rattling of the gate. It was Govind, the oldest boy in the neighbourhood, and by extension, a bully.

'Aye Tappya, what are you doing here?' he yelled. 'You broke our team of eleven, you—'

Tappu didn't wait to hear the rest of it. With a hop, skip and jump, he sprinted away.

Govind ran after him, chasing him down the street. 'Come here, scoundrel! There are still ten of us. We'll all whoop your ass when I catch you.'

Meenakshi laughed with her hand on her mouth, as if trying not to laugh too much, even as Tappu ran a-flying to the gate with profuse apologies.

Govind reached out and held Tappu, caught him by the ear and gave him a thwack on the back of his head, while showering upon him the choicest of abuses. And then he heard Meenakshi laughing and stopped.

His hold on Tappu loosened and the boy ran away.

But Govind's gaze was locked on Meenakshi now. Something began to tingle inside her, and she could suddenly feel every fibre of her sister's clothes that she was wearing, which, even though loose, contoured over the curves that she had developed of late.

Govind came up to her and brought his lips together in a whistle.

'Looking beautiful, Meenu!' he said in his typical crude way. And then he winked.

Meenakshi, stunned at the sudden praise, fled into her house and stood blushing by the door, her breath stuck somewhere in her throat.

2

The Unfortunate Suitor

'*H*arikumar Jaywantrao Deshmukh.'

The young man sitting respectfully next to his mother introduced himself.

From behind the human wall created by her sisters, Meenakshi tried to peer into the room. She snatched glimpses of him through the slits between their bodies. A man quite sophisticated for these parts, surely, dressed in a crisp checkered shirt and well-fitting trousers, unlike the ones stitched by Mangesh Kaka, the village tailor. He smelled nice as well. She had heard that men from the city wore perfume. There were special scents made for men! His hair was sleek as well, parted neatly at one side of his head, not one strand out of place. And, oh God, he had no moustache!

She heard her father's voice.

'Good, very good,' said Shantaram Patil. 'You are so clearly a city boy. A clear and authoritative voice, just like a man should have! I have been to Bombay once, about twenty years ago. Is that right, Renu?'

Renuka tittered appropriately.

The boy's mother chipped in. 'Do visit again. This time, stay at our place.'

An awkward silence followed. It took a few moments for the boy's mother to realize the impropriety of her invitation. One just didn't invite folks from the daughter-in-law's place to stay over. She quickly rectified herself. 'Patil bhau, we are forward-thinking people. All these old-fashioned rules don't mean much to us.'

Shantaram laughed uneasily as though they meant nothing to him either. 'But will you be okay with a girl from Vatgaon? Everything in your city will be new to her.'

'We are okay if you are okay,' said Harikumar's mother. 'As you know, Hari has no father, God bless his soul. I just want him to get settled with a decent girl who will look after the house while he focuses on his business. I have asthma. Gets terrible sometimes. Everything will be in the hands of the children. When Holkarbai referred Manda, Hari liked her instantly, and Holkarbai is a family member to us.'

Meenakshi searched for Holkarbai, the marriage agent who had brokered the match. There she was, sitting plump on the sofa, smiling like a well-fed kitten.

Mrs Deshmukh leaned forward. 'We don't expect anything from you. Hari does well for himself, and—by God's infinite grace—his father has left us well off.'

'All that is fine,' Shantaram said with a wave of his hand. 'Good education and fine business and all that, but does he know our traditions?'

There was a mischievous smile on Shantaram's face as he said that. Standing in that faraway corner of the room, Meenakshi recognized it as the indulgent smile he often had when he tested his daughters.

'Yes, sir,' said Harikumar. 'I do pujas and keep upwaas.'

'Last solar eclipse, he fasted the whole day,' Mrs Deshmukh waxed eloquent. 'He keeps shravan fasts too. Who does that in today's times?'

Renuka raised her brows at Shantaram. It was a look of caution that said, *Don't needle him too much. He's a good boy.* She cast a sideways glance at Manda. She was sitting there, occupying as little space as possible, a smile hidden on her lips. It was surely a preordained match. Renuka threw a silent prayer up to the skies.

'Okay!' Shantaram slapped his thigh. 'We like your family too. It is true—matches are made in heaven.'

'Of course, of course!' Harikumar's mother laughed.

Then Shantaram shuffled in his chair and assumed the pose

of someone with authority. He asked, 'Son, do you know how to make a patravali?'

Harikumar balked. He looked at his mother, who looked equally lost.

Meenakshi smiled. Here was the test!

Renuka came to the rescue of the flustered boy. 'Patravali… you don't know? The plates we make out of sal leaves for eating meals on special occasions?'

'Oh, that!' said the boy's mother. 'It scared me when bhau said that so unexpectedly. Of course Harikumar can make them. He's good at craft.'

'I wonder if he can make one now,' said Shantaram. 'You see, in our village, there is this small custom. The prospective groom makes a patravali when he proposes. I made one too in my time.'

'It's an old stupid custom and it's okay if you don't want to—' Renuka began, but she was cut off when Shantaram glared at her.

'He says he can make one,' Shantaram laughed without mirth. 'So let him. It will be pure fun only, all right?'

Harikumar wiped away a sudden train of sweat from his brow. 'Of course!'

A plate of large green sal leaves was brought to him. Eleven pairs of eyes, ten of them female, looked at him as he folded his sleeves and prepared for the task. Meenakshi took a step forward too. This was going to be fun.

Next came a tray with a reel of thread and a needle. The needle wasn't threaded; threading the needle was part of the test.

Harikumar smiled at everyone, and as his mother tapped him lightly on his back, he picked up the needle. Squinting, he tried to pass the thread into the needle and missed. The girls tittered. He tried again. More titters. After he missed twelve times, the titters vanished and gave vent to frustration.

'There's some breeze coming in from somewhere,' his mother reasoned.

One of the sisters ran up to the windows and closed them.

'*Saavkaash*, Hari,' said his mother. 'You will do it now.'

He wet the thread with his lips, squinted, and tried again.

And then it happened. The needle pricked his finger, but he did it.

Shantaram released a long sigh of relief. 'Now, the leaves. You have to fold and stitch them.'

As the room fell silent once again, Harikumar tried various combinations and arrangements, folding the leaves and holding them in place. Renuka shuffled in her seat (she looked more uncomfortable than Harikumar was), and Shantaram signalled her to stop fidgeting. Meenakshi saw that gesture; it was a gesture of confidence. Her father knew the boy would do it.

Harikumar began. He put the base—the largest sal leaf—and deftly folded six other leaves and made a circle. Then he went on to stitch them in their positions. Slowly, sighs of relief passed around the room.

When he was done with one side, now much more confident, he turned the whole thing over, and started to make the other layer of leaves.

'I will need more leaves,' he said.

'Sure, sure,' Shantaram said, and then yelled, 'Meenu, go run and get more leaves from the tree outside.'

Startled at the sudden mention of her name, Meenakshi gathered her bearings and bounded away.

The afternoon sun was up. Meenakshi looked with disdain at the fallen leaves of the sal tree, which had already turned brown. She could not take those for the patravali; they would crumble to bits the moment a needle was driven into them.

She looked up at the tree. Fresh green leaves, now lustrous in the reflected sunlight, mocked her. She tried to reach them, but couldn't. Hitching up her skirt, she tried to jump, but apart from the tinkling of her anklets, nothing happened.

'Companion, don't be so miserly,' she said, nettled. 'What's a few leaves?'

But the tree had decided to make some mischief.

With childish petulance, Meenakshi picked up a stone. 'If you don't give me the leaves,' she said obstinately, 'I'll hit your boughs till they break and fall down.'

The tree, spread like a mammoth over her, looked down at her, but nothing happened.

Meenakshi shut one eye, took aim, and hit a bough.

The tree still did not move.

'You are petty, Companion,' she said and sat down right underneath the tree. 'I will sit here till you give me your leaves. I cannot just go inside and say I did not get them. There are new people inside. Maybe he will even be my brother-in-law. I won't be insulted. I won't go from here.'

At that, one leaf broke off and fell into her lap.

'What will I do with one leaf, you miser of a tree?'

Then another leaf fell, and before it could touch the ground, a third came down, and then a fourth and a fifth, and soon there was a shower of them falling all over the girl. She wiped her tears, laughed, and picked them up till she could hold no more.

'Did you strip the whole tree bare?' Shantaram asked as she walked in with the leaves.

Without answering him, Meenakshi entered, the leaves held in the folds of her skirt. She came in like that and dropped the leaves on the table.

That was when Harikumar really noticed her.

His gaze first fell on her bare legs, and then he saw her face. It was a brief glance, but the gaze lingered for a split second over the part of her body that her mother had told her to keep well-covered.

Meenakshi withdrew, now aghast, as if she had committed a crime.

The young suitor silently worked with the leaves that Meenakshi had brought in, but this time, he began sniffing at them too, as if taking in the scent of the person who had held them not so long ago.

When he put the last stitch into the patravali, and held it up for display, there were sighs and gasps. This was not a masterpiece by any standards, but it exceeded expectations. It was a rare moment when Shantaram praised someone openly; this time he did.

'Son, you are precisely what I am looking for. My Manda will be truly happy with you. You have your head in the sky, but you are a true son of the soil.'

Mrs Deshmukh giggled like a schoolgirl. 'I told you so!'

'So, Mrs Deshmukh, as father of the daughter, I ask you,' said Shantaram, 'how do you want the wedding?'

'Any way you suggest, Patil bhau,' said the boy's mother. 'We are open to options. What do you say, Hari?'

Harikumar cleared his throat. 'Aai...I wish to say something.'

'Well, sure! It's turning out to be your day, after all.'

The young man's gaze scanned past everyone in the room. Everyone looked at him too, with their bright eager eyes, as if waiting for him to just say the word, and then they would jubilate.

Harikumar's gaze rested on Manda. 'You are a nice girl, Manda,' he began, his words steeped in diplomacy, 'and someday you will make your husband very happy.'

Shantaram shuffled in his seat. The smile on his face was wiped off with those words and replaced with a frown that made his daughters take two steps back.

'What do you mean, young man?' he asked.

'Sir...I don't know how to say this except with total honesty.'

'I don't like preambles, young man.'

'No preamble, sir...but...'

'*Kaay aahe tujhya manaat,* Hari? (What's on your mind, Hari?)' his mother chipped in. 'Speak your mind.'

'Aai...I like Manda, but...but I like *her* more.'

And, just like that, Harikumar raised his forefinger to point at Meenakshi, who was now standing at the heart of the crowd.

The girl, when she realized what had just happened, shrank into nothingness.

'WHAT!?' Shantaram shot up. 'Are you out of your mind? She is just fifteen.'

'Sir,' Harikumar stood up too, but slowly, politely. 'Please listen to me. I am not making an obscene request. I am only twenty-two myself. I am prepared to wait for your youngest daughter till she comes of age.'

'What is this madness?' Renuka stepped forward and faced Harikumar's mother. 'What is your son saying?'

'Madam, I have fallen in love with your daughter,' said Harikumar hesitantly and yet with a strange boldness underlining his words. 'I have never seen her before today. But she just walked in now and something stirred in me like it has never done before. And now I feel that if she doesn't become my wife, my life itself is a waste.'

'HOLKARBAI!' Shantaram screamed for the marriage agent, who was sitting silently, aghast at the sudden turn of events. 'Tell this fool to get out of my house immediately.'

Radhabai Holkar stood up at that command and grabbed the man by his hand. 'Have you gone insane? What are you blabbering? She is a child—'

'You don't understand—' Harikumar protested.

Shantaram flung the towel that was on his shoulder to the floor and stormed out of the room. 'Renuka, get everyone out of my house right now,' he yelled and disappeared.

❧

Meenakshi shut herself in her room and did not open it until evening. Shantaram locked himself in his room in a wild temper too, and when he came out hours later, no one spoke above a whisper. Renuka sat sobbing in a corner, cursing whoever it was that she cursed on such occasions.

But if anyone would have seen Meenakshi then, they would have seen the fear creeping within her.

The girl had not moved an inch from afternoon till evening. She stood fixed at one spot in that closed room, in front of the mirror where the girls used to dress up, and she kept staring at herself. She didn't know what was going on with her; such a benumbing feeling had never overcome her before. Perhaps it was because of the way the man had looked at her. Or because she had seen the silent censure in her sisters' eyes. Or because she sensed the admonishment that would come from her parents.

In a fit of rage and utter helplessness, she messed up her hair and whatever little makeup was on her face. Her eyes bled kajal; her lips bled lipstick. Thus, she stood like a rock, refusing to even let tears flow out of her unblinking eyes.

She had hated the man's trembling finger, pointing at her, singling her out. She did not know what that expression was, but it reminded her of Tappu's face when he saw the sweetmeats at Kopre Dada's sweet shop. Or the look on that ruffian Govind's face whenever he came across her, which was often. It reminded her of those same sick drooling faces with those misty, desirous eyes. Like a dog drooling over a piece of meat.

Why? What was in her that men looked at her thus? No one looked at her sisters like that.

She stared at her reflection in the mirror, trying to locate that one thing that was different in her. Aai said she was too full for her age; maybe that was it. Perhaps. Who knew what men thought! Meenakshi might be a teenager, but she understood things like breasts, and she knew there was something about them that attracted men. But was it only that? How could men be so shallow?

Why was she growing into this woman who scared her? Why couldn't she be like her sisters, all docile and demure? Wasn't that what was hammered into little girls since childhood? Then what was happening to her?

'It's because you are special.'

Meenakshi felt her blood going cold in her veins. It was a voice. Almost human. Not some vague thought; they were real words. Spoken right into her ear, slowly but firmly. It made her fingers turn cold.

'Who is it?' she turned to look. But apart from the howling wind, there was nothing.

✤

Around dinnertime, her mother knocked on the door.
'Come out, eat something,' she said curtly.

Quite in a stupor, Meenakshi opened the door.

'What have you done to yourself?' exclaimed Renuka, throwing her hand to her mouth.

And then Meenakshi broke down. She threw herself into her mother's arms and hugged her as tightly as she could.

'*Bas, bas.*' Renuka patted her head. 'It's not your fault.'

'But why, Aai? What is happening to me?'

'You are growing, that's all.'

'But why like this? None of my sisters—'

'Every girl is different, Meenu.' Renuka sat her down on the bed. 'You will not understand now, but you are maturing fast. A man who does not know you will not believe that you are just a child. Don't ask me how this is happening, but it is.'

'I don't want this—'

'Why, child?' said Renuka in a soft voice, much different from what it was a few hours ago. 'Think of this as a gift. Slowly, you will learn to use it well. We mustn't cry about the gifts we have.'

'It is not a gift. It is a curse. I don't want it.'

'No, Meenu!' Renuka admonished. 'Don't say that. You are my most beautiful girl.'

'But what if something bad happens to me?'

'Nothing will. I am there for you. I will take care of you.'

'And…Manda Tai's wedding?'

'We'll wait for another opportunity. That man was stupid anyway.'

A faint trace of a smile appeared on their lips.

✤

Renuka's words put Meenakshi's mind at ease. For the rest of the day, she was her usual self, prancing about the house, even giggling a few times. Things changed again after dinner, though, when Shantaram went back to his room and Renuka took his plate inside.

Meenakshi was sitting on the kitchen floor with her sisters, having her dinner. The sisters spoke in hushed tones, and Meenakshi wanted to say something too, but this was one of those occasions when anything you said would come out wrong. And she had always been considered a pariah by her sisters. Or maybe they were just in awe of her. If these had been just vague notions so far, today they hung in the atmosphere so thickly that they could be cut with a cast iron knife.

'Manda Tai, Aai said that man was stupid,' she said eventually.

Her sisters' talks came to a grinding halt.

They turned to look at her, all except Manda, who continued to hide her face and now broke into a fresh set of tears.

'You don't talk too much,' said Suparna, the fourth sister, 'this is all because of you.'

'Because of me? How?' Meenakshi quipped.

'The way you go about, strutting like an apsara! Which man will not slip? Hasn't Aai told you how to behave like a woman? Look at Kumud. She's also a child, but see how decent,' Suparna spat out.

'Am I not decent?'

'Go away, Meenu. It is all because of you that Manda Tai lost such a good match.'

The other sisters said nothing, but they did not have to. Suparna was known for her acerbic tongue. Whenever any of the sisters picked a fight, they sent Suparna ahead, and she sallied forth with the end of her dupatta tucked into her waist, as if for a battle. Meenakshi had always admired how her Suparna Tai never flinched from confrontation, but today she was the target.

She couldn't bear to sit with her sisters any longer. Pushing her plate aside, Meenakshi stood up and stormed out of the kitchen.

In blind anger, she rushed into her room to lock herself in

again, but stopped when she heard the soft voices of her parents coming from their bedroom.

Curiosity overcoming everything else, she stood by the slightly open door and pressed her ear as close to the slit as she could.

'She is still young; she doesn't know,' her father said. 'You have to teach her.'

'Aaho, I try,' said Renuka. 'I try the whole day. What do you think? Just this morning, she was wearing this shirt and I had to tell her to change it. She just doesn't understand. I am telling you, there's something wrong.'

'Wrong? What's wrong?'

'I am a woman. I know. She is…growing up very fast. Do you know about her woman's thing? She started at just ten, imagine. Why else do you think I don't take her to the temple on some Saturdays? But it is so precise that it astounds me. It always starts on a Saturday morning and dries up that same night. She bleeds just for a few hours every fourth Saturday. That's not natural!'

'Well, you know your womanly things better. Should we take her to a doctor?'

'Doctors don't know anything. I talked to my old Aatya about her. She said every girl grows differently.'

'She might just be large?'

'No. She is in full bloom. She is a fully-grown woman in a child's body.'

'What does that even mean?'

'Make Manda and Meenu stand side by side,' said Renuka, 'and then ask a stranger to tell who is older. You are their father. You won't see all this.'

Shantaram pondered. 'But she's only a child. Our child. We have to do what is best for her.'

'Of course. That's what I am worried about. It's not just about her growing so rapidly. See, I have noticed something happens to men when she is around. I don't know why. Those neighbourhood boys…I have stopped her from playing with them. That day I caught them standing behind the wall of our compound, looking at her. They...had their hands inside...oh God, I cannot say this.'

Shantaram glared.

'There was that rowdy Govind too with his ugly smile...I wanted to shout at them all, but what could I say?' asked Renuka.

'You have to—'

'You don't understand. Nothing has happened with our other daughters, has it? We give them the same food that we give Meenu. Same bhaat-bhaaji (rice and vegetables). I am telling you...we need to be cautious. If anything happens tomorrow, we won't be able to show our face to society.'

Meenakshi reeled. Her parents were thinking she was a freak. Was she? What was that her mother had said—a fully-grown woman in a child's body?

What did that even mean?

She ran into her room. There was no sleep for her that night.

3

The Waterless Well

*M*eenakshi missed out on wishing her Companion the next morning.

It was mid-morning and she was still in bed. Her sisters had already bathed and were dressing up for their schools and colleges. Her mother came in once to wake her up for school, but she firmly turned to the other side and pretended to sleep. Missing school was nothing new for her.

When she heard the last of the sisters wishing their mother goodbye and slamming the door behind her, Meenakshi finally opened her eyes. She went out into the garden with a lota (mug) of water and went to the corner designated for the morning ablutions, and then visited her huge leafy friend.

'Companion, everyone is bad,' she fretted, not caring if her voice carried into the house. 'You are my only true friend. You will never hurt me, will you?'

Meenakshi blinked back her tears and peered at the tree as if it would give her some sign. There was no sign though, except that the flower hoods seemed to be exceptionally droopy that day.

'See, I knew it!' said Meenakshi. 'You are sad because I am sad, isn't it?'

When she went around the tree once, she felt it under her foot.

'Oh, good!' she said, and picked up the gold coin of the day. 'You never fail to cheer me up.'

❧

That afternoon, after lunch, Renuka sent Meenakshi to a store with a shopping list of three items—sugar, soap and tea, the barest necessities. At the shop, Meenakshi ignored the usual smiles of

Debu, the boy who sat at the counter, and stuffed the things into her bag. When she brought her purchases to the counter for billing, she felt his hand graze hers. Twice.

She quickly paid him and walked out of the shop without giving him another look.

But no sooner did she come out of the shop than she heard muffled laughter behind her.

There were voices. Boys. She felt their eyes on her.

A wave of anger mixed with fear overcame her. In an instant, her armpits went clammy with cold sweat. Every male gaze had started to evoke that sick feeling in her.

She tried hard not to turn and look. She knew exactly what kind of boys they were, and what they were doing. They were probably standing in a group, ogling her rear with those disgusting grins on their faces. At times she felt like going right up to such boys and slapping them across their faces, or something more—digging her fingernails into their mouths and tearing their lips clean off. Then they'd be grinning forever, wouldn't they?

'Go now. Don't be a sissy!' she heard one of them say.

'Going...don't push!' said another, and this voice astonished Meenakshi.

The next moment Tappu came up to her quickly, trying to match her step for step.

'How are you, Meenu?' he asked.

It took Meenakshi a moment to register that it was Tappu, and then she began breathing easier. It was only Tappu, after all.

'What happened to you re, Tappya? Why are you dressed in these funny clothes?' she said.

The funny clothes were a full-sleeved checked shirt that was all buttoned up and a pair of tight crotch-hugging jeans hitched up with a leather belt that had a flashy oval buckle. He wore black sunshades, totally meaning business.

'Nothing. Where are you going?'

'What's wrong with you? Why are you acting strange?'

Tappu laughed. 'Don't I look all grown up? You like it?'

Meenakshi laughed. 'Is a girl coming to see you?'

'No, no, no girl. What girl?'

'You look nice.' Meenakshi winked. '*Ekdum* hero.'

A broad grin appeared on his face and he turned as if to look at someone. Meenakshi turned too, but could not see anyone.

'Anyone there?' she asked.

'No, no one…'

'But I heard you talking to someone.'

'It's no one, *aai shapath*!' He moved closer. 'Meenu…I wanted to tell you something…'

'Wanted? Means you don't want to tell anymore?'

'No, no, I have to tell. I mean…I will tell now.'

Meenakshi let out a huge belly laugh, which made her upper body shake. 'You are really an ass today. Okay, tell.'

Almost dancing on the balls of his feet, Tappu let it out. 'Meenu, will you come with me to the viheer?'

The viheer. The well. The common village well where the village sourced its water from. On its embankment were dense trees and plants of all kind, growing on the soft cool soil. That is where people hung out, with their families in the evenings, with their friends in the mornings and afternoons, and—as everyone knew—with their lovers at all times of the day. No one saw the lovers, as they stayed well-hidden in the shrubbery, but everyone knew they were there. It was the unofficial dating spot of Vatgaon.

'Viheer? Why?'

'Just like that. We'll do some timepass.'

'What timepass?'

'Arre, come…'

'Okay, like a picnic? Pindya, Abdul, Nisha…they are also coming?'

'No. Just you and me. Like we used to play alone when we were kids? We will play and chat. Just fun, nothing else.'

'I don't know, Tappya,' Meenakshi grew thoughtful. 'I am not in the mood today.'

'Please...'

'Okay, let's go...'

'Really?'

'Yes. Let's go.'

He whooped with joy but stopped abruptly when he realized it was weird.

'But I have this shopping bag with me. I'll keep it home, tell Aai I am going with you, and then—'

'No, no need. If you go home, your Aai will not let you come out again.'

'Then why don't you go with someone else today? We have so many friends...I'll come tomorrow.'

'No. I want to go only with you. Or not go anywhere at all. Ever!'

'Arre, Tappya, oh okay, don't start crying now!' He was actually tearing up. 'Okay, come. But no mischief, okay...'

'Mischief? What mischief?'

There was no answer. The next moment, they turned and walked towards the well, Meenakshi taking the lead. She did not see Tappu turning back and giving a gentleman's salute to Govind, who was hidden in the bushes, applauding him with a thumbs up sign and a wink.

❦

They could not see the water in the well from the mound they were sitting on. All they could see was the foliage of the many lantana bushes that were around them, with their clustered crimson-yellow flowers shining gloriously in the post-noon heat, and that gladdened Meenakshi's heart.

Unable to resist herself, she ran up to the nearest bush and picked up a cluster. 'Aren't these flowers lovely, Tappya?' she said, holding it up. 'So small and delightful. Like they are smiling, all at once.'

'You look nice,' said Tappu, ignoring the flowers.

He was comfortably settled on the mound already, his knees

drawn up, his arms locking them.

'How many times will you tell me that?' Meenakshi laughed. 'Chal, now, are we going to just sit here?'

'Let's sit for a while,' he said. 'I'm a bit tired after all the walking. Then we will play.'

'Okay, what will we play? I know…hide-and-seek. It will be fun in these bushes.' Meenakshi looked all around as she said that, and then something grabbed her attention. 'But oh…see that!'

She threw the cluster that was in her hand away and romped back to the bushes. She returned with a ripe drumstick in her hands.

'You always need to have something in your hands, don't you?' said Tappu with a grin.

'I cannot sit idle. I am not like you, mhatara!'

Tappu did not take offense at being called an old man. In fact, something quite contrary was happening to him right now. His eyes were now on the drumstick, which suddenly had a different meaning as the girl held it in her hands. He knew he mustn't stare, but he could not avoid looking at her soft, grown-girly fingers moving on it. Her forefinger came to the tip of the drumstick and tapped it gently, and something happened to him—something that had started happening often lately, for which he had to run to the bathroom, leaving whatever it was he was doing. And usually, when that happened, he would be thinking of Meenakshi.

Drawing his legs closer, he moved up to her.

'You watch movies?' he breathed hard.

'Sometimes.'

'Which? Tell me the names.'

She rattled off a few.

'Ae Meenu, we look like the hero-heroine of a movie, sitting alone like this.' His hand came over her shoulder.

She didn't seem to mind it. He drew closer.

'You like that…that stick?'

He placed his hand over hers, guiding it to squeeze it gently on the drumstick.

'Leave me, Tappya. What is this?'

'Just teaching you a game.'

Then he forced her hand and put it on his jeans and sighed, 'Touch it, please.'

'TAPPYA!' Meenakshi screamed and pulled her hand away. She stood up, horror written all over her face.

In an instant, the boy's excitement died away. An unfamiliar fear crept on him, of a kind he had never experienced before. Oh hell, what was this! Even as he sat there, looking at the horrified face of the girl he had just outraged, he felt the blood draining out of his groin and rushing frantically into the organ that needed it more—his brain. And he just knew, something bad, something very bad, was going to happen.

The regret of a misdeed may have rarely hit anyone as hard as it smacked Tappu right across the face that afternoon.

There was something in Meenakshi's eyes now. For once, he looked beyond her chest and hips, at her face. It was grimmer than his mother's when she had caught him masturbating, and more forbidding than his father's when he had caught him puffing on his discarded cigarette.

'Sorry, sorry, Meenu…I didn't mean…'

But she only stared at him now, with an expression that belied all definition. She did not even look like Meenu anymore. Suddenly, a vision flashed in his mind, the vision of his Kusma Aatya who had fallen to her knees midway during a procession to Pandharpur and started swaying rhythmically like a crazed woman. It had scared him to death, but the men had started pounding their dhols and chinking their taashas, encouraging her to continue her eerie dance, while someone said aloud, 'We are blessed! Mother Goddess has entered Kusma's body.'

He could not tell why this look was similar. He hoped it was not.

What would he do if some Devi had really entered this girl's body now to punish him? He had heard tales of that kind of thing happening.

'You should not have done that,' said Meenakshi. It was a grown, womanly voice now.

'I am sorry.' Tappu fell to his feet, and lay prostrate on the ground, rubbing his nose in the mud. 'I will never do it again.'

But Meenakshi had gone beyond all reason. The thing that was growing in her eyes was complete now. Two red disks had replaced her black-brown irises. And she continued to stare accusingly at her offender with those bloodcurdling eyes, her big bust heaving like it were lugging a heavy load up the five hundred steps of the Ambabai peak.

❦

When Meenakshi neared the house, the evening sun had already begun its descent. Her tiny fingers curled around the shopping bag handles, she walked in a daze, unmindful of the two street dogs that had been following her all the while, trying to sniff at her bags.

When she reached the gate, her reverie broke. Suddenly realizing the hour and seeing the bag in her hand, she felt that sense of panic that she should have felt two hours ago. Shooing one of the dogs with all she had and sending the other packing behind it, she broke into a run.

She jumped over the gate rather than opening it with the infernal creaking noise that it made. She stood still to assess the atmosphere inside the house. Was her father sitting in the verandah, fretting and fuming? Was her mother peering at the path outside, panic-stricken? Were her sisters running all over the place, asking for her?

Nothing seemed to be amiss. So far so good. Her folk probably hadn't even realized she was not back home yet, and for once, she was happy no one cared for her much. She was the seventh daughter, after all. Probably by the time her parents had reached the point of giving birth to her, all their love had dried out. How much love can humans have in their puny hearts anyway?

Looking at the sal for reassurance, she tiptoed into the house.

Her mother was preparing dinner in the kitchen. She could hear the pots and pans. The sisters were at their schools and colleges. And her father, as usual, was invisible.

She kept the bag down on the dining table and ran directly into her room.

But that night, Meenakshi found out her absence hadn't gone unnoticed. The girls had just finished dinner, and after washing their plates, were preparing to move to their common sleeping rooms. Meenakshi was about to follow when she heard a voice calling out to her with an unfamiliar undertone.

'Meenuye...'

It was her father.

The other girls hastened to their rooms and Meenakshi felt a tingle run down her spine. She had been summoned, and that could never be good.

She looked in the direction of her father's room. He was wiping his hands with a towel. Her mother came out of the room with his dinner plate in her hands and rushed into the kitchen without even looking at her.

Meenakshi had no recollection of when she had entered her father's room the last time. With calculated steps, as if she were entering an uncharted cave, she walked in.

'Yes, Baba?' she asked.

'Sit down.'

Her father was dressed in his usual all-white kurta and pyjama. It contrasted with his dark complexion and made him look larger, almost spectre-like in the near-darkness of that room. Did he look like this now? Meenakshi hadn't yet seen those thin gray strands in his sidelocks. As she was scrutinizing him, he belched and then began.

'Meenu, you know you are my favourite daughter, right?'

Meenakshi did not know that. She could not remember when her father had expressed anything like this to her directly.

'As a father, I am not supposed to be close to my daughters,' continued Shantaram. 'That's how our tradition goes, and that's your mother's duty anyway. But I try to express my love as much as I can.'

Meenakshi nodded.

'But you must know that a father's love is different. A mother's love is built on concern; a father's love is built on hope.'

Meenakshi busied herself in picking a string on her dress.

'Your mother tells me that you are growing. Growing up is a good thing, but she is concerned. She says you are still a child and you are growing too fast. Are you, Meenu?'

'I don't know, Baba.'

'Look at that mango tree in our garden. You know how the cycle goes. The fruits first come out, little, green, very bitter. In a few weeks, they become ripe and yellow and sweet. Now imagine if one of those fruits did not follow the cycle. Imagine that some parts of that fruit grew rapidly while the other parts remained immature. Think of a yellow ripened fruit with its tart juices still inside. That would be odd, no?'

'I…don't understand.'

'Oh, I cannot explain well. But your Aai tells me I should talk to you. Meenu, I see you as someone capable of doing great things. Other fathers in our village restrict their daughters. I don't. But you have to be careful.'

'All right.'

'This is a crucial time of your life. You have to be aware of the people around you. Especially boys.'

'I always am, Baba.'

'You don't understand, child. Monsters will never show themselves as monsters. They will come hidden in many disguises. Sometimes they will look beautiful and tempting.' Then his tone suddenly changed. 'Your friend, that boy, Tappu…is he back home yet?'

She felt a jolt of electricity running down her spine.

'What happened to him?' she asked, hoping her voice wouldn't break.

'His mother had come looking for him while you girls were eating.'

'I haven't seen him today,' Meenakshi said with a straight face.

'He is your age too,' said Shantaram. 'See what I mean? He's probably gone off somewhere, not caring for his folks at home. Look how distressed his mother is now.'

'I don't know anything about him.'

'I am not saying you do.'

At that moment, Renuka walked in again. She had been standing at the door, eavesdropping. 'Where were you this afternoon then, Meenu?' she asked. 'You took two hours to return from the grocery store. You walked in silently like a mouse, but I saw you.'

The pang in Meenakshi's young heart grew more intense, and she hoped it didn't thump so wildly as to be noticed. Treacherous tears prickled in her eyes.

'Why are you crying now? What did I say?'

Meenakshi tried to look up at her mother, but she could not. All she could see was the corner of her saree tucked into her waist and her hand poised on it firmly.

'I...I really don't remember, Aai.'

'Didn't you see Tappu at all?'

'No...' Meenakshi looked at her father. His head was bowed down as if in shame. Something broke her heart at that gesture from the man she had looked up to, and she said meekly, *'Ye-es.'*

Renuka roared, 'Why did you lie then?'

Now the tears came out freely like a bleeding wound that had not started clotting yet. Along with it came spit and mucous and a lot of wheezing. 'I'll tell you the truth, Aai...but you won't believe me. I was returning...from the store. Tappu met me outside. He asked me to go to the viheer with him.'

'Viheer?' Renuka's eyebrows disappeared in her hairline. 'Why?'

'He said we'd play. I went, but I didn't really want to go, Aai. He insisted.'

Shantaram said quietly, 'What happened after that?'

'I sat with him. We talked for a while and then...he came close to me.' Meenakshi started sobbing louder as she said this. The sisters came to the door, but Renuka shooed them away and shut the door.

'What happened then, Meenu? Did he touch you?'

Shantaram shot a look at his wife, but she waved him away, and waited for her daughter's reaction.

Then, slowly, but with purpose, Meenakshi nodded.

'And?'

'Then I don't know anything. I went blank. Believe me. It was like I fell asleep, Aai. When I woke up, I was near our house gate and it was evening.'

Renuka and Shantaram shared a look of disbelief.

'You don't remember anything?' asked Shantaram.

'No.'

Shantaram stood up. He walked up to the door and began to put on his chappals.

'Where are you going now?' asked Renuka.

'To their house, where else? I have to see if—'

Renuka went closer to him and held his arm. 'Listen to me, don't go.'

'Why? His mother is looking all around the village. We have to tell her...'

'Look at her.' Renuka pointed to Meenakshi. 'We don't know what happened. People will come and question our girl.' She lowered her voice. 'She says she blacked out. You believe that? She is hiding something.'

Shantaram sat down. 'But the boy—'

Renuka waved a hand of reassurance at him.

She went to her weeping child and patted her on the back. 'Sit here,' she said. 'I'll make some sherbet for all.'

Renuka was still putting the deep red kokum concentrate into water when a loud sound from the neighbouring house shattered the silence. She almost dropped the glass and went running up to her husband. 'What was that? What…?'

Shantaram shoved her aside and strode towards the gate. He opened it with a loud screech that set the dogs barking, and disappeared into the neighbours' compound.

'Oh my God!' exclaimed Renuka, clutching her bosom. She stood like that with bated breath, and when Meenakshi went up to her and kept her hand on her shoulder, she started.

For nearly ten minutes they stood like that, and then they saw Shantaram returning from the darkness he had vanished into.

Renuka ran up to him, 'What happened, ho? Why did you go there? Did they find the boy? Is he all right?'

Shantaram returned home, sat down in the verandah, took the glass of sherbet, and sighed. All his daughters were around him now; Renuka could not shoo them away any longer.

'He has been found,' said Shantaram, and Renuka went ecstatic. 'But—'

A suffocating silence followed.

'He is not himself. He is delirious, sort of. All dazed and stunned. I saw him, and nobody will go see him right now, you hear? His mouth is open. Like stuck open by some force. His tongue is retracted all the way down to the throat. The vaidya is trying to pull it out, or the boy might choke to death. His eyes aren't closing either. Dazed, like he saw something horrible and turned to stone. The boy is colder than the lake in winter.'

'Oh my God!' said Renuka again and looked at Meenakshi. The girl looked on with an expression of fear.

'Why? What happened to Tappu, Aai?' asked Manda.

'You girls don't talk now,' Renuka chipped in. 'He has been found, that's all. He'll be better tomorrow morning.'

The girls quietly went to their rooms, speaking to each other in muted whispers.

'Why are you here? You go too.'

Meenakshi turned and followed her sisters.

After the girls left, Renuka sat next to Shantaram, rubbing his hand, which had gone cold too.

'Don't worry. It will be all right,' she said. Her words meant nothing.

'You don't understand,' said Shantaram. 'If the boy comes to his senses tomorrow, he will tell exactly what happened to him.'

Renuka felt her heartbeat quicken. 'Oh!'

'We don't know what happened, do we?'

'No, we don't,' said Renuka. 'Meenakshi does not seem to remember. Or she does...who knows? But what if the boy talks about it tomorrow like you said? What if this is something we cannot control?'

The couple had no answer. They sat like that up to a late hour in the lingering darkness, enveloped by the frantic sounds from the neighbouring house.

4

A Mother's Concern

*I*t was two in the morning when Renuka finally moved to go to sleep. She glanced at her husband, who had fallen asleep on the cot in the verandah. Leaving him there, and ensuring that the gate was locked, she poked her head into one of the two bedrooms that her girls shared.

As her eyes acclimatized to the dark room, she could see four outlines of differing sizes sleeping on mats on the floor—four of her daughters.

Quietly shutting the door, she walked to the adjoining room, where her other three girls were.

Here, she spread a mat woven out of dried coconut-palm fronds on the floor, mumbled a prayer that came from memory and not intention, and laid herself down. She could hear the ancient ceiling fan above that made all the noise in the room, and it slowly began to lull her into sleep.

She was half asleep when she was awakened by a clear voice that cut through the darkness.

'I never wanted to be here.'

Her eyes opened wide. She sat up abruptly, ignoring that painful snap somewhere in her back.

In the farthest corner, sitting up now, was Meenakshi.

She seemed to be in a trance, like she was looking at something in the distance. Renuka could faintly see the girl's heaving chest and hear her breathing, that sounded like bellowing. Her hair had come off and was now streaking down in two thick bunches on either side of her head. Then Renuka saw the one thing on her child's face that made her remember God again—a twisted smile.

Such an emotion rose in her that she momentarily lost her ability to breathe.

'Meenu...' she whispered. 'Who are you talking to?'

Whether it was at the mention of her name, Renuka could not tell, but at the next instant, Meenakshi fell back on her mat, turned over, and went still.

Renuka had no sleep the rest of the night.

❧

When the rooster crowed, Renuka opened her eyes and sat up, suddenly alarmed by the faint light of dawn in the room. Had she really slept? She felt like she had just shut her eyes a minute ago and it was dawn already.

Her eyes wouldn't close again. The memory of last night came back to haunt her, and whatever sleep she had lost vanished into a distant land.

Her girl wasn't on the mat.

In a flash, Renuka sat up. Then she stood up and saw the vacant space where Meenakshi had been sleeping. Her bed covers were now curled into a big O, resembling a nest where her sleeping form had lain all night.

It was just ten to six. The thick haze of the previous night still hung in the atmosphere. Renuka went to the corridor. Seeing it vacant, she hurried along it, her bangles making enough noise to wake up the neighbours.

As she ran, she pinched her forearm in hope. Oh, what would she not give to realize all of this was just some bizarre nightmare, and she would wake up from it and see that her youngest daughter was back with her in the form in which she loved her the most—those chubby cheeks, those widely-staring inquisitive eyes, and that hair neatly oiled and bundled in two tight plaits!

'Meenu!' she screamed when she reached her husband sleeping on the cot in the verandah. The man did not stir.

She heard a faint giggling sound.

Clutching her breast, Renuka ran in the direction of the laughter. *She's laughing,* she told herself. *Laughing is good.*

She spotted her then, under the boughs of the sal in the garden, playing gleefully and jumping and prancing on the fallen leaves.

Renuka stopped.

Had last night been a dream?

Meenakshi was hopping on the ground under the tree. Time and again she would pick up a huge bunch of the fallen leaves and throw it upon herself. As the leaves—different shades of green and yellow and brown—cascaded down, she laughed merrily like a child on a merry-go-round for the first time.

A fond smile grew on Renuka's lips. What was the cause of her worry? Here she was—her Meenakshi—as youthful as possible, engaged in something that amused her, something totally harmless.

Renuka showed herself. 'Meenu…'

Meenakshi's smile mellowed. She clutched the leaves and hid them out of sight behind her back.

'What are you doing, Meenu?'

'Nothing, Aai… Just sitting here.'

Renuka came up to her and stroked her cheek. 'My dear girl… All right, I won't bother you much. But why did you get up so early?'

'I just woke up.'

'I see…' Renuka was not gasping any longer. Last night seemed like a distant memory—that adventure of the missing boy, the sleep-talking; it was like it never happened. 'Okay, don't dirty yourself too much. Come back inside. I am heating up water for your bath.'

'Yes, Aai.'

Renuka smiled again, and then jangled her bangles all the way into the house.

Behind her, Meenakshi slowly dropped the leaves she was holding in her hands. They fell, one by one, till none were left, and yet, there was something that remained in her hands.

Meenakshi examined it closely.

It was yet another gold coin, unmarked and unsigned, like

they always were. A fat ungainly man's face was engraved on it. She had never cared to know who that fat man was. The yellow rays of the rising sun shimmered on the surface of the coin and reflected on her face. They gave her an ethereal look, which became all the more resplendent as she broke into another of her pure, unadulterated smiles.

✿

That afternoon, Renuka changed into a fine saree and slipped into her good chappals.

'Where are you going?' Meenakshi asked as she was about to step out.

'Just visiting the Namdars' house,' said Renuka.

'Tappu's house?'

'Yes,' Renuka smiled. 'They are our neighbours. It is not good if I don't pay them a visit.'

'But Baba said—'

'Baba doesn't know about such things.'

Renuka set out. As she turned away from Meenakshi and faced the Namdars' house, her heart again began to beat like a war drum.

At the Namdars' gate, Renuka paused to scope the environment. It was quiet now. She crossed her heart, hoping that she was doing the right thing.

Renuka saw Savitri, Tappu's mother, coming out with a bundle of clothes for drying. She made a gesture at her, which was midway between a smile and a look of grave consternation.

'How's Tappu?' she asked.

Savitri kept the clothes down, went up to the gate, and undid the latch. 'Come, Renu. See for yourself.'

Renuka walked into the house. She waved a cautious hand at Tappu's old grandfather who was sitting on a cot in a corner of the verandah, looking every bit like he was ready to die, just the way he had for the last twenty years. Then the door swung open and she entered.

Renuka could not see Tappu right away. She first saw his three brothers, naked except for short cloth rags around their privates, playing with a plastic toy train that was missing several wheels. Then she saw Tappu. He was on a low bed by the wall, and she knew at once that he was not all right.

His stiff body reminded her of the electrocuted lamb she had seen near the powerhouse once. His hands were raised skyward, just like the lamb's tawny forelimbs, and his eyes, glazed and glassy, were staring in the distance. The boy's mouth was open as if in a scream, and his tongue was pulled all the way back inside the open mouth.

The only sign of life in the boy was the slight rising and falling of his chest.

'Oh my God!' Renuka exclaimed in horror.

One of the children made a loud 'Wheeee!' at that point and Savitri screamed at the top of her lungs, 'Get out and play, you good-for-nothings! Don't you see, your brother is half-dead?'

The children rushed out of the room at once.

'Sit,' Savitri pushed a stool towards Renuka.

Renuka sat on the stool and Savitri sat on the floor, wiping invisible tears with the end of her saree.

'What did the vaidya say?'

Savitri sniffled. 'What will he say? This is not his job.'

'What is it then?'

Savitri's eyes grew large, like she was to narrate a horrific tale with relish. 'Agga, you know the stories of our village, no? I used to tell this good-for-nothing Tappu, "Don't go here", "Don't go there". Never listened. He must have walked under the peepal tree at noon.'

Renuka only nodded.

'I told him pretas rest in the peepal trees in the afternoons. He must have disturbed a dead spirit. That's what! A ghost got to him. See how he looks. All *zhapatlela* (possessed).'

'So...he has been stunned by a ghost?'

'What else, Renu?'

'Now what?'

'His father will bring a priest today. We don't understand these things. Let the priest do whatever he wants to do. I have kept fat roosters for sacrifice if he asks.'

Just then, Renuka looked at the boy and there was a flicker in his eyes.

'I…I think…he's moving.'

'Don't mind that,' Savitri said. 'That keeps happening. Yesterday he smiled at me too. It's the ghost in him that's making him do that. Don't look at him. He might hypnotize you too.'

'You are sure it is a ghost?'

'What else?' Savitri laughed uneasily. 'Yesterday I was so worried, I thought he'd die. But then Ajoba told such possessions happen commonly and exorcisms are done all the time. So I am not worrying. Anyway, thanks for coming. Who visits anyone nowadays? You are a good neighbour.'

That remark hit Renuka. A 'good neighbour' was hardly what she was being at the moment. In fact, she was mumbling silent prayers to let the boy stay in that condition. *If he never comes out of it, he'll never be able to tell what happened.*

'Okay, I'll see you,' said Renuka abruptly. 'There's so much to prepare for dinner. I'll come again.'

'Yeah, come again, haan?'

Renuka found her way out of the house. It bemused her how a mother could be so carefree about a son who was practically dead. She was not educated herself, but she had scant faith in rural superstitions and even scanter faith in ghosts and spirits. It was a kind of contradiction, as her mother used to say when she was alive. *'Renu, you believe in all the Gods, but you don't believe in the demons? How is that possible? Foolish girl, Gods cannot exist without demons!'*

But she was not complaining now. Let them think there was a ghost. It served her purpose.

Renuka was walking thus, on the short path that led up to her house, when she saw Meenakshi at the other end. Suddenly, her feet stopped.

She thought of calling out to her daughter. Words of reprimand as to why she was out of the compound were on the tip of her tongue when she heard a boy's voice. Quickly, on an impulse, she hid herself in the bushes.

It was an older boy's voice. 'Ae Meenu…wait, no…'

The boy appeared in front of Meenakshi. Was he that rowdy Govind?

'Meenu, listen na…I have something to tell you…' Govind ran up, huffing. 'I know what happened to Tappya.'

Renuka's heart stilled. But despite her worry, she didn't fail to notice how her girl did not flinch in the presence of the local ruffian.

'You should know. *Your* friend, after all,' said Meenakshi with surprising boldness.

'I know *everything*,' said Govind insistently. 'I know how he got zapped. His parents are fools to think he is possessed.'

'Then what is it?'

'Oh, you don't know?' Govind had a smirk on his face now. That smirk sent shivers down Renuka's spine.

He grinned. 'I was there. I know you went together.'

'Go away, Govind,' said Meenakshi in a firm voice. 'Go away and don't bother me.'

Good girl, Renuka thought. *Fight him.*

But Govind grabbed her arm. 'Ae, Meenu…you have something in you, re. That Tappu is a child; he could not bear it.'

'What are you saying?'

'Ah, don't act so innocent!' said Govind. 'You don't know? Look at me at least…'

'I have no time for this.' Meenakshi turned to leave.

'What's Tappu's fault?' he said, obstructing her path. 'You look like a film heroine. Even I—'

Renuka saw her daughter's fist balling up. If that hadn't

happened, she would have herself jumped onto the scene and smacked that Govind right across his cheek, but now she was intrigued. She wanted to see what her girl would do.

But the moment passed. The fist uncurled. A smile appeared on Meenakshi's face, and that made Renuka's mouth run dry. It was not like any smile she had ever seen on her face. Hell, right now she did not even look like her daughter.

Renuka found herself staring at her daughter's hand, the one that was a fist just a moment ago. But what was this? Something was happening, something that was way beyond her understanding. Something she would remember for the rest of her life with a brainfreeze.

There was a transition brewing in her daughter beginning with the fingers. They were becoming darker and longer. Something flashed through her mind…her old grandmother's wizened fingers, shortly before she had died. But Renuka knew, she just knew, this was all in her mind. How could this crazy thing be happening?

'MEENU!' Renuka yelled out loud. 'Why did you come out of the house?'

Upon hearing her voice, Govind backed off, and seeing who it was, turned and began to run.

Renuka ran after him. 'Where are you running off to, you bastard? Have balls, then turn and face me! You cross paths with my daughter ever again…'

But the boy had fled out of earshot.

Renuka came running to Meenakshi and held her tightly in her arms, squeezing her hard as if trying to stifle the transformation that was coming upon her. The next moment, she released her from her grip, and smothered her face with kisses.

She wanted to deny everything—what she had seen and what she hadn't. She had suspected there was something wrong with her daughter, but now she wanted to turn a blind eye to it. And that would be the best thing to do because if she saw her daughter in that form again, she was sure she would blind herself.

5

The Man of the House

The man of the house woke up at ten, a late hour by his standards; and what irked him was that he was still in the verandah, on that blessed cot his dear departed father used to sleep on once upon a time.

The first thing he did was call out to his wife, which led him to the realization that she wasn't at home. That explained a few things, like why he was still on the cot in the verandah. Slowly, he rose, watered the sarsaparilla that had graciously climbed on the verandah's railing, and then headed to the bathroom.

When he reemerged and still didn't find Renuka, he dressed up and proceeded to the outside world where his work beckoned him.

Shantaram Hanumantrao Patil belonged to that generation of a once-rich family that did not have to practise an active occupation to keep the household lamp burning. Three generations of his forefathers had slogged (the first generation the hardest) to build and retain the ancestral bungalow that his family lived in now, along with the garden and the host of trees surrounding it, and a few other small properties across the village that raked in a considerable amount in rent.

This rent and the income generated by selling fruits of their trees were what the Patils lived on. Until a few years ago, that had been more than enough for their sustenance as well as for putting something aside for a rainy day.

But, of late, the rainy days had been many. With seven daughters, whatever savings existed were earmarked for their nuptial expenses in fixed deposits and were strictly not to be touched. As the number of members in the household increased over the years, the income became inadequate to the point that the family now lived a hand-to-mouth existence.

That day was the first of the month, when Shantaram made the rounds of his rented properties. He would return by evening, his pockets stuffed with enough cash to just about manage to run the house for the month, provided an ugly quirk of fate didn't decide to rear its hood. Cursing himself for harbouring a negative thought, he shrugged and left the house.

By afternoon, Shantaram had collected the rent from his tenants. A few had courteously asked him in for tea, which he had firmly refused. He did not enter the houses he leased on principle, but the truth was that he did not want to see how others were handling his properties. Even if a king would have lived in one of his houses, plastering the walls with gold, Shantaram would have felt uncomfortable seeing it. It was not the fear of having his property damaged that bothered him; it was the fact that his possession was not really his anymore.

He sought reprieve at a roadside inn on the highway for tea. This was safe territory, for it was between his village and the next, right on the arterial route where only trucks and private vehicles passed by, most of them making their way to the city of Kolhapur forty miles away. The tea came in a small glass. He dunked the biscuits into it and ate them leisurely.

After fifteen minutes, Shantaram got up and was about to walk away when he noticed a familiar face sitting in the corner of the establishment.

It was Harikumar, the suitor.

Shantaram had to peer to make sure it was really him. There was something painfully different about him—his hair. It was all gone, and there was but a short stubble on his scalp. Just then, Harikumar turned to look at him too, and the next moment he came running up to him.

'Patil sahib, so nice to bump into you like this. Good afternoon,' he said with all the politeness he could muster.

'Good afternoon.' An awkward pause followed, and then

Shantaram said, 'So you are still here?'

Harikumar looked at his feet. 'I…I came back. For another visit.'

'I see.' Shantaram turned. Disinterest in both the person and the conversation showed on his face. Yet, he asked, 'Did something happen?'

Immediately, tears began glistening in the young man's eyes.

'What's wrong?'

'Mother passed away last week,' Harikumar said in a choked voice.

Shantaram stepped forward with such suddenness that his leather Kolhapuris stomped on the ground. 'Last week?' he shot out. 'But you were here just ten days ago.'

'Yes. We returned to Bombay after that. Couple of days later, she got one of those asthmatic attacks. Only…only this time it was terrible. I saw her…her face all bloated and contorted, as if trying to grasp at something. "Air, air," she yelled and opened her mouth and shut it repeatedly. "Air is all around you, Aai! Breathe," I said. But she couldn't. She just couldn't. There…right there…in front of my eyes, her face turned blue. I saw her die, and I was just standing by. That is the worst thing—seeing someone die and not being able to do anything about it.'

Shantaram took it in. 'But why are you here? Shouldn't you be conducting her last rites?'

'All that is done, sir. I have an aunt in the city who was with me throughout. Not a real aunt, but closer than one.'

Shantaram placed a hand on the man's shoulder. 'Please accept my condolences. She was a good woman.'

A cry escaped Harikumar's lips, but he quickly stifled his mouth with a handkerchief.

'Do you have some work in the village?'

Harikumar lowered his head. 'No, sir,' he said. 'I'll just stay here for a few days.'

'Business?'

He shook his head.

'Visiting a relative?'

'No one. I have booked a room at Apsara Inn.'

'But, really, *why*?'

'Actually, I was hoping to meet you again, sir...'

'About Manda?'

'No, sir.'

Shantaram looked at him with puzzled eyes. A curious flicker of worry passed across his face. Without responding, he turned and began to walk away in a huff. He had almost hailed a State Transport bus on the highway when Harikumar came running up again.

'Patil sahib...wait...'

Shantaram stopped. The bus passed him by.

'Sir, please,' said Harikumar. 'Did you think about what I told you the last time? About...your youngest daughter...Meenakshi?'

Now, if the man had been in a better state of mind, Shantaram would have punched him in the nose; instead, he said calmly, 'There's nothing to think about.'

'You don't understand me, sir.'

Shantaram's eyelashes fluttered with worry, rage and shock. 'What the hell are you saying?'

Harikumar looked straight into Shantaram's eyes with a stony gaze. There was no smile on his lips.

'She is just fifteen,' seethed Shantaram.

'What is age, sir?' asked Harikumar. 'I will keep her like a queen. I have a huge house—no, *houses*—in Bombay and have a family business that my father left me. I earn more than most people. Why do you object?'

'SHE IS JUST FIFTEEN!' Shantaram repeated.

'Is it about dowry? You don't have to give me anything. In fact...' Harikumar fell at Shantaram's feet. 'If you allow me to marry her, I will give you five lakhs as a present.'

'Get up, Harikumar,' said Shantaram. 'I know your qualifications and eligibility, and that's the reason I agreed to see you for my older daughter. If you want Manda's hand, take it any day. But Meenakshi is off-limits for the next five years. I cannot do anything about it.'

Shantaram stopped another bus. It slowed down and he got in without turning back.

※

Even as Shantaram proceeded to open the gate of the compound, Renuka ran up to him.

'How did you know I have returned home? You are no less than a sniffer dog,' said Shantaram.

'I'm not a wife for no reason. Wives have to be sniffer dogs and more,' said Renuka, without skipping a beat.

'Of that I have no doubt.'

Then the tirade came. 'Where were you all day? Don't you just go walking around like that without telling anyone. If anything happens to you, what will I do with these seven girls on my head?'

'Oh, calm down, Renu. Today is the first of the month. Do I have to tell you every month?'

Almost instantly, Renuka softened. 'So you brought money? Good. I have to tell you something too. Today, I visited the Namdars' house and on the way back, I saw—'

'OH, DO BE QUIET!' Shantaram yelled. It was uncharacteristic of him to raise his voice. However, anger and concern had been brewing in him all afternoon, and now it spilled out.

Renuka backed off. 'What happened?'

'I am sorry,' he mumbled. 'I should not have—'

'That's okay. Screaming is good sometimes. Tell me, what happened?'

'I met Harikumar.'

'*Harikumar?*'

'Yes. He is staying at Apsara. There's bad news. His mother's dead.'

'Oh! How? She looked so well...'

'You can never tell what people hide inside them, can you?' said Shantaram.

Those words, and the way they were said, sent a shiver down Renuka's spine. 'Why is he here?'

'Take a guess.'

'Meenu?' Though her tone was interrogative, it wasn't really a question. A man going out of the way, crossing all levels of sanity to meet her daughter—it was not new to her.

'He begged. Fell at my feet, almost rubbed his nose into the ground. Just so that I'd agree to his proposal.'

Renuka made a sound that was almost a groan. She recalled the adventure with Govind that morning and a sense of alarm proliferated in her mind.

'But why? Why only her?'

'I told him,' said Shantaram. 'I repeated that we are ready to give Manda to him. But he wouldn't listen. Age doesn't matter, he says.'

'Oh! This is not good. Not good at all.'

'I saw something in his eyes, Renu. A longing that I have only seen in the eyes of people who pine and waste away. Remember that jilted Narayan who just used to sit and drink by the viheer till he died? This Harikumar was a fine man just two weeks ago. Today he's a beggar, wasting away like a vagrant. All for what?'

Renuka came closer to Shantaram. 'Look, we must not tell Meenu this. Nothing about Tappu either.'

'Now what about that Namdars' kid?'

'I overheard someone today. Our Meenu was with Tappu. But there is something more.'

'What?'

'I don't want you to get worried, okay?' said Renuka. 'But I have to tell you. There was this guy teasing her on the street. At first, Meenakshi ignored him and reproached him like any self-respecting girl would. Then something overcame her. She became different. I mean, really, she began to change. A dreadful smile broke out on her lips and she began to talk in a seductive voice, a voice that no mother should ever hear on her daughter. It scared me so much, and then—'

'What?'

'Her hands began to turn. Change, I mean. Like she was turning into someone else.'

'What are you saying?'

'I am telling you what I saw.'

'Then?'

'I jumped in and chased that guy away. I just ran and held our Meenu tightly. But it was not a hug of love; it is just that I did not want that other thing inside her to come out.'

'Other thing?'

'Don't you see it yet, Manda's father?' said Renuka. 'I have never believed in superstitions, but our Meenu is not ordinary at all. There's something inside her. Today I saw it with my own eyes.'

Shantaram sat down on the cot, wordless.

It was a cold night, the beginning of winter. But despite that nip in the air, Renuka broke into a sweat. Wiping it away with her palloo, she said, 'Do you...think it's because something went wrong that night?'

'What night?'

'*That* night, when she was still in my womb. When we did the yajna. Something horrible happened that night, I know.'

6

Naked Man in the Grove

*L*eaving the room where her sisters were still lost in sleep, Meenakshi skulked up to the sal tree. The sun was just beginning to rise, tempting the skies with golden streaks. Seizing the moment, she sat down beneath the shadowy boughs of the tree and took a leaf from the hundreds scattered on the ground. She looked at it closely, as if she were reading something in those veins. Then with her nails—which were surprisingly back to being long and sharp, though her mother had trimmed them just two afternoons ago—she began to carve something on it.

Her fingers ran along the contours of the leaf, applying added pressure on the veins as they began carving out a shape. She had nothing on her mind; she let her fingers guide her.

For a long time, she sat engrossed in her art, and then something distracted her.

There was a noise in the vacant garden space ahead of her, which was overgrown, with many bushes. No one, except stray animals, visited there anymore, and there was the fear of snakes too. Meenakshi stood up and looked. But when her scrutiny yielded nothing, she went back to her leaf carving.

It happened again. This time it was a definitive crash, like someone was trying to break something. The leaf still in her hand, she walked with measured steps to the corner. Everything was silent now, even the chirping of the morning birds, as she entered this untrespassed spot of the garden with great care and caution.

Meenakshi looked furtively for the source of the crash. Perhaps a dog or a cat had strayed and had fallen from a tree branch and was now stuck in the bushes. Perhaps it was struggling for its freedom. That thought pained her and she began to look more closely.

Then she saw it.

It was not an *it*, though. There was a man crouching in the bushes.

Backing off several steps, Meenakshi let out a gasp.

The man stood upright, and in a swift reflex, she shut her eyes. The man was stark naked and completely unbothered by that fact. He hid nothing; he flaunted nothing. He just stood there in the form nature had given him.

She opened her mouth to scream, but something told her she must not.

This was the first time that she was seeing a grown man naked. It scared her. She shut her eyes and tried her best not to look. It was small mercy when the man stepped back into the bushes and the leaves covered his privates. That was when she looked at the rest of him, not scared anymore, and then was struck by how handsome he was.

His hair, a shade of burnished brown, fell like waves over his shoulders, which were like two blocks of the finest marble ever crafted. His chest was flat like a slab of the same marble, with chiselled grooves in all the right places, and from the sides rose a pair of the finest arms she had laid eyes on, well-sculpted manly arms that could make a graceful dancing mudra or even pull an entire bullock cart if it came to that.

She dared to look at his face, and, quite surprisingly, it was a kind face with a welcoming smile on it. That smile, contained within such perfect jaws, could not belong to any earthly man. And the eyes were the colour of a summer river; the longer she looked into them, the more she felt like she was slipping away somewhere.

Unknown to herself, she stepped closer to the man.

'Don't! Stop!' he said.

Meenakshi stopped. 'Who are you?' she asked.

'I have come to meet you.'

'But who are—'

'I am Kritaveer. Call me Krita,' he said in a firm voice that was both authoritative and friendly. 'I am your friend. You are becoming a woman now, and I need to tell you that I am here for you and you should not worry.'

As if released from a stupor, Meenakshi said, '*What* are you?'

'What I am and what you are—these are questions whose answers will be revealed in due course of time. Right now, let it suffice that I come from a faraway place, and you do not belong here either. This, your earthly life in the body of this girl, is your cage, your prison.'

Something told Meenakshi that the man was not talking to her now. His kind eyes were looking at her body, and his compassionate words were falling on her ears, but the person he was addressing was not her.

'I think you know a few things,' Meenakshi said. 'Why are these things happening to me? Everyone thinks I am a freak. My mother, my father, my sisters—'

'They don't matter,' said the naked man. 'They are people of this world, limited by their ignorance and arrogance. You are trapped inside the body of this girl, and until you are released you will remain who you are. You are cursed to grow with this girl.'

'Cursed?'

'Yes, you have forgotten where you come from. That is part of the curse. But you will remember. Until then, you will be inside this girl, Meenakshi.'

Dawn broke, and Meenakshi had an acute realization—she was not alone. There was someone inside her. She had felt it for long; she had heard those voices all around her. But now she knew those voices were not *around* her; they were *within* her. They had been speaking to her; now she *knew*. And now, that someone was struggling to get out, trying to claw at her from inside and emerge from her body.

The words that came out of her mouth were not hers.

'I am alone. No one understands me here.'

'Don't worry,' said Krita and smiled again, a smile that sent a ripple through her heart. 'There are many companions here to help you complete your human birth. The humans here do not know who you are. That's how it is meant to be.'

'Who are these companions?'

'There are many,' Krita's face lit up. 'I am one. I will come when you really need me. But even if I am not there, there's always another you can bank on.'

At that, Krita turned to look behind her, and Meenakshi realized he was looking at the sal tree.

'*Companion?*'

'So you know it already,' said Krita. 'Nature is your friend. Trees, birds, animals, they are your helpers.'

Meenakshi nodded.

'But I will not fool you. After the calm comes a storm. A storm has to come in your life too, a terrible tragedy, or perhaps a spate of them, and you have to face them. That's part of the punishment.'

'*Punishment?* Why am I being punished?'

'That's not for me to say now. You will know.'

The man then disappeared; his job was accomplished. Gasping, Meenakshi found that she had broken into a sweat that was now pooling in various regions of her body.

When she could breathe again, she realized she still had something in her hand, and her fingers ached. She raised her hand to see what it was, and she saw the leaf.

The carving was now done; her fingers had moved by themselves. In the mesh around the veins of the leaf, she could see a hazy shape of a proud figure, staring haughtily at her.

It gave her quite a start—this was the fat man engraved on the coins.

7

Festival of Snakes

A week later, Suparna took Meenakshi and Kumud to visit the snake charmers' jatra, on the occasion of Nag Panchami, at the nearby village of Battis Shirala. Suparna had taken it upon herself to convince her parents to take her younger sisters along, and they were now her responsibility.

The village of Battis Shirala was populated by families who had been snake charmers for generations. Every year, in the prelude to Nag Panchami, the festival of the Snake God, these families made a beeline to the Goddess Ambabai temple to partake in an interesting tradition. They were each given a flower, which was to be placed on the head of the Goddess' idol. If the flower fell to the right, then that family earned the privilege of catching and nurturing a snake and presenting it in the grand procession that year. This was a noble responsibility that brought the family a significant amount of social repute.

The procession had begun when the Patil girls reached the village.

The snakes, well-fed and worshipped by their families, were being led into the procession. Colours and music rent the atmosphere; songs from Hindi and Marathi movies blared on loudspeakers. People dressed in their finest clothes danced to the tunes in the middle of the road, ahead of the snake exhibits that rolled out on vehicles. Along the sides of the road were stalls selling trinkets and edibles for the crazed revellers, making the whole show quite carnivalesque.

Meenakshi craned her neck to see the first snake that she could spot, a common krait. It was led by a family and followed by a dozen other people. The men of the family opened the basket and the snake hissed, waiting for the right opportunity to strike.

A boy from the family flashed an orange cloth in front of the krait. That sudden change in its environment unnerved the reptile and it darted its head in every direction and lashed precariously close to the boy who easily sidestepped it.

The audience clapped and cheered. A folk song blared from a loudspeaker attached to a tempo which moved ahead of the crowd.

'Come on, Meenu, let's have that candyfloss!'

Meenakshi turned her head away from the snake and looked at Suparna pointing at a cart by the roadside, where a lady was sitting with several of the pink stringy sweets.

'Yes, let's!' said Kumud.

'You two go,' said Meenakshi. 'I don't want it.'

'Sure?' said Suparna. 'I want to see those bangles too.'

'Yes. You go. I'll be here.'

The sisters scrammed, leaving Meenakshi to enjoy the show. Snakes were much more fascinating than stupid bangles and candyfloss anyway.

Meenakshi saw a vast array of snakes—kraits and vipers and rat snakes, each of them more menacing than the other. Every time a snake lunged, there was deafening applause, and the family would puff up in pride for having climbed another notch in their social standing.

Then, in the distance, a crowd erupted in a loud cheer. This was followed by an explosion of colours and music that increased in volume till the zestful strains of that live band—from drums and trumpets to tambourines—overtook every other sound. Meenakshi craned her neck to see. It was a large open truck, its front painted red and orange, a group of young men and women dancing ahead of it with total abandon. A banner proclaiming Nag Devta Mitra Mandal shone amidst dancing lights. The other snakes paled in comparison, for the showstopper had arrived. Someone splashed colours on the dancers. Young boys took their shirts off and danced, and women laughed merrily, but no one stopped or paused. As the procession inched its way towards Meenakshi, the number of revellers swelled up and the music reached such a crescendo that she could not hear her own mind.

Almost clapping now, just like the others in the crowd, Meenakshi stood on her toes to get a better view.

There were men ahead of her and behind her, and all of them were trying to look at one thing, everyone practically trying to climb over each other in their quest.

Meenakshi did not mind the men touching her. In a place like this, pushing and pulling and jostling was expected.

A man climbed up on the roof of the truck and announced on a mike, 'Folks, here's what you have been waiting for! Nag Devta Mitra Mandal brings to you our beloved Snake God. Cheer loudly for the family who has brought him to us this year—the Gorse family, the pride of Battis Shirala. Back off now, and feast your eyes, as we show you the king of snakes—the king cobra.'

There were sighs and gasps, and people cheered loud enough to puncture eardrums.

The show was about to begin.

A man with a white stubble, evidently the head of the Gorse family, came to the front of the truck. On his forehead were various marks of devotion. Another man, a younger one, brought out a round earthen pot whose mouth was covered with a smaller pot. Everyone held their breath as he placed the pots on the floor of the truck. There was dead silence now; even the music stopped.

The Gorse patriarch bowed low and joined his hands in reverent worship to appease the Snake God who was in the pot. Standing in that crowd, Meenakshi's heart began to thump. This would be the first time she would see a cobra—a well-appeased, well-fed cobra at that.

The younger man moved in, and as cautiously as he could, raised the smaller pot.

Hearts were on the verge of stopping at this point.

Thence arose the king cobra, first bringing his majestic head out of the pot, glistening black and brown all over except for the white bands across his neck. He came out without fear, with a sense of monarchical pride, and lashed his forked tongue out. The tiny beads that were his eyes darted all around, and his head swayed on all sides.

'God! God is here!' chanted Gorse. There were tears in his eyes. 'Bless us.'

Gorse undid a red cloth that was tied around his waist. It was a slow, calculated movement. His eyes were on the snake at all times. He took the cloth in his hand, bent defiantly close to the snake, and swept it gently along his body.

That did it. The snake raised his head again, and the next instant, his glorious hood went up.

The crowd burst into a tumult. Some of them started to dance, but Gorse gruffly warned, 'People, be quiet. Do not excite the Snake God.'

But the Snake God *was* excited. Gorse led him on with his cloth, flashing it here and there, making him turn his hood in confusion at the people standing on all sides.

Standing ahead of the crowd, Meenakshi suddenly began to feel dizzy. She had been staring too long at the swaying snake's head and did not realize when the crowd went from awe to frenzy.

The men suddenly seemed to be closing in on her, their breathing very prominent. She tried to look at the snake's hood and the proud gleaming face of Gorse as he led the snake, but something was changing within her. She felt it—it was the throbbing under her skin that had begun to scare her these days.

The breathing of one man in particular stood out. It hit right into her ear.

'Look behind you, fool!'

There it was again—that voice from inside her. It stilled her heart.

She realized she was pinned against someone.

The man right behind her was touching her. She was scared

to look, but she felt his grubby hand on her waist now. Creeping. Crawling. How oblivious she had been! Blame it on the crowd or the show, but she hadn't realized it until she had been warned by her inner voice.

But now she knew. It was happening, and then she felt that man's erection pressing into her buttocks. She looked back and saw his grinning teeth, and a whiff of his bad breath ran up her nose. He nodded and winked at her, as if to say—*You are enjoying it too, aren't you?*

'*The bastard...*'

No, she did not say that! It was the voice, the voice.

'*You stay put, Meenakshi. I will take care of this.*'

The next moment, she felt a tingling in her fingers.

She could still see the swaying hood of the snake at a distance. Gorse had found his groove now; he was dancing in front of the reptile. There were others on the floor of the truck, people from his family, and they took turns in taming the animal.

And then the music began to play.

Meenakshi could not breathe. The man's hand had moved upward, having gone from her waist to her breast.

Her fingers! They were throbbing now. Moving on their own. They felt heavy, scabby. She felt the skin of her hands becoming taut, stretching, threatening to crack. She looked down at her fingers and was horrified.

This was not her. This dark clammy skin, these popping fingernails...these were not her hands!

She was still looking at her hands when a shout passed through the crowd. The loudspeaker blared, 'MOVE ASIDE!'

Meenakshi turned to look at the truck, and she ducked just in the nick of time.

She barely escaped the king cobra, who had ejected himself from his pot like an arrow shot from a bow.

Even as she fell, she saw the fangs of the cobra jutting out from his mouth, and she saw them cutting an arc in the sky above her and clamping right into the chest of the man who had been molesting her.

The man collapsed instantly. He began to quiver even before he could reach the ground. His arms stiffened as if he was trying to fight something, and then they fell loose.

Forever.

White foam streamed out of his mouth and spread in the mud.

Meenakshi looked aghast and then felt something soft touch her feet. It was the cobra, now nestling comfortably between her feet, looking as harmless as if he were her pet snake.

'The man is dead!' someone yelled into the stunned silence. 'THE MAN IS DEAD!'

❦

Suparna and Kumud came rushing to the spot to find Meenakshi being accosted by a group of irate people.

'Why was the snake at your feet?' a woman asked, her face inches away from Meenakshi's.

'What kind of sorcery is this?' said the younger Gorse. 'This has never happened before. What did you do to our Nagoba?'

Nagoba was safely in his earthen confinement now, definitely not pleased. The pot shivered with furious thudding sounds, the sounds of an angry hood beating against its insides.

'I didn't do anything!'

'Don't tell us that,' said the woman. 'We have been taming snakes for centuries. This has never happened. Snakes have never flown out like that. A flying snake! Who can believe it?'

'Where are your parents, girl?' asked Gorse.

Her sisters, who had come up now, looked on helplessly. Especially Suparna, for she had brought Meenakshi there at her own risk.

Then Meenakshi unfroze. Suddenly, she appeared to be taller. The townsfolk gasped, and this time they did so even more loudly than they had done when the king cobra had been unveiled.

For there was an unmistakable glow in the girl's eyes. Something was glinting there, sparkling, like those eyes could think on their own. She wasn't the same anymore, and didn't look like a sweet girl in a strange town. It was as if she belonged there; no, it was as if she owned the place.

Suparna's mouth fell open. Kumud began to sob. Everyone took two steps back.

'I am not of this town,' said Meenakshi. Her voice was different too. Older, more daunting. 'Now I am going to turn around and leave. Whoever tries to stop me now will do so at his own risk.'

She took a step forward, towards her sisters. Without a word the people parted, and a gulf opened up between them.

'Come, Tai,' said Meenakshi, grabbing Suparna's hand, who instantly felt the warmth in it.

They picked up a now-disconsolate Kumud on the way and walked forth. All eyes were on them, and slowly the people broke into whispers.

Meenakshi reached the end of the crowd before she turned again, and this time she looked at the man lying dead on his back.

Then she turned away and made her way out.

8

The Night Visitor

*I*f Meenakshi had been a stranger to her sisters until that day, she became an alien now, a species they could not fathom. Kumud was too scared to recount the events of Battis Shirala to their parents. Even Suparna did not talk about it. But they gossiped about it to the other sisters. Meenakshi felt her sisters' eyes following her wherever she went, and there were whispers that stopped as soon as she came within earshot. With time, the sisters stopped inviting her to the things they did together. With a feeling of dread, Meenakshi realized that she was being ostracized in her own home.

A few mornings later, Meenakshi was sitting beneath the sal, comforted by its shade. Her game involved digging up earthworms and placing them on large leaves. The worms had no fear of her; they climbed right up on her arms. Their clumsy, slimy gait tickled her and lifted her spirits.

She became aware of her mother's shadow creeping up on her. 'Meenu, what are you doing here?' she said.

'Just playing.'

Renuka sat down beside her. 'Meenu, we haven't talked in days. How are you, girl?'

'I am well, Aai.'

'I don't think so. You have changed since you came back from Battis Shirala. Did something happen there?'

'Nothing, Aai!' Meenakshi went back to playing with her earthworms. 'You people worry a lot!' she mumbled.

Renuka let out a laboured breath. 'Look, Meenu, it was a wrong decision to let you go there. Anyway, you are not going anywhere now.'

'Okay.'

'I just hope it's not something like what happened with Tappu,' said Renuka.

'What has that got to do with me?'

'I really hope it has nothing to do with you.'

❦

That night, Meenakshi overheard her parents again. After her sisters had gone to sleep, Meenakshi went into the garden, and pressed her ear against the wooden window of her parents' bedroom, which didn't close all the way.

'So, what will you tell him now?'

It was her mother's concerned voice.

'I don't know. It's only a matter of time before he comes here again,' said Shantaram.

'Oh, that should not happen.'

'It will. You haven't seen him recently. He's desperate, raving like a lunatic.'

Meenakshi moved closer, trying to hear their words better so that they made sense to her.

'It's not right,' said Renuka.

Shantaram did not answer immediately, and in that brief moment of silence, Meenakshi's pulse went racing.

'Don't tell me you are considering it,' said Renuka.

'Of course not,' said Shantaram finally. 'What do you think? Am I a monster to give up my girl to a grown man? That's not going to happen. I won't stand for it. I will deal with that fool if he lands up here again.'

Meenakshi smiled, but it was laced with worry. Her juvenile mind put two and two together. They were talking of the suitor who had asked for her over her sister. She forced herself to recall his face, but it just wouldn't come to her. And what was his name? Hariram. No, Harikumar. Yes, that was it.

She felt proud of her father for standing up for her. It was not like child marriages didn't happen in the village. Just last year, her friend Lata had disappeared. People were told that she had been sent to her aunt's house to study. But everyone knew she had no aunt. They knew she was now in Sangli, living in her husband's house, a rich middle-aged landlord.

She saw this frail man—her father—in a new light now. But more than that, she was relieved. Relieved that she was not being dumped on another man. For she did not know what the demoness living inside her would do to the next man who came into her life.

❦

'Shh…hey, Meenu…'

Meenakshi turned around.

She was still outside the window, standing in complete darkness, with only the moon shining overhead. The lights of a few neighbouring houses were still on, but it was long past dinnertime.

There was no one moving about. The sal tree was on the other side of the garden, and Meenakshi could see it swaying lightly in the night breeze, but she knew it could not speak to her, at least not in the way humans did.

'Here, Meenu…'

This time she caught the direction of the voice. She saw a figure jump off the wall and land in the bushes below.

She recognized him only when he came closer to her.

'*Govind?* What are you doing here?'

There was a sheepish grin on his face. 'Shh…don't be so loud. I just saw you from the fence and came over.'

'You get out now. My Baba is right in there.'

'He won't come out. He sleeps at this time.'

'How do you know? Have you been keeping an eye on my house?'

'No, Meenu. Only you.'

Meenakshi was thunderstruck. That sick feeling crept up inside her again. That loathsome grin, that lustful look, that fidgeting with the body…

'Get out now, or I will scream.'

'No, you won't!' He clamped his hand on her mouth.

She struggled, but was no match for his might.

With shocking ease, he shoved her against a sturdy palm tree and pinned her hands behind her back.

'I know what you did with Tappu,' he spewed. 'But he's an idiot. Got himself paralysed. All this that you have…was too much for him.'

Govind was unrestrained now. A carnivore who had smelled blood. His eyes lingered on her body like he'd devour her that very instant.

Meenakshi screamed, but the sound died somewhere behind the wall of his sturdy, tobacco-stinking fingers.

'None of the women I have been with had a body like yours,' he said. 'What do you eat, girl? Why are you so…so yummy? You drive men to sin, you…temptress!'

She bit his hand. He laughed.

'Sorry, but I am not normally like this. Women love me. Why don't you? Why won't you have some fun with me? Who will know?'

Meenakshi shook her head vigorously. Stray words fell out of her mouth.

'You…don't know…what will happen…'

'Bah!' he said with lustful twinkles in his eyes. 'Real men don't think of what will happen. Come, let me make a woman out of you. Trust me, you will enjoy it.'

Meenakshi saw the zipper open and shut her eyes.

Looking at the sal tree, which was just beyond her, she mumbled a prayer. 'O Companion…do something…'

And her Companion did not let her down.

The tingling began in her fingers. Even as they were clasped in his grip behind her back, she felt the blood begin to bubble underneath the surface of her skin. Her fingers went warm, and she felt them throb like they had never done before.

Perhaps he felt them too. His grip on her loosened.

'What are you doing? Stay calm. Just having fun.'

She could not see them, but she was sure her fingernails were growing. She could feel that searing, burning pain in her fingertips. Like someone was poking the flesh under the nails with a cutter blade, but from within.

She knew that from beneath her nails new cuticles were sprouting forth. What was inside her wouldn't stay inside anymore.

'Step back now. This one is mine.'

The voice had spoken. Meenakshi lost control of herself.

❦

Govind was smelling her hair, with his front pressing on her with all his force, when his nose felt the matted spot on her neck.

He moved back. 'What is this? Do you have some skin prob—'

But his words died midway. He had just opened his eyes and what he saw curdled his blood.

He had a glimpse of those eyes—those blazing red orbs—that were now staring back at him. Below them, the lips that he meant to bite on were now puffed and fleshy, reminding him of the tumescent protuberances on his cancer-afflicted grandmother's body.

'Meenakshi, relax. He won't be able to harm you.'

The voice dissolved in a grunt, and then there was a jab and a wet squelch.

Meenakshi looked with horror at what she had done—at what SHE had done—and screamed.

The searing cut was on his groin. A bleeding tear that had slashed him from one end to the other.

'Oh no oh no oh no...' he said, unable to even scream, as he saw the gash widening and blood beginning to spill out. 'DAMN! BITCH! What did you do?'

The girl was beyond hearing anything now. She stood like a colossus, her neck as thick as the trunk of the tree behind her, her arms hanging downward like drooping boughs. Her waist had grown considerably, with a belly the size of a large water pot, and ended at a navel that stuck out, the size of an onion. Her clothes were tatters on the ground now, and the hair in her armpits and over her nipples looked like smears of cattle dung. And then he saw the vagina—a slimy mound of loose-hanging flesh, a death trap for anything that might dare to enter it.

'Who...who are you?' he stuttered.

It was too late. Govind, the young man who had climbed over the fence for a quick round of excitement, would never get any answers anymore.

As his innards spilled out of him, he flopped, and then keeled over and fell, right at the feet of the thing that was, at times, a young girl named Meenakshi.

9

The Deal

*I*t was dawn when Meenakshi woke up and found her clothes in tatters under the palm tree. Scenes of the previous night reappeared in her groggy memory and the remnant shreds of sleep vanished.

That boy! He had jumped over the wall. And...?

'You don't remember, Meenakshi?'

Quick as a flash, she sat up. Her heart went into its wild thumping mode once again.

What had she done to the boy?

A stray dog came up to her, sniffed at her eagerly and scooted into a clump of bushes outside the kitchen wall. Meenakshi turned to see what was happening, and froze. There it was—a huge ugly swathe of blood.

'Oh my God...' she muttered breathlessly.

Her steps turned to the red blotch.

There it was! *There!* Just as she had feared. Something welled up inside her. She retched up a stream of vomit in the bushes.

He was dead in the bushes; lying on his back. The eyes, like stones, staring vacantly into the space above. The mouth, open, with the sneer still on it. Flies buzzed around his midsection, where the blood came from, attracted to something pink and fleshy. Meenakshi squinted to see what it was and puked again. A portion of his colon was jutting out of the fatal wound.

A wound that she had inflicted.

'You should be pleased.'

Meenakshi twitched.

'Aren't you?'

She beat her chest. But that detestable nagging voice wouldn't stop.

'What wouldn't a woman give to be able to put an end to bastards like this one? Didn't you enjoy tearing apart the belly of the man who tried to force himself on you?'

'Shut up! *Shut up!* SHUT UP!'

Suddenly, Meenakshi was warm and sticky all over. She looked down at herself.

There it was. Right there, glistening crimson in the light of the recently risen sun.

Blood. *His* blood.

'Don't weep, you fool, this blood is of an evil—'

A rooster crowed, cutting off the voice. Meenakshi was nothing more than a teenager now—unsure, fearful. This was not her fault. But there would be questions. Blame. Reprimands. Punishments. What would she say? What *could* she say? She went numb. All processes within her stopped, and there was a blank white space in front of her eyes, a white space that told her nothing, suggested nothing.

But something *had* to be done. Fisherwomen used this garden route as a shortcut to reach the other houses to sell their fish. Why, someone might be coming up the path even at this very moment!

'Tell me, what do I do with this body now? Did you think of that?'

There was silence.

'Speak now, you murderess, you who says will put an end to my troubles.'

She saw the sal. It was rustling, calling her. She ran to it, her naked feet falling on twigs and getting scratched and pierced and cut, but she ran, and hugged the tree till she felt the warmth of its huge brown bark.

And then she turned her head and saw the pit.

The pit.

That dung hole had always been in the garden.

But she did not see it as a pit now; she saw in it the hope she needed. The green spot on her white space.

She ran crazily along the length of the garden, praying that the pit would be suitable for her purpose.

It was just a step away from the patch where the naked man had appeared that day, the desolate unused corner of the garden. Only, right now the place did not smell of manly scent as it had done that day. Right now, it smelled of…

…Shit.

Literally. The hole was filled with refuse and dung and manure from the farms, and she recalled her father telling her that it was a compost pit. A *compost* pit. *Fertilizer.*

This was perfect! What better place to return a body to its elements than a pit that is built for that express purpose?

Without losing another moment, Meenakshi ran up to the dead boy and grabbed him at his ankles.

He was too heavy for her, and for a whole minute she just tried to get the right grip on him. She grunted and tried again, and that stray dog came again to look. But the corpse wouldn't move, and then—

'What would you do without me? Here!'

Just like that, she felt the strength surging into her arms. They were still the same, soft teenage arms, but she felt the added strength in them.

The corpse moved effortlessly this time.

Minutes later, the hapless corpse was in the bubbling compost pit. It went in bit by bit, that jutting intestine going in last. As the bubbles rose—the sign of a zillion bacteria getting excited and ready to consume this feast—she smiled. Her father had told her that bubbles meant decomposition. In a few days, nothing would be as it was now.

Leaving the body to the care of the bubbling methane, Meenakshi went up to the well in the garden and washed herself. Then, praying that no one in the house was astir yet, she ran up to her room and pretended to sleep.

Later, when she went to look, there was no sign or shred of him. From within, she heard the voice:

'His ass is grass.'

'Literally!' said Meenakshi, and laughed.

❦

With school being out of bounds for her, Meenakshi's folks stopped waking her up at all, and she continued to sleep much beyond her usual time. Her sisters dressed up and left for their schools and colleges, no one as much as turning to look at her sleeping, much less wondering why she wasn't going with them. Only Suparna went on two occasions and nudged her, but Meenakshi pulled the sheet over her head and slept till it was almost lunchtime.

A few days later, she woke up at noon with her mind blank, bereft of any thoughts. Renuka went up to her and said, 'Woke up at last? Your sleep is getting longer and longer these days.'

Meenakshi yawned and stood up.

'Wait…where are you going?'

'To the well to wash.'

'Okay. Get dressed soon.'

Something pinched Meenakshi's heart. 'Why?'

'We are going to have a guest shortly.'

Meenakshi wanted to ask who, but she knew ignorance was bliss. Turning on her heel, she began to walk away.

'You won't ask who?'

She turned again. 'Okay. Who?'

'You remember Harikumar?'

Meenakshi's heart stilled. 'Why is he coming here?'

'To talk about you.'

There was a look of concern on Renuka's face even as she said that. Meenakshi welcomed the frown; it told her that her mother wasn't entirely happy about it either. But she felt the jab in her heart nevertheless.

'What is there to talk?'

'Your Baba knows.'

Meenakshi silently walked up to the well and washed. All the way, she thought of various things that could have gone wrong. She recalled the look of resolve on her father's face. She remembered feeling proud of him, of the fact that her father wouldn't just give her away to some man.

She rushed to the kitchen and accosted her mother.

'Aai, why is that man coming to talk about me?'

Renuka took her girl's face in her hands. 'Meenu, you know you are my most sensible daughter, right?'

Meenakshi brushed away the platitude. 'Why?'

Renuka's tone changed. 'Meenu, let me tell you the truth. I am proud of you. Both your Baba and I are. There is something special in you, but you are our girl, and we will do what's best for you. It's as simple as that.'

Tears pooled in Meenakshi's eyes but they refused to spill over. 'What went wrong, Aai? From a few nights ago to now, what went wrong?'

'Which night?'

'I overheard you and Baba. Weren't you speaking about that man Harikumar?'

'Shh…you mustn't take his name.'

'Why?' Meenakshi screamed. 'He's not my husband.'

'Quiet, Meenu. He's not your husband now. But who knows what lies in store?'

'Why are you even talking to him, Aai? Why open this thing up? I don't—'

'MEENU!' Renuka shouted now, the only way she knew to end discussions with her daughters. 'We are your Aai-Baba. We will never do anything wrong by you. When the entire village was going on and on about how we had only daughters and no son, we scoffed at them. We are proud of our seven girls. We are not like the other families in this village that are marrying their daughters off at ten and twelve. We won't do that. We won't send you away with *any* man. I don't know why I even told you that he's coming. Forget it!'

'Fine,' Meenakshi huffed. 'You people talk to him then. Don't call me to see him.'

❦

Meenakshi had no intention of seeing any man in the world ever. At this moment, she even hated the man with the brown locks, that Krita. They were all the same, all vultures trying to pounce on female flesh.

She decided to sit quietly under the sal tree, and respond to no one.

But when the gate squeaked open that afternoon, teatime for most families, she could not throttle her curiosity.

Nimbly she came out of her sulking and tiptoed around the walls of the house to take a look at the man again.

'Why are you even going to look?'

'You be quiet!' she said in an angry whisper. 'Just want to recall his face, that's all.'

Staying hidden behind the last bend of the wall, Meenakshi cocked her head to get a better look. The boughs of the sarsaparilla kept her concealed, but she had a fair view.

Yes, he was the same man—that clean face and those sympathetic eyes—but he looked different now. All his slick hair was gone. He was also thinner. The gauntness suited him better.

Harikumar stood at the gate and looked around, and for a brief moment Meenakshi felt that he had spotted her, but then her father came out to greet him.

'Come in, Harikumar. Tea awaits us.'

'Thank you, sir. Thank you for agreeing to see me.'

The gratitude was genuine. The handshake was firm. The handshake of two men who have signed a secret pact.

'What is going on here?'

Meenakshi put a finger on her lips to silence the voice. As if that could happen.

She edged closer to the walls to listen to the conversation. She heard her mother come out, offer her condolences, and sit down to join the men.

'I don't see Meenakshi,' said Harikumar. 'Is she not at home?'

'No,' said Renuka with a misplaced laugh.

'Oh. I thought she'd be—'

'Lusty bastard.'

'It's okay,' said Shantaram. 'It's adult talk we are having here. It's good that *children* are not around.' The subtext in that was so thick it hung in the air.

Renuka said, 'Look, son, we know why you are here. We have talked about it long and hard, and we think you must leave for your city. You have nothing to gain here, at least not what you are asking for. You know Meenu's age and we cannot marry her off. Let me repeat what my husband must have told you a hundred times—we will gladly marry our daughter Manda with you. You have seen how beautiful she is, and she goes to college. She is perfect for you.'

Harikumar smiled. 'Madam, if it was about Manda, wouldn't we have been married already? I'd probably be treating you like my parents and serving you in my huge house in Bombay already.'

'You are being irrational,' said Shantaram with an edge in his voice. 'Do you even know that marrying an underage girl is illegal?'

'Sir, if I have your permission, I will take care of the legal aspects. All that you have to decide is whether you agree to give me Meenakshi as my bride. And, madam, let me tell you this. It cannot be any of your other daughters. In fact, if I don't marry Meenakshi, I won't marry anyone else ever. That's a vow I take.'

'Oh, my dazed stars! What a fucking fool!'

Meenakshi was stunned. The bough of the sarsaparilla seemed to close in upon her. Here was a man taking a vow for her. She was too naïve to understand the implications of it, but she knew what vows meant. She had read of Bheeshma's unbroken vow in the Mahabharata. But this shocked her. She did not deserve this. She thought of running up to the man and beating him up for the awkward situation he was putting her parents in.

'*What a sucker! What a fool!*'

'Shut up, shut up!' Meenakshi breathed.

'Are you out of your mind?' said Shantaram. 'We agreed to meet you because we thought we could drive some sense into your brain, as you don't have any elders to guide you. But this is preposterous.'

'Preposterous?' said Harikumar as politely as he could. He reached into his briefcase and produced a bundle of papers. 'Look at this and tell me if it is preposterous.'

'What is this?'

Shantaram picked up the papers and unfolded them. It did not take him long to understand what they were.

'Oh God!' he exclaimed. 'This is clear proof that you are mad.'

'What is it?' asked Renuka.

'These are his property papers. Of his house in Bombay. It's a property of...how much...'

'Forty-three lakhs,' said Harikumar. 'And it is yours. Just give me Meenakshi.'

Shantaram slapped his head. His fist rolled up and it seemed like he'd sock the obstinate man's jaw, but then the fist uncurled. The hackles went down.

'Son...this is unimaginable...'

'What is, sir? This is only a small proof of how much I love your daughter. I will have no one else. Usually girls pay dowry. Here, I am. Why is that wrong?'

'Where will you keep her?' asked Shantaram. 'I mean, even if—'

'Don't worry about that, sir. This is only one of my three houses in the city. She'll be a queen.'

'Your business pays you so much?'

'It's a family business. My wealth is not just mine; it has been built by three generations before me,' said Harikumar.

Meenakshi could imagine her father's brain-wheels turning. She did not know numbers, but this was a lot of money. One night she had heard her father tell her mother about all their assets, and they were not even close. But this was her father. She believed in him. Any lesser man...

But there was also doubt.

Would her life be traded away just like that? Hadn't Lata's father loved her a lot too?

She could not hide herself any longer. 'Baba, no...' she said, emerging from the bush, tears clouding her eyes.

'Oh, there you are, Meenakshi,' Harikumar stood up, overjoyed. 'You don't know how desp—'

'Stop there, son!' Shantaram arrested his progress. 'I am too small a man and this is too big a sum. We have to think. You must leave now.'

'Okay, sir! I will leave,' said Harikumar in all politeness. But there was a smile of contentment on his face, the smile that only comes to someone who knows everything is going according to plan. That smile scared Meenakshi.

As he walked to the gate, he stopped for a brief moment next to Meenakshi. He reached out and wiped away her tears. 'I am not a bad man, you know,' he said. 'Think it over. We could have a great life together.'

Shantaram took a step forward. Harikumar walked out of the gate.

❧

Renuka rushed ahead and held her girl by her shoulders.

'Meenu, we are here for you,' she said.

They lie. Trust no one.

Meenakshi brushed her mother away and turned to face her father. 'Baba? You too? What did you tell that man? Will you give me away, Baba? Say something, Baba!'

Shantaram sat down, his head lowered, his mind far away now, adrift in thoughts that the little girl would not understand.

'You were against this,' said Meenakshi. 'What changed then?

I see. He made an offer.'

'It's not like that, Meenu,' said Shantaram.

'But *you* called him here. You are entertaining him with tea and talks and...'

'Renu, please take her away.' Shantaram pressed his temples with his fingers. 'I see a migraine coming.'

Renuka grabbed Meenakshi's arm. 'Come on, Meenu. Let your Baba rest.'

'It's all about money, I know!' Meenakshi jerked her mother's hand off with such force that it swung all the way to the back. 'That's all that matters now. That's all—'

'Good, Meenakshi, good. Tell them off.'

She fell silent for a moment, and then she frowned again. 'Is it? Is it all about the money? In that case, wait...'

'NO! I know what you are thinking. I forbid it.'

Ignoring that voice and leaving her parents looking at her in puzzlement, she turned and ran into the house. She ran all along the corridor on the sandstone, and then paced up the stairs. She went to the farthest corner of that corridor and climbed the stairs to the loft.

The loft was only high enough for her to stoop and walk. Its musty smell marked it differently from the rest of the house. There were cobwebs all around, and even as she entered, her feet traced prints in the soft dust that had gathered on the floor.

The girls had been forbidden to enter the loft, and none of the others did out of sheer fear anyway, but Meenakshi had a little secret here. *Her* little secret.

'I forbid it, Meenakshi. Smother the thought!'

She crossed the length of the loft and came to its farthest corner. Here, in a worn-out iron trunk, was her secret.

She went down on her haunches and, heaving, she threw open the lid of the trunk.

All at once, the loft was illuminated.

In the trunk were dozens and dozens of gold coins, now

glittering, shining, moving as if they were alive.

This was her collection, gifted to her by the sal, one each on many mornings, and she had carefully preserved them here. She knew they were valuable but had no idea what their value was. Yet, she knew instinctively they must be kept carefully for the right time. Perhaps the time had come.

She took one of them in her hand and looked at it. It had an imprint of the sun on one of its faces. Other coins had waves and the moon and elephants on them.

She turned it over. This other side, like all the other coins, had the mysterious fat man's face on it.

'Don't, Meenakshi!'

She had no idea how many of them would be forty-three lakhs' worth. She scooped up as many as possible, but then abruptly stopped and took her hands out of the chest.

Something was happening below. A loud shout stilled her heart. Then there were more shouts, and in that moment, she knew something terrible was going to happen.

10

The Blue Slipper

$\mathcal{M}$eenakshi stood by the dust-stained window of the loft, looking down. It was a crowd of people, around a dozen, entering the garden through the little iron gate, which protested with its usual hellish squeak. Men and women walking in without niceties. No smiles on their faces. Two of the men even carried stout lathis.

A sense of foreboding gripped her. Then she saw the person at the head of the crowd and lost her footing.

It was Govind's mother, who was an influential doctor with a private practice in the village. The board outside her clinic proclaimed her name—Dr (Mrs) Vilas Jamblekar—embossed in a sans serif font with a string of degrees under it.

The doctor stormed into the house with her white apron still on, as if she needed to remind people of her profession. Behind her stood a trembling Savitri Namdar, Tappu's mother.

'Shantaram bhau,' Dr Jamblekar began, 'my son has not returned home in five days. We have looked for him everywhere and now his friend says that he saw him near your house the evening he went missing.'

Renuka stepped forward before her husband could reply. 'Doctor bai, we haven't seen Govind at all. He's missing? What happened?' She said that with clenched teeth and in quick words even as the memory of Govind accosting Meenakshi on the street invaded her mind again.

'Why will his friend lie?' said Dr Jamblekar. 'This was the last place where he was seen.'

'Agga Doctor bai, what does that mean?' Renuka's voice rose. 'Are you implying that we are hiding him?'

An older man from the crowd spoke up. 'It's not like that, Patil bai. We are just frustrated. Not finding him anywhere. Just got a tip that he might have come here. Would you mind if we looked? Yours is a large garden.'

'Well, look all you want!' said Shantaram, stopping Renuka from saying anything further by raising his hand. 'Go in the house, courtyard, garden, anywhere. We are right here.'

The crowd dispersed. The women marched into the house while the men scattered to various corners of the garden. Meenakshi looked nervously from the loft's window. The scenes were playing out in her mind now—Govind straddling the fence and then jumping in. Walking up to her. Smiling with his lustful eyes. Unzipping his pants and…

…after that, it was a blank.

Until the next morning, when she had—

'Don't worry. They won't find anything.'

Meenakshi did not reply. She was too numb.

Her eyes followed the men as they looked in the garden. Some looked in the well and behind the trees. Meenakshi's heart sank when one of them thumped wildly on the bark of the sal tree. Several leaves fell, and she could hear the tree groaning in agony. The men with the lathis walked up to the corner of the garden near the compost pit and her breath quickened in panic.

'Don't worry. Humans are blind. They cannot see what's right in front of them.'

The man who went to the pit pinched his nose. He said something to another man, and they laughed. They circled round the pit, and one of them, seeing that no one else was around, went and pissed in a corner. Then they walked away.

'I told you so.'

'Shut up!' Meenakshi said breathlessly.

'What are you doing here alone?' The voice came from behind her, human, this time, and it made her jump.

She turned and saw Tappu's mother standing in a half-crouch at the door of the loft, holding the beam for support.

Meenakshi's reflex was to look at the open trunk. She quickly put the cloth over it.

'Nothing, Aatya!' she said. 'I just came up here to play.'

'Play?' she repeated idiotically and looked her up and down. 'You play here?'

'I…I just…'

'Forget it. Have you seen Govind?'

'No.' It was a curt, easy lie.

'His friend says he came in here.'

'In the loft?'

The woman stood, silent, and looked all around the loft. It had sparse furniture, all old and rotting, except for the trunk, which was where her eyes lingered for a while. Then she firmly looked away and said, 'Well, come downstairs. This place has mould. You will fall sick.'

Meenakshi heaved a sigh of relief, and then asked, 'How is Tappu, Aatya?'

The woman gave her a long stare and then, with an expression of great distress, walked out and went downstairs.

❦

'What did you find? Tell me, what did you find?'

Renuka was now confronting the crowd, standing them off even as they prepared to leave.

'Why are you getting so defensive, Patil bai?' said Dr Jamblekar. 'We are looking everywhere. Any clue, we go and check. It's my son who is missing. I should be the one panicking.'

'That's not it, Jamblekar bai,' said Renuka, dropping the 'Dr' tag without hesitation, and ignoring her husband who was trying to signal her into silence. 'You bring a mob to search my house. You treat us like criminals.'

Meenakshi came down and stood silently in a corner.

'We are sorry if we offended you, bhau,' Dr Jamblekar addressed Shantaram directly. 'I hope you understand such things have to be done when a child goes missing.'

'Child? You son is an adult horse!' Renuka simmered. 'He must be out somewhere, hanging his tongue out at some girl like he always does.'

'What are you saying, woman?' Dr Jamblekar moved forward with menace in her eyes.

'Aai, please...' Meenakshi protested.

'You be quiet, Meenu!' Renuka thrust a hand in her face. 'What do these people think? They will come and treat us like criminals and we'll allow it? Ae Jamblekar, don't you know your own son?'

'Don't you dare talk like that about my son!'

'Why shouldn't I?'

Tappu's mother chipped in. 'Renu, I have been quiet until now, but please. What Doctor bai means to say is that we must all take care of our children.' As she said that, she looked directly at Meenakshi.

'Why are you looking at her?' Renuka took two steps forward, her hand now raised threateningly.

Shantaram reached her in the nick of time and grabbed hold of her hand. 'Have you gone mad, Renu?' he asked.

'Get out of here!' Renuka yelled at the procession that had stormed into her house. 'Never show me your faces again.'

Dr Jamblekar lurched forward with rage in her eyes, but the old man grabbed her. 'He's not here,' he said. 'Come, let's go and look elsewhere.'

❦

After the mob left, Meenakshi walked up to the point where she had buried Govind.

There she stood, at the rim of the compost pit, not minding the smell in the least. Something had consumed her attention—it was a blue slipper that had emerged out of the deluge and was now bobbing up and down slightly, its bottom end slapping the sludge.

That was everything Meenakshi needed for the memory to come back to her. She remembered refusing to look at his face, and instead looking down at his feet, at his slippers.

Those same blue slippers.

*'Didn't I tell you humans are f****** blind?'*

'Shut up, you murderer!' Meenakshi yelled.

It was that yell that made her parents turn to look at her sharply. For once, there were no words.

But a moment later, Renuka lost it. 'That slipper! It's that bastard's! I saw it the day he was molesting my Meenu.'

❦

Shantaram quickly ran up and clamped a hand on his wife's mouth. 'Shh, Renu! What are you saying? Those people haven't gone far.'

Tears streamed down Meenakshi's cheeks as she sobbed, 'Baba, he was here. He was here that night. And he tried to—'

'He tried to what, Meenu?' Renuka asked.

'He tried to force me.'

Renuka, fit to burst into another scream, said, 'See, I told you. Didn't I tell you? That bastard was after my Meenu.'

Shantaram slapped a hand on his forehead.

'Then what happened?' Renuka asked.

'I don't remember, Aai…I pushed him or something. Then I went all blank until morning…'

'Control your sobbing, you idiot girl!' said Shantaram. 'What happened in the morning then?'

Meenakshi didn't have words. It was like the thing inside had caught her tongue and tied a knot in it. But there were flashes. Terrible flashes. Govind's body slumped in the garden. Bleeding. His intestines jutting out…

Shrugging off those glimpses, she turned and looked at the slipper. Her bewildered parents stood behind her, holding each other's hands, holding their breath.

'Is that slipper that boy's?' Shantaram asked.

'Yes.'

'What? What happened here?'

And then what Meenakshi said changed the way her parents looked at her forever.

'I dragged his body and dumped it into the pit. He is…he is still in there.'

A moment of stunned silence later, Shantaram burst out. 'BODY?'

'Oh my God! What did you do, girl?' Renuka wailed.

'I didn't do anything,' said Meenakshi, now defiant.

'Then who?' Renuka blabbered.

'*She* did it.'

There was a laugh inside her as she said that, a laugh that only she could hear, and it drove her mad.

'I'm actually enjoying this. Aren't you, Meenakshi?'

The afternoon froze. Both man and woman felt a chilling wind brush past their necks and into their clothes, and their blood ran cold.

'She…' said Renuka in a voice that wasn't above a whisper. 'She who?'

'She who lives inside me.'

Shantaram went up and held his girl, and then, feeling awkward, pulled back. 'Meenu…oh my Meenu…'

'She protects me. I don't ask her to.'

Renuka grabbed Meenakshi's shoulder. 'Protects you from what?'

'Men.'

Renuka gasped.

Meenakshi went on, 'He came that night. He forced himself on me. And…something happened. My nails…' She looked at her nails, ungainly and untrimmed now. 'They began to grow. My hand moved on its own… No, she made it move. And thrust it right into his stomach.'

'And then?'

'I woke up in the morning. He was covered in blood.'

'Where?'

'By our kitchen wall in the garden outside. I dragged him and put him into the pit and cleaned the blood.'

❧

The three sat for an hour in the garden. Wife and daughter sat on the bench and Shantaram squatted on the floor, his head buried in his palms. Then he got up, full of purpose.

He patted his wife's back reassuringly. 'Renu, Renu, we have to control ourselves now. It won't do to panic. See, he's already inside. He won't come out. This is a compost pit, a decomposition pit. Put a bull in there and it will turn to pulp in a fortnight. The boy is gone. No one will find out about him if we are careful.'

Renuka sniffed away her remaining tears and steeled herself. 'You are right. Meenu, you have to…to be very quiet about this. Don't even tell your sisters.'

Shantaram broke a branch off a nearby tree and tore away its leaves. It was a thin stick now, with which he prodded at the slipper, and pried it out. 'This is rubber. It won't decompose. We will bury it in a separate hole. Let me also find the other slipper. Meenu, what have you led us to?'

11

The Witch

After that fateful morning, Meenakshi was homebound. The gulf between her sisters and her had widened. But she could not blame anyone. At times when she sat silently, weeping under the sal tree, she would question her existence itself.

But she liked the solitude. Where humans were out of favour, nature won. Gradually she learned to comfort herself, and instead of just wasting away under the tree, she began to communicate with the beings of the garden—talking to the trees, playing with the worms and insects, and even with the very wind that seemed to caress her face with sympathy these days.

Three afternoons after the mob incident, Renuka asked Meenakshi to accompany her to the grocery store. The girl's mood suddenly changed when her mother called her. She went running up to the gate, her pigtails flying. It made her look quite gauche, and Renuka noticed that her little daughter was now an inch taller than her.

Renuka admonished her. 'Stop skipping on the road like that and walk like a decent lady.'

Meenakshi fretted, but obeyed her Aai.

Mother and daughter made a beeline for Debu's store, where they equipped themselves with bags of food. With the rent money, Renuka ordered rice and oil. They asked Debu to send the stuff over to their house.

Then Renuka offered to buy Meenakshi a saree. It was nothing short of an occasion, for it would be the girl's first saree. Renuka insisted on buying Meenakshi one, for she now had the height for it, and she would teach her how to drape it. In her words, a saree would look elegant on her. So they walked to a saree shop, and started looking at a few of them. But it was only when her nails began to tingle did Meenakshi realize what was happening. The shop attendant who was draping the sarees on her was getting too close, grazing his fingers against the smooth skin of her belly as he tucked the folds in, and smoothing the creases over her curves. Alarmed, Meenakshi pulled her mother out of the shop as soon as possible.

❦

While walking homeward, they took a brief reprieve at an old man's sugarcane juice cart.

So far, Renuka had strangely behaved out of character. Her guard was down, and it was as if she had forgotten the incidents that had come to her notice only a couple of days ago. There was a body decomposing in her garden, but there was absolutely no talk or discussion about it.

But Renuka knew what she was doing. She had taken refuge in denial. Over the days, she had rationalized to herself that this wasn't something that she could control. She forced herself to believe that the worst was already behind them. And it was wise not to behave any differently. People were already scrutinizing them. Tappu's mother's behaviour had changed, which was a profound indicator. There were no more greetings from her; instead, there was a scowl on her face whenever their paths crossed.

'Aai, you haven't had a sip!' said Meenakshi.

'Oh yes.' Renuka quickly came back to the world she was contriving, the world of denial and fantasy.

Out of the corner of her eye, she saw two women at the adjacent sandwich stall. They were speaking in hushed tones, but loud enough for the sound to carry to her.

'That's her,' said one of the women, 'the Patil girl.'

'Her? She is *fifteen*?' said the other woman.

'Doesn't look like it, does she?'

'She looks at least twenty to me. Her blouse size is bigger than my sixteen-year-old's.'

'Isn't it?'

'I believe all that they say now. She looks the type.'

'What type?'

'You know.'

'Yeah, I understand. First that Namdar boy. And now Dr Jamblekar's son.'

'Oh!'

'And I heard that during Nag Panchami—'

Renuka turned back sharply. Clasping Meenakshi's hand, she gave the two women such an angry glare that they walked away, leaving behind the glasses that the vendor was handing out to them.

❧

But the ordeal was not over; it was just beginning.

As they walked along the bend that led to their home, they heard a woman from another neighbouring family, the Manekars, shouting out loud.

'Ae Keshva, come inside. Why are you standing in the porch? Get into the house!'

Renuka and Meenakshi turned to see a teenage boy being slapped by his mother on the back and led inside their house. Once the boy was safely inside, the Manekar woman stood at the door, glared at the Patil ladies, and then slammed it shut with all her might.

'Why were you staring at that girl? Don't you know she is cursed?' they heard Manekar shouting from the window of the house. 'She does something to boys like you. People say she ate up that Jamblekar's son. Ate up, you hear? She's a witch! Next time you stare at her, I will break your legs and lock you in the house.'

'Witch, Aai?' Meenakshi asked her mother with a tear in her eye.

'Forget it, Meenu,' said Renuka. 'You know how the villagers are. They just need something to talk about.'

They walked the rest of the way in silence.

Renuka had managed to tell her daughter something that would quieten her for now, but her own mind was in disquiet. She did not know what she could do about it.

But something else was waiting for them.

When they reached the house, they saw the mob in the garden again, with Dr Jamblekar leading them. And this time there were stronger men with them, men with bulging biceps and flaring nostrils and wielding lathis.

'Ahaaa! Here she comes!' Dr Jamblekar began the tirade.

Renuka could see her husband. On his face was a look of utter helplessness. What could he do against this mad mob? Their daughters stood behind him, simpering, and they were no help in the situation either.

'What is it now, Jamblekar bai?' Renuka stepped up, pushing Meenakshi protectively behind her.

'Ask your daughter where my Govind is,' she asked.

'Who, your son, that sleazebag?' said Renuka calmly. 'Go look in the brothels outside the village.'

'Hey, hey, mind your tongue!' Dr Jamblekar came forward threateningly. Tappu's mother held her back.

'You mind yours. What can we say about your son, the great shining beacon of our village? How dare you come up and ask about him again? What proof do you have that he was here?'

'Ae Shirkya!' Dr Jamblekar shouted. 'Come here.'

A scrawny boy in only a vest that went down to his knees stepped forward. He was no more than five.

'Shirkya, tell this blind woman what you saw.'

Shirkya wiped the snot off his nose with his wrist. There were tears of intimidation in his eyes.

'Tell, re!' Dr Jamblekar slapped him on the back.

'I...I...'

'So now you will threaten a poor child?' said Renuka.

'He…climbed that wall,' the boy stuttered. He pointed to the wall that Govind had scaled that fateful night.

'What?' Renuka thought quickly. 'Someone entered our compound at night? Are you sure it was Govind?'

'Yes.'

'Suparna, Manda…go inside this very moment and check if all our cash and jewellery is safe,' Renuka screamed. 'What are you standing here for? Go inside, I said!'

'Don't change the topic!' said Dr Jamblekar. 'We are calling the police if we don't find him by evening.'

'Oh, by all means, do!' Renuka moved her arms in a dramatic manner, right in the doctor's face. 'Now I have proof that he entered our compound, and I was actually looking for my gold mangalsutra yesterday. You remember that, don't you?' She looked at Shantaram, who nodded nervously. '*We* have proof that your son broke into our private property. What proof do *you* have?'

The crowd was stunned at the sudden turn of events. The men standing behind Dr Jamblekar, who thought themselves to be wiser than women in matters concerning the law, began to whisper among themselves, and Renuka caught them nodding.

'Meenu, you go inside *now!*' Renuka waited for her daughter to obey her command, and then looked at the befuddled doctor. 'Lady, we have tolerated your transgressions twice. You may be the much-respected lady doctor of our village, but right now you are behaving like a common vandal. The next time you come here to question my daughter without proof, it won't be good for you, or…' She looked at every member of the mob and swept her forefinger across all of them. '…for anyone who dares to come here with you.'

A man whispered something in Dr Jamblekar's ear, but she waved him away.

'You want proof?' Jamblekar asked Renuka, her hands firmly in the pockets of her apron. 'All right, next time we will bring it. Solid legal proof. And not us. The police will bring it. You hang on there, Patil bhau.'

The last sentence was directed at Shantaram, who stood in his verandah, cowering.

With the issuance of that final warning, the mob moved out of the premises.

12

The Grave Robber

The sisters were huddled together in one room, and Meenakshi was the centre of attention for once. The sudden spotlight made her nervous.

It was Jaishree, the second sister, who did most of the talking this time. 'Is something going on in the house that we don't know about, Meenu?'

Meenu felt a warm current running down her throat. 'What's wrong?'

'All these people marching in,' said Jaishree, 'and talking about you.'

'I don't know.'

'Oh, my Meenu, there's a reason why we don't take you out with us,' continued Jaishree. Manda hushed her, but she went on, 'Anyway, what's this whole thing about Govind?'

'What about him?'

'She won't tell!' said Jaishree. 'Now see what problems she is creating! Doesn't she care about Aai-Baba? Tomorrow the police might come at our door. Can you imagine that?'

A tear prickled Meenakshi's eye. But her attention lay elsewhere. The familiar tingling sensation had begun to grow in the tips of her fingers again.

'Well, let's sleep then, sisters,' said Jaishree. As they went out, she said to the others, 'Mark my words—this girl is a bag of problems. Stay away from her. She will drag and drown us all along with herself.'

The sisters went to sleep in their rooms and turned the lights off. Meenakshi could not sleep, though; she tossed and turned in bed long into the night.

'They will abandon you. One by one, they will all abandon you. And then you will be alone. Only I will be with you. Do you hear? Only I. And you.'

Meenakshi wanted to scream in order to shut that voice out, but the darkness would not let her. She got up and walked out of that claustrophobic room.

※

There was no sleep in the parents' room either.

'What will we do?' asked Shantaram. 'Now you have gone and incited them. They are already furious. Don't you have any sense? Can you even imagine what they might do tomorrow?'

'Why scold me?' asked Renuka. 'What else could I do? Should I just hand over our girl to them?'

'Stop talking nonsense. There are things you cannot control, but you mustn't complicate them. What if they really bring the police?'

'Let them come, no? Even they will not find any—'

'Stupid woman! These are the police. They are not stupid villagers who will not see a dead man's slipper in a compost pit. They are going to see everything. Even dig into the pit. They might bring sniffer dogs if they have so much as a suspicion. You know that bastard woman, that Jamblekar, she has a clout. She will pull the strings. Something's up her ass.'

'Well…' Renuka sat down, dumbstruck. 'I don't know what to say when you put it like that. But you tell me what we can do.'

'I don't know.'

Neither of them heard the soft footsteps turning away from the window. As Meenakshi walked away from there, she wiped the tears clouding her eyes.

※

A few hours later, when the family was sleeping, Meenakshi woke up, startled.

Rutuja was sleeping beside her, her hand on her belly.

Meenakshi softly moved the hand away and sat up.

The rasping voice breathed in her head:

'*Get up. You have work to do.*'

That night was different in so many ways.

The sense of foreboding that had been gnawing at her had now reached its peak. She had never been awake at this hour—the clock told her it was past three—but she was wide awake now, and she knew it was futile to try to sleep again.

She moved forth silently and slowly, not so much walking as gliding. When she reached the door, her hand moved to the handle and opened it, and she slid out without turning back to look at her sleeping sisters.

Her conscious mind had left her now; the being in her had taken over, and it guided her steps.

'*You have work to do.*'

In the darkness of that long corridor, as Meenakshi sallied forth in her deadened shell, her skin began to alter. Gone was the smooth flawless skin of her arms. It was replaced now with a ribbed reptilian skin, hardened and warty and untouchable. The transformation was sporadic. It worked fitfully, starting in patches and moving upward from her fingers, till it reached the elbows and the shoulders and then covered the entire body.

As the skin began to transform, her body grew in size too. In minutes, she looked intimidating, with her head reaching the nineteenth-century rafters holding up the ceiling of the house. That giant figure, looming thus in the corridor, was a sight that could wrench out a healthy man's heart. She stopped growing when her head hit the ceiling, and then moved on, not minding the rafters that pulled out her hair as she dragged her scalp along them.

By the time she reached the main door of the house, her clothes had fallen off. It was a cold night, but that did not daunt the creature from boldly walking into the night, naked and unashamed. The only thing that covered her vitals was the profuse hair that grew on it. But nakedness was the least of her concerns now, if she was indeed a *her* anymore.

She glided through the garden effortlessly, only stopping for a moment near the sal tree—which shook its leaves with some mysterious sentiment—and then moved on to the far end of the garden. There she stood as if frozen.

The monster stood still, staring in the vacant distance, unmindful of the barking of the dogs that had begun to gather around her. In the darkness, she even towered over some of the trees, and stood like an untimely effigy of Ravana, to be immolated at Dussehra. She would have been visible from three compounds away if people had been awake.

That, combined with the fact that her eyes hadn't blinked since the transformation had happened, the stench emanating from her body, and the nostrils that flared repeatedly, made her one of the most terrible things to ever walk on the face of the earth.

Then she sat, not all the way, but on her haunches. Her eyes swept over an arc and then lowered on a spot ahead of her—the compost pit. Sitting like that, she looked very much like a gigantic frog waiting for some unsuspecting prey to come up close. And then she made the move.

Her right hand made a fist and it came down with such abruptness and speed that it caused a small explosion in the air. It dug into the compost pit, and it moved inside in a swirling path, going round and round, and then it stopped.

It had found its quarry.

With a little grunt, she splashed through the decaying muck and pulled it out.

The days-old corpse was now in her large hand. The compost pit had done its job well—the bacteria and other microorganisms had spared no expense in ravaging the fibres of this new entrant into their ecosystem. The body was reduced to half, the bleeding sores open and gaping, and bones jutting out, them being the last things to decompose.

The creature looked with interest at the corpse covered in muck, knowing full well that it was still evidence for anyone who might stumble upon it. This would not do. This is what she had come to take care of.

She knelt on one knee then. She placed the body on her thigh, with its half-spine resting on it. The body reposed thus, she curled her fingers to resemble the claws of a huge bird, and, with a bloodcurdling yell, she dug her talons into the gaping abdomen of the corpse.

With great rapidity, she proceeded to rip the body to shreds, tearing away fragment upon fragment, and throwing it back into the compost pit. She ripped it away as if it were just a trussed chicken, and the pieces she tore off were no bigger than the slivers of meat one might throw to a cat.

When only bones remained, she stopped. With a grin on her grotesque face, she brought her elbow down with resounding force upon the skull, which smashed into smithereens like it were a crumbling cookie. The ribcage came next. Then she snapped each limb into many pieces.

She threw the bones, crumbled and splintered, into the compost pit. Those shreds would be decomposed even before the sun came up.

There would be no telltale signs even if someone decided to swim in the pit.

The job done, she stood up and started walking back to the house.

And the moment her foot entered the threshold, she shrank, and, over the minute, regained her unblemished complexion. By the time she opened the door, she was Meenakshi again, shivering, wondering why she was naked, and her clothes scattered on the floor.

13

Flaming Torches

*O*nce again, making sure that Meenakshi was asleep, Kumud softly latched the door from outside and ran back to her parents' room. She joined Suparna there, who had just finished narrating the tale to her bewildered parents.

'Why did you hide all this from us till now, Suparna?' said Renuka, breaking the thick silence that hung in the air.

'We didn't know what to do, Aai,' said Suparna nervously. 'But now with all this talk about Govind—'

'And that man died?' asked Shantaram.

'In front of the entire village, Baba.'

Renuka stood up, popped her head out of the door, ensured that the corridor was silent, and then turned back towards them inside the room.

'Look, Suparna. Don't tell this to anyone else,' she said. 'Let us keep this within the family. Meenu is ours, and we have to see that no harm comes to her.'

Then she turned to Shantaram. 'It is good that this happened far away in Battis Shirala. If it had happened here, the whole village would have come up to torch the house.'

'Is Meenu a witch, Aai?' This was from Kumud, and it made everyone turn sharply towards her.

'No, of course not!' said Renuka, a smile firmly fixed on her face. 'What a stupid thing to say!'

'But all my friends say there is something wrong with her,' said Kumud. 'They say she looks weird and does weird things. When she was in school, she used to talk to herself and keep staring at the walls.'

'That's how she is,' said Renuka, not sure what she was saying.

'You don't indulge in such talk.'

There was a noise in the corridor outside. Someone had probably woken up and was moving about.

'All right, now you two go back to your room,' said Renuka. 'Your Baba and I will decide what's to be done. Remember, do not breathe a word to anyone.'

❧

The moment the girls left, Renuka turned to her husband, blinking in the morning light that was now filling the room. 'What are we supposed to do? That Jamblekar too...'

Shantaram's head was bowed, looking at the floor tiles. He shook his head in despair, and then he looked up.

'I love my daughters equally, don't I?'

'Yes, you do,' said Renuka.

'Then why am I beginning to see Meenu differently now? Am I a bad father?'

Renuka did not reply. What could she say? She was beset with such thoughts too. Some of her thoughts were such that she could not speak them out loud to even herself.

'Kumud...why did she say that, Renu?'

Renuka's chain of thought was broken. 'What?'

'That Meenu is a w-wit—'

'Witch?'

The ease with which his wife could pronounce that word shocked Shantaram.

'You know how children are,' said Renuka.

'How can you be so—'

Renuka cut in, 'You know...I think what you...we were thinking a few days ago might be the solution.'

'What?'

'You know,' said Renuka. 'Don't make me spell it out. Think about it. He's rich and besotted with her. He will take Meenu to Bombay and then it is their life. Our other daughters will have a brighter future. And, truth be told, do you think you will be able to find a better match for Meenu when she becomes an adult?'

Shantaram heard it all out in pensive silence. He did not object this time.

❧

Dr Jamblekar barged in with her posse of a dozen people at half past nine that morning. Leading the procession with her were two constables and an inspector.

Shantaram shuffled on his feet when he saw the khakis. 'Doctor bai, what is this?' he asked coldly.

'You wanted proof. You shall have it,' said Jamblekar with an exaggerated shaking of her head. Thrusting her hands firmly in her apron pockets, she added, 'Here's a warrant to search your house.'

'WARRANT?' said Renuka, coming out. 'You really brought policemen to our house?'

'Step aside now,' said Dr Jamblekar, a gleeful smile dancing on her lips. 'Let Inspector Awchat do his work. You cannot stop us.'

Without a word, the stern-faced policemen stormed into the house. The other people in the group stood back and watched, doing exactly what they were supposed to do—add weight to the proceedings. Shantaram looked around helplessly for a minute and then resigned himself to sitting on the cot in the verandah.

Meanwhile, Renuka stood simmering in a corner, trying not to listen to the heart-wrenching sounds of her cupboards being opened and utensils being upturned. Her nostrils flared with both anger and shame—shame at the most intimate bits of her life being thrown open thus.

For Shantaram, the twelve minutes that the policemen were inside their house, throwing his wife's and daughters' clothes out of the cupboards, were moments of eternal shame. He would never be able to live them down.

Finally, they came out, their deed done, but devoid of any result. The crowd sighed in disappointment.

Savitri Namdar stepped forward. 'Aaho, Inspector, don't forget to check in the lawn and the garden. Patil bhau has a huge property.'

Quite obediently, the policemen walked into the garden. Meenakshi's heart stopped when they trampled upon the fallen leaves of the sal tree, crushing the dried ones and squishing the raw ones. They walked up to every tree, looking behind them, prodding into the loose soil with their sticks and shuffling through every heap of dried leaves.

Then they went up to the compost pit.

'What's this?' said the inspector, prodding the sludge with a stick.

Renuka hurried forward. 'That's our compost pit,' she said in helpless rage. 'We make fertilizer for our plants.'

'Look everywhere, Inspector!' said Dr Jamblekar.

The inspector wordlessly pinched his nose and went down on his haunches next to the pit. The Patils held their breath as the inspector went up to the spot where they had buried the slippers two days ago. For those few seconds, every frown and wrinkle on the Inspector's face was carefully observed. Then, one of the constables produced a long branch of a tree and stuck it into the pit. Immediately, a rank smell of decay permeated through the surroundings, and everyone covered their noses, even the girls who were standing far away in the verandah.

'How can the Patils live in this shit?' asked one of the men. Dr Jamblekar scoffed in response.

The Patil couple looked on with horror as the policemen moved the stick in the pit, as if stirring some thick broth. At any moment, they felt, the stick would hit something harder than the manure it was in, and then there would be a shout of exclamation. The next moment, the body—surely a partly-decomposed horror—would be dragged out for all to see.

But moments passed and nothing happened. Bewildered, the Patil couple looked at each other, and Renuka silently mumbled something.

Meenakshi was dazed, though, with voices playing in her head.

'We did a good job, Meenakshi. These bastards won't find a mortal cell in there!'

'Nothing here, Doctor bai,' said the inspector.

'Please look everywhere! Look again!' Dr Jamblekar screeched.

'We looked. That too, in your presence. There is no sign of your son ever being here.' The inspector turned to Shantaram. 'Sorry, Patil sahib. We had to do this.'

Shantaram stood up. 'I understand.'

Before Renuka could go up to Dr Jamblekar, which she intended to do with a pronounced swag, the latter turned and left the place in a huff.

❦

The Patils kept on sitting in their places for a long time, even the girls. No one moved or spoke or thought of their humanly needs. They just sat and wondered, zapped by what had just happened. Their house was an upside-down mess, and the whole village—the people who were in their garden and the crowd that had gathered outside—had seen the police ransacking it. Even if nothing was found, suspicion was thick in the air. There was the sense of impending doom.

It was Shantaram who stood up first.

'I am calling him,' he said.

Renuka nodded.

'Who, Aai?' asked Meenakshi.

There was no answer.

'Tell me, Aai. Baba. Who? Who are you calling?'

Without answering, Shantaram walked into the house.

Meenakshi kept on looking at her father with tear-filled eyes. She knew her father meant the man from the city. She wanted to stop her father, but what could she say to calm him down? Never before had she seen her father being humiliated to this extent. For the self-respecting man, it was nothing less than being stripped naked and paraded in the village square. The pillar that held up her life was crumbling to dust. There were no words she could form now, nothing she could say that would make sense.

❧

Later, at dusk, Renuka stepped out into the courtyard to bring the spices in. It had been a sunny day and she had put the yearly rations out to dry. The garden—still fresh with the footsteps of the mob and the policemen—now had saffron patches of turmeric and the crimson of crisp chilli peppers. She came out, sat next to the whole spices, felt them and shook her head. They weren't dry yet. But the sun had set and she had to take them inside.

Deftly, she picked up the large aluminum tray carrying the turmeric sticks and placed it in a safe spot inside the house. Then she went back to pick up the chilli peppers.

She was still attempting to grip the tray when she saw the shadow of a person standing in the courtyard.

Immediately she stood up and her mouth opened to say something, but she had gone speechless.

It was Tappu Namdar.

The boy was standing on his feet, badly wobbling and shaking. He looked no different from a goblin, not even able to stand erect. He tried to open his mouth, but only managed a quivering of his lips. His eyes darted everywhere, and he raised an arm with much effort and pointed…

Renuka turned to see what he was pointing at and saw Meenakshi just coming out of a door in the house. The boy's trembling forefinger was pointing at her, as if stabbing her with blame.

'S-sh-she…she d-did…this…'

The words that issued from his mouth were a slurred hiss, like the sound of water droplets vaporizing on a hot plate.

Then the boy collapsed into his mother's arms, who, Renuka saw now, had been standing behind him all this time like the shadow of a ghost.

'Bring a chair!' said Savitri. 'Someone go!'

Then the mob came forward. They had sent Tappu ahead to identify his culprit, and he had done his task. Now that his job was done, the crowd moved forth.

Renuka found her voice. 'Suparna! Jaishree! Manda! Come out, all of you! Now! Call your father too.'

Meenakshi, now frozen in her corner, noticed that her mother had not taken her name.

'What are you yapping about?' said Renuka, sallying forth, dauntless.

A man stepped up with a chair. Making the trembling boy sit on it, he said, 'Oho Patil bai, this is enough now. Didn't you see? Tappu just pointed at your girl. We asked him to go point at the one who put him in this state and he showed us your girl. What does that mean now?'

Renuka tried to find words to say something.

'Our Govind. Tell us where he is,' said another man.

'Why are you back again?' said Shantaram, adjusting his kurta as he came out of the house. 'Even the police found nothing.'

A voice came from the back. A strong female voice, and its strength lay in the anger and the determination that it was laced with.

'The police were a mistake.'

Dr Jamblekar was not wearing her coat now, as if hinting that she was not in the mood for saving lives today. She wore a dark sari that blended with the twilight, making her a part of that endless canvas of the sky.

'This thing is out of the realm of police affairs.'

'What do you mean?' said Renuka. Her eyes were wide with fear now, and she felt something bubbling in her chest, a feeling of impending doom. The secret she had borne for long was now going to spill out.

'Ask your daughter about the Nag Panchami at Battis Shirala,' said Dr Jamblekar with enough venomous spite to kill the king cobra that had been the star of that event.

'Wh-what happened at Battis Shirala?' said Renuka.

'Your daughter showed her true colours, that's what!' said Dr Jamblekar. The other people in the crowd nodded. Even Tappu raised his hand and placed it on his mother's hand more firmly.

'What true colours?'

Darkness swept the garden at this point. Someone from the back of the crowd lit a matchstick and then a flame went up, a flame at the end of a stick. Renuka's heart sank. The people were carrying wooden torches, and now they were lit.

'Patil bai, how long will you hide your daughter's disease?' said Dr Jamblekar. 'I don't blame you, because you are a mother. But don't you see? Your daughter is a patient of the mind. She is a danger to this society. To you.'

Renuka choked, weighted down by the possible truth in the allegation. She looked at Shantaram, who stood helplessly silent too.

'There is something very wrong with your youngest daughter,' said Dr Jamblekar. 'You know it too. Do you not worry about the well-being of your family?'

'But...Meenu is a child,' said Shantaram.

Renuka looked up sharply at him, aghast at her husband's faux pas.

'No. Not a child.' said Dr Jamblekar coldly. 'Don't you see she has stopped being a child long ago? Men, what do you think of this? Is this girl really a child?'

Dr Jamblekar looked at the men in the mob and moved away. Each and every set of male eyes, filled with pure greed, were now fixed upon Meenakshi. The lights of many torches shone on her. The sight was a frightening one; that of a row of able-bodied men held in a wide-eyed trance.

'See what I mean?' Dr Jamblekar looked at Renuka and huffed. 'This is what your daughter does to men.'

'This is not right,' Tappu's mother broke in. 'A girl holding men in lust like this? Hurting them?' She placed her hand on her son's head. 'She is dangerous to our village.'

Dr Jamblekar nodded. 'I don't know, and perhaps will never know what she did to my son. But—' Then she yelled, 'O brothers! Men! Wake up!' She took a torch from the nearest man's hand and swayed the flame in front of their eyes. The men flinched and snapped back to reality.

'She is a witch, don't you see?' Dr Jamblekar finished.

At that, Renuka burst out. 'What? Do you even know what you are saying?'

'Don't listen to her!' the doctor screeched. 'Go on. We have to take this girl with us.'

The men, who had probably been waiting for this, ran forth. A pair of hands first grabbed Shantaram, and about the same time, another pair held Renuka. And as if the men's hands were not enough, their threatening, flaming torches held them back. The girls immediately went into a frenzy, but before they could even react, they were all bundled into their room and bolted from outside. It was like all of this was a synchronized and well-rehearsed manoeuvre, planned by the mob before they had entered the garden.

Amidst all the screaming and shouting and thumping against the locked door, there was Meenakshi, now rooted to her spot in the verandah.

'DON'T ANYONE DARE TOUCH HER!' Renuka yelled.

Dr Jamblekar looked at the squirming Renuka but said nothing. Working up an expression of disgust on her face, as if she were approaching a worm, she went up to Meenakshi and scrutinized her.

'Leave her! What's her fault?' cried Shantaram.

The men moved ahead. Emboldened, they came closer to Meenakshi too, as if she were a thing of wonder, and stood around her, staring, gawking. The lights of their torches gleamed on the girl's body, highlighting the glistening lines of sweat that were streaking down from it.

But Meenakshi stood firm, praying inwardly, hoping against hope that the tingling in her fingers wouldn't happen again. Not now. Not in front of all these people.

'Why stop me now? Don't resist. Let me come out. Don't you also want to kill all these drooling bastards? Bash their skulls in? Bury them in the same pit as their sleazebag relative?'

And she prayed harder, like she had never done before.

Even as she joined her hands in prayer, she felt the balls of her fingertips press against each other, and she opened her praying eyes for just a moment and saw—the skin was moving by itself. She thought of the cataclysm she might unleash right there in her father's verandah, and create a night that would go down in history as the worst night in Vatgaon. No, no, that should not happen. She willed the monster inside her to go back; she willed with all her might.

'No, I will not let you come out...'

'Don't try to stop me. You have no power over me.'

'You have caused enough trouble as it is. I will stop you, even if I have to kill myself.'

Meenakshi stretched out her hand to grab hold of one of those torches. How easily her cotton skirt would catch fire and end this all!

But then it happened.

A miracle.

Through the crowding chaos of the lecherous male faces, Meenakshi saw a face—another face, behind them all—that glowed with a serene smile, brighter than the torches. He was standing some distance away, in the desolate clump of bushes near the compost pit, the same place where she had seen him the first time.

It conveyed an instant calm. Meenakshi felt that everything would be all right. Then, just as abruptly as it had appeared, it vanished.

And the chaos was back.

Meenakshi became alive once again to the screams and shouts and the thuds and thumps all around her. She heard the pitiful cries of her mother and father and the angry yelling of Dr Jamblekar. And she felt—

—the touch of one of those men on her shoulder.

The skin was cracking. She saw the blood streaking through in lines, and she wrung her hands to hide her blight, but she knew it was coming. There was no way to stop it.

'*Here I come...*'

This time she feared she wouldn't black out. She would see what she was going to transform into.

Everyone would see.

She could not hide her hands anymore. The skin had begun to turn harder, thicker, drier, just like the matted, moulted skin of the reptile she had seen a few weeks ago. The tips of her fingernails became pointed and sharp, and though Meenakshi could not look at those tips in the melee, she knew it was a sight she didn't want to see.

Then, uncontrolled, and with great ferocity, the hand lashed out.

And up.

Right at the chin of the man who had dared to touch her.

Even as Meenakshi stared at that man's face with eyes that seemed to be made of glass, a trickle of blood spurted from his chin, and then it increased to a flow, and kept on till it became a stream.

He screamed, and that pushed all the other men back.

In the moment that the man stood stunned, she grabbed his torch, and then brought it perilously close to her face.

Dr Jamblekar stopped yelling.

Her mother's protests stopped. Instead, she began to wail. It was a loud piercing wail of helplessness.

Dr Jamblekar found her voice. 'She's a witch. I told you! She's a witch.'

The torch came right into Meenakshi's face, its naked flames curling on her cheeks. But Meenakshi stood unfazed by those lashes of fire.

Instead, she stooped, and then, by some involuntary force, her mouth opened. Before she knew what was happening, a large volume of air blew out from her mouth.

'I won't allow you to kill yourself, you see?'

It was not a mere gust of air that issued from her mouth, though; it was a hurricane.

In that hurricane, the first things to go out were the torches. And then, the men, who were swept backward by the sheer force of it.

One of the men hit his head on the fencepost of the garden and collapsed. Another came and fell right at the feet of Savitri Namdar, making her keel backward.

And then—

'Step back!' came a man's voice from behind them.

Everyone turned to look.

'Unhand the girl,' said the man who had just spoken. And everyone fell silent, for they saw him. His uniform, rather. He was a policeman.

'We found these chappals at a brothel in the nearby village,' the policeman said. 'Recognize these, Dr Jamblekar?' He threw a pair of blue chappals on the ground.

'These are…'

'Your son's. He was there with a prostitute for a couple of nights and has now run away. Stop tormenting this family right now or I shall have to book all of you.'

Shantaram looked at Renuka, befuddled. Only Meenakshi could see the patch, though, the patch where her father had buried the slippers. It was all dug up now.

'But…you saw what she did!' Dr Jamblekar protested.

'I also saw what *you* did,' said the policeman, 'and how all these men cornered that girl. Why, even now some of your men are holding the Patils captive!'

The men released Shantaram and Renuka from their clutches right away. Renuka, now unstoppable, moved ahead. There was a ton of confusion, but she didn't care about it right now. 'Arrest this bitch of a woman right away, sir,' Renuka screamed, fighting back her tears. 'She has—'

'You rest, Mrs Patil,' said the policeman. 'And the lot of you, vacate the premises right now.'

'But...what about...' Dr Jamblekar stuttered.

'Your son has run away from home. Maybe run away to the city or...who knows? He's an adult, and nothing can be done of it. I suggest you give up on him too. If this was such a problem, you should have taken care of him when he was younger. Get out now.'

With those words of the policeman, the people filed out one by one. Savitri helped Tappu get up on his feet and held his hand as he hobbled away.

Renuka turned around with tears on her face. 'Thank you...'

But there was no one to thank.

The policeman had vanished.

As the aghast family turned to look at Meenakshi, her frown disappeared. Recognition had dawned upon her.

The policeman was the naked man from the grove.

14

The New Life

*H*arikumar sat across the Patils in their verandah the next morning—an uncharacteristically silent one. Even the morning birds seemed to have forgotten to sing their melodies. The men had teacups in their hands, and while Shantaram slurped on his tea occasionally, Harikumar held it steadily in his hands till it went cold.

'So, yes,' said Shantaram. 'We see merit in your proposal. Your doggedness wins. We agree to hand over our Meenakshi to you, provided you marry her at the earliest.'

'I accept,' said Harikumar. He looked around and saw Meenakshi hiding in the room but trying to peek out nonetheless. 'Do not worry, Patil sahib. I wish for nothing more. We will marry whenever you want us to.' He looked unashamedly in the direction of Meenakshi as he spoke that last line.

Shantaram looked at Renuka, and then she spoke, 'But our worry of her age persists…'

'Don't let that bother you,' said Harikumar, still staring at the slight sliver of her face staring at him from the room.

'Will you take care of her?' asked Shantaram.

'I assure you; she'll have as good a life with me as she has with you,' said Harikumar with obstinate confidence.

'So, you are sure?'

'Never been surer of anything else. I will marry your girl and keep her like a princess. Come to Bombay whenever you like. Meet your daughter. I will be happy to serve you both.'

Renuka beamed. It was her first genuine smile in several days. 'Harikumar,' she said, holding his hand, 'we apologize for what we told you here a few days ago. You have a heart of gold. It is difficult for us to keep Meenu here and there is no one we can entrust her to. Somehow, despite everything, we feel you will genuinely look after her. Please, do take good care of her.'

'Goes without saying,' said Harikumar, and kept the cup down. 'Have you asked her?'

'What will the poor thing say?' said Renuka. 'She is still trembling like a leaf. What is her fault in all of this? But...' There was a sudden change in her tone. '...she will be fine once she is away from here.'

'So, when do you want to get us married?' asked Harikumar.

'Tomorrow itself, if you are willing,' said Shantaram. 'With great difficulty, a pundit has agreed to perform the ceremony. Is that all right?'

'Sure,' Harikumar beamed. 'I could not be happier.'

'It shall be only us and the girls,' said Shantaram. 'Do you have any guests you'd like to invite?'

'Guests?' Harikumar laughed. 'No. I will come all by myself to claim my bride.'

※

There was only one being Meenakshi had to say her goodbye to. As soon as Harikumar left, she came out of her hiding and ran up to it.

'O Companion!' she said in a choked voice and hugged the huge trunk of the sal. It looked more benevolent this afternoon. 'Make me one with you and let me live here forever. Just like you stand here. No one can ever make you budge an inch.'

A few leaves rustled. Meenakshi looked up and saw a crow flying away from them, probably going to some unknown place in a faraway land.

'Do I really have to go?'

Upon that question, a leaf fell directly by her feet. She picked it up. It was a fresh leaf, still green and healthy. There was no reason for it to fall off the tree like that.

But there *was* probably a reason. As Meenakshi absentmindedly twirled the stalk of that discarded leaf, she felt her fate to be strangely similar to the tree's.

❧

The wedding was the sorriest affair the village temple had seen in decades. It was a Tuesday afternoon when the stage was set in the temple courtyard around a ritual fire. As the flames began to rise in the sky, Meenakshi was brought to the scene, led by her father. Her mother and sisters followed in the procession. Meenakshi looked dazed. Even as the nebulae of the flames danced in her black bead-like eyes, she showed no effect. All she could do now was to trust her parents, who told her they were doing the right thing.

Then why did it feel so wrong?

But she thought of her mother and her father in the grip of the angry villagers. She thought of her sisters confined in that room by the angry mob, flames of fire dancing on their faces. Of how she had come close, this close, to unleashing her inner demoness in front of so many people.

She had brought her family and her village on the brink of slaughter.

Someone tugged at the end of her saree. It was the pundit, tying a knot with her saree and the man's shawl.

The man. Her husband.

He was there now. Smiling at her. Breathing so hard that even she could hear it.

Unbidden, a nasty picture rose in her mind—of him on top of her. His naked body pressing against hers. His thing between her legs. And she would have to yield. For he was her husband, wasn't he?

The bridal rounds began in a daze. As the pundit solemnized the vows, Meenakshi's eyes turned blurry till she barely knew where she was going. Renuka had to hold her twice and redirect her as she almost walked into the fire.

At last, with the chant of *Shubha Mangala Saavdhaan,* the

ceremony was over. 'You are now husband and wife,' said the priest in great exultation. 'Go forth and lead a pious life in the service of God.'

The bridal couple bowed and walked slowly towards the gate, beyond which a new life beckoned.

Only her mother cried, and it was a wail that would have been more at home in a funeral procession.

❦

All through the journey in his red car, bedecked to befit the nuptial vehicle that it was, Meenakshi sat in funereal silence. She sat next to him as he drove, adorned in her bridal finery. No one from her family accompanied her on this maiden journey to the city. Their goodbyes had been bidden at the house gate itself, with tearful assurances that they would soon come to visit.

Harikumar drove on for an hour without a word, focusing only on the road ahead. But Meenakshi knew that every time she moved, every time her ornaments clinked, he stiffened. She snatched looks at him, never daring to look at him directly, but in the various tiny mirrors of the car, and she saw his mouth beginning to form words but not say them.

When it was nearing evening, he spoke the first word to her. 'Hungry?'

She hadn't known she was hungry until he asked.

He drove the car down the highway onto a service road and stopped at the first decent inn he could see.

'Stay in the car,' he said. 'I'll be back in a minute.'

He returned with two plastic meal boxes in his hands. Opening the car door, he sat in the driver's seat and handed her one of the boxes.

'Best to eat in the car,' he said. 'Dhabas are sleazy places this time of the night.'

Meenakshi opened her box and looked at the food. It was different from what her mother prepared. She didn't even know what half the things in them were. Silently, she put a morsel in her mouth.

Harikumar, meanwhile, had found his groove. He proceeded to describe the foods to her, and then spoke about how he was a good cook too, and about living in some hostel, not many years ago, where he had picked up those skills.

Meenakshi did not really listen to his words. She looked at his eyes, and she thought that they were gentle eyes. But then she recalled the lustful looks they had the first time he had seen her, and she cringed.

Somewhere, in the middle of all the talk, one of his sentences stood out, especially as there was a pause after it. As soon as Meenakshi realized what he had said, she registered it. 'I will never hurt you.'

She looked at him with unblinking eyes now. 'Hurt?' was the only word she said. Her first word to him as wife.

He smiled. 'May I call you Meenu?'

She nodded.

'You will always be happy with me,' he said. 'I am a good man. I don't drink, I don't smoke. No bad company. My business is legit. Meenu, you have nothing to worry about.'

Meenakshi's heart warmed as she heard those words. Maybe that was the normal state of things. Girls lived with their parents only up to a certain age and left their homes to make new ones with their husbands. She had heard her friends talk about the uncertainties concerning the kinds of husbands they would find, and here she had found one who was, even though by his own claim, a good man. Shouldn't she be happy?

He took the emptied meal box from her, went out of the car and threw it in a corner. Then he came back promptly and started the car.

There was no more talk the rest of the night.

❧

It was early dawn when Meenakshi opened her eyes, and the world seemed to have changed. They were now driving through a street teeming with people. Her quaint unpeopled village seemed to be in a different world altogether. People here were busily running around even at this hour, when even the cows didn't stir in her village. The roads were shiny and filled with strange cars. Men and women dressed in strange clothes looked into the car, and she felt conscious about still being in her bridal saree.

Then she realized that she had slept on the shoulder of the man, her husband, and he had not bothered to wake her up. She jerked up suddenly and saw she had left a patch of drool on his shirt.

'Welcome to Bombay,' he said.

The panic hit her full force now. She grabbed his arm, and then realizing that that was making him lose control over the car and it had begun to swerve, she left it and grabbed his thigh.

'Please!' she said.

'What? What is it, Meenu?' He narrowly missed a newspaper boy on a cycle, who shouted a terrible curse word that Meenakshi had never heard in her life.

'You have to let me go,' she said.

'What are you saying, Meenu?'

'You don't know anything! All the men who have touched me have met terrible fates. I don't know what Aai-Baba told you, but I am cursed.'

'Fuck cursed!' said Harikumar, and Meenakshi was suddenly struck by his change in tone. Maybe the city had changed him too. Maybe he would show his true colours soon, after having been gentlemanly so far.

'I don't care,' he said, softer now. 'It's our life now, Meenu. What is past is past. Here, in the city, no one believes in curses and hexes. No one has time.'

'Are you...are you...going to...'

'Am I going to what?'

Meenakshi looked away. She could not bear to look at him

anymore, the swearing man with gentle eyes. She only said, 'Touch me?'

Harikumar laughed aloud, so much so that he swerved again. 'Oh, foolish girl! Of course, I will touch you. I am your husband. But do you think marriage is all about husbands and wives touching each other?'

Meenakshi felt a warm sensation rise in her fingertips and she muttered under her breath, 'Oh God, no...no...not now!'

'What are you mumbling?'

Meenakshi hid her hands away from sight, and she told him, 'You say you will not hurt me? But don't you see? You can never hurt me. I am worried that I will hurt you.'

Harikumar turned to look at her, at her face, and the look of lust seemed to be back, if only for a moment. 'Are you trying to scare me?'

'You don't know...'

'Don't worry,' said Harikumar. 'Neither of us is going to hurt the other.'

He drove his car into the gate of a compound. Meenakshi's heart beat faster as she saw the cubbyhole apartments of the building. She could see through the windows of some of them, which looked smaller than a room in her old house. She saw shirtless men standing at the windows and brushing their teeth, she saw women in loose cotton maxis doing their stuff, and children getting ready for school.

And there was one more such room in this building where she would be touched tonight. By this man.

Harikumar parked the car and went running to open her side of the door. 'Well, come out!' he said. When she did, gingerly, measuring each step, he ran to the back of the car and brought out the suitcase containing her clothes.

'Is this...' she began.

'Your new home, yes,' said Harikumar. 'Come with me. I promise you, all your fears will soon be quelled.'

As she stepped out of the car in her red clothes, every head turned to look. She walked slowly, with the veil covering her face, and allowed herself to be led by him into a narrow corridor. He made her stand in front of something that looked like a cage, and pressed a button. Despite her mental state, she could not stop being curious. She recalled a friend telling her about things called elevators in city buildings, cages that you walked into and they took you wherever you wanted to go.

The elevator dinged and Harikumar pulled the door open. 'Well, get in,' he said. 'Don't be afraid.'

She stepped in, looking everywhere she could through the veil drawn over her face. He pressed the number 4 on some kind of a light board. The cage started moving upward and she gasped.

When it stopped with a jerk, she gasped again. Harikumar laughed and guided her out by holding her hand. They were now in a corridor with many doors. He pressed a doorbell.

Meenakshi looked around to see where the sudden chirping of the birds had come from. Harikumar chuckled again and pointed at the doorbell. She looked up and saw a picture of Ganpati stuck above the door frame. Just like in her old house. Village or city, some things didn't change. She could make new companions here. Like the Elephant God himself, perhaps?

'Who lives here?' asked Meenakshi.

Before he could answer, the door opened.

It was a middle-aged woman, dressed in a soft white saree with a dulcet green border. She squinted through the grills of her door, and then her face broke into a huge welcoming smile.

'Arre, Hari! You are here early! Come, come... I thought it was the cablewallah!' said the woman.

Harikumar took his shoes off and stepped inside. He tugged at Meenakshi's saree and she did the same.

'Tara Aatya,' he said. 'This is Meenakshi. Meenu.'

The woman named Tara stepped up and pushed the veil off Meenakshi's face, and placed a hand on her chin as though spellbound. 'Oh God, Hari! She is every bit as beautiful as you described. Are you sure you will be able to keep up with her?'

Harikumar laughed uneasily. 'Really, Tara Aatya!'

'Come in, Meenu,' said Tara. 'Don't wait at the door.'

Meenakshi saw a little more of the house. The room she was in was a hall with a seating arrangement in a corner near the window. She missed a beat when she looked down and realized how high above the city she was.

'Sit, Meenu!' Tara pointed at a soft couch, the kind Meenakshi had never seen before. 'I have started with the tea. If you want to freshen up, the bathroom's that way.'

Harikumar closed the door behind him and guided Meenakshi to sit on the couch as Tara disappeared into the kitchen. He sat on a low stool, facing her, but at a respectful distance.

'Is she your aunt?' asked Meenakshi.

'No, not by relation. I call her Aatya out of respect,' said Harikumar. 'Actually, Tara Aatya is like a mother to me. She is not related, though. She was my tuition teacher when I was in school. Her affection for me was boundless even then, as it is now.'

Meenakshi looked around and she saw something that made her feel a slight pinch. Directly above the TV, on the wall, was the garlanded picture of a man.

'Tara Aatya lost her husband many years ago. She has no children,' said Harikumar.

Tara came out with three cups and some biscuits on a tray. 'How old are you, Meenu?' she asked pointblank.

'I…I will be sixteen next month.'

'Which means you should have finished with your tenth standard by now. Did you go to school?'

'I did. But I didn't complete—'

'Oh, all right. You don't have to tell me everything right away,' said Tara. 'We will take care of it.'

The next few minutes were spent with Tara recounting episodes from Harikumar's childhood when he was her student. She laughed as she narrated his little misdemeanors and glowed with pride as she listed his academic achievements. When tea was done, Tara stood up. 'Come with me, Meenu. Let me show you your room.'

'My room?'

'Just come,' said Harikumar and guided her.

Tara walked ahead and opened a door. It was a small room, neatly done up with sparse furniture, and a single bed along one wall.

'This is where you will stay, Meenu,' said Tara. 'Hope you like it.'

'But...'

Tara heard the apprehension in Meenakshi's voice and then glared with big, round eyes at Harikumar. Then she lunged at him and pulled his earlobe. 'Hari, you rascal! Have you not told her yet?'

'Ow, ow, Tara Aatya! You tell her!' he laughed.

'Okay,' said Tara, 'what this idiot hasn't told you yet is that he is not going to live with you. For now, you will live with me and get an education. I have no one, you see, and we will have a wonderful time. I will make a fine lady out of you. All here at my place. Private education.'

'But...what about...he's my husband...'

'That he is,' said Tara. 'Hari, you tell her. This is your department. I am going to look at lunch.'

Harikumar closed the room and sat Meenakshi down on the bed. He took her face in his hands and said, 'It will be torture for me, Meenu, but I am not a monster. Did you think I will harm a child? The marriage is just a formality, and a rural marriage means nothing legally, to be honest. I did it so that I could bring you here, away from those people. Or else, I was prepared to wait. You will live here now, and I am still your husband. But we will officially marry only when you turn eighteen. And till then, I will not touch you in any way that you fear. Tell me if this arrangement is all right with you.'

Meenakshi was speechless, tears now threatening to spill out. Then she flopped down at his feet.

'How can I ever express my gratitude to you?' she said, still fighting back her happy tears. 'Oh, how mistaken I was! You are the kindest man I have ever met. How will I repay this debt?'

Harikumar jerked his legs away, aghast at the gesture. 'Get up, Meenu. Stop this nonsense. You will never touch my feet again, you understand? Just because I am your husband, it does not mean I am God. I am as human and as prone to making mistakes as you are. And I will commit a lot of them. Honestly, whenever I see you, lustful thoughts enter my mind. I fantasize about you. But I have steeled my mind to do the right thing. I want you, but not now, while you are still so young. Even now, I cannot resist the temptation to pin you against that wall and do things I have never done before. You don't know how much I have been struggling against myself the entire journey to stop that urge from taking over. And...and I am...just a man.'

He had her face in his hands as he said that, and now he raised her chin. For a frightening second, Meenakshi felt he would kiss her and everything would be undone.

But then he retreated. 'This is not right, Meenu. I am sorry. I cannot control myself any longer. I am leaving now.'

Meenakshi ran to the door. 'When will you be back?'

'In time,' he said. He stepped out of the door and paused. Then he looked at Tara, who was now standing behind Meenakshi. 'Aatya, just make sure no other man sees her,' he said. 'You know why I tell you that.'

'I know,' said Tara and bid him goodbye. Then she looked at Meenakshi and gave her a reassuring smile.

Part Two

The Blossom

Year 1999

15

Letters from the Starved

Sitting on a couch in the apartment that she had called home for three years, Meenakshi flipped through the pages of *The Times of India*. Her special interest, however, was not the news. Turning over the pages, she came exactly where she wanted to be—page 3 of the *Bombay Times* supplement.

Her finger moved over the curves of the one-eighth-page picture of a model in a body-hugging evening gown, and she smiled to herself. One of these days, if Tara Aunty allowed her, she would get such a gown too, and wear under it what the fashion-savvy people called 'lingerie'. It had taken a while for her to learn to pronounce that word.

Tara came and joined her for tea. She peered into the newspaper and laughed. 'What's that thing Madhu Sapre is wearing? Looks like it will fall right off her shoulders.'

Meenakshi retorted, 'This is fashion, Aunty!'

'Ah, don't you talk to me about fashion! When I was in college, I modelled a bit too.'

'Really? You modelled?'

'Why, look at me! Don't you see the spark even now?'

Meenakshi looked closely. 'Well, now that you say it—'

'Humph! You and your mockery. Go and find some strapless sackcloth like your favourite model is wearing in the name of fashion.'

'Well, don't fret, Aunty! Let's have our tea.' She picked up her cup and took a noisy uncivil sip. When Tara scowled at the indecent sound, she took another sip, this time silently elegant.

'Better,' said Tara. 'Being sophisticated is not just about replacing "Aatya" with "Aunty". It comes from within.'

'Yeah, yeah, *Aunty*. Point noted.'

On the table, the main newspaper began to flap. The breeze was strong at this time of the morning. Meenakshi took a tissue box to keep as weight, but then she saw something on the page.

She picked up the paper and whistled. 'Wow!'

'What is it?' asked Tara.

'Listen: *A premier ad agency is looking for new female models aged eighteen to twenty-two for an international shampoo brand. Payment on par with global standards. Walk-in interviews at—*'

'Why does that interest you?'

There was the lustre of wide-eyed wonder in Meenakshi's eyes. 'Oh, Aunty, don't you see? It's a great opportunity. I am good-looking and smart, and I will be eighteen in a month. I really want to do something now.'

Tara looked away. 'Cannot happen, Meenu.'

In a flash, her mood changed. 'Why not?'

'It just cannot.'

'Why did you teach me all that stuff then? Now I am on my way to graduating. But what use is all that if I am only supposed to sit at home?'

Tara took Meenakshi's hands in hers. 'I am not the one to decide this, Meenu. Your husband has entrusted you to me. He is the one you should ask.'

'So I'll ask him!' said Meenakshi with an edge to her voice. 'Call him here.'

That suggestion had the predictable result—silence.

'You can't, can you?' Meenakshi scoffed. 'Even if you do, he will not come! Of what use is such a husband who has not come to see his wife in five years? Only gifts, letters and phone messages—'

'MEENU!' Tara raised her voice, a rare thing for her. 'Take back your words about Hari this instant.'

Meenakshi only stared back.

'Take it back, Meenu. You know Hari does not deserve that. Not now, at least, when his self-imposed exile is coming to an end and he's making plans to start his life with you.'

Meenakshi knew that too. She had lately begun to look at the calendar a lot, counting the days down to her eighteenth. Each day brought a new wave of panic in her.

'I take back...' she said haltingly.

'Good!' said Tara. 'When he comes, *you* ask him. After that, you don't need to ask me anything. Ever.'

'Oh, Aunty, don't do that now!' Meenakshi shifted closer to the lady and put an arm around her shoulders. 'I know you don't like drama...'

'Of course I don't!' Tara stood up. 'Now get up. Let's do some work around the house rather than just sitting here talking about things that cannot be done.'

✿

Later, when Meenakshi was in the privacy of her room, she sensed hundreds of thoughts bubbling in her head, something that had been happening a lot lately.

Bombay—now politically renamed Mumbai—had put a new spin on her. She had gone out in the city, always under the careful protection and tutelage of her guardian, Tara Aunty. She had been awed by the buildings, some of which made her tilt her head all the way back to see where they ended. She had been in trains (in the ladies' compartments) and she had been in monstrous double-decker buses, and she had sat in autorickshaws, with Tara Aunty making sure that she wore layers of dupattas. Those dupattas had become a part of her whenever she stepped out of the house, no matter what outfit she wore.

But the biggest intrigue of the city was its people. Never before had Meenakshi seen such a large variety of people in one place. They were light-skinned and dark-skinned, tall and short, thin and fat, all kinds. A few of them were wearing the kind of clothes she had seen back in her village, but most of them wore outlandish things that she could not have dreamt of even in her wildest imaginations.

Once Tara Aunty told her, 'You mustn't just look at people's clothes, Meenu, but try to look at what's inside. Look at their emotions. Like that girl sitting all pretty with that guy there is probably feeling so out of place. Or that old man in his happy shorts and T-shirt gobbling up that frankie there. He's probably challenging his cholesterol levels, hidden from his family. And that man in the swanky business suit over there is probably full of worry about whether his meeting will go well. You need to learn to look within people and you'll hear so many stories.'

'Then why do you make me wear these dupattas?' Meenakshi once asked her.

'Because people are shallow.'

Such doublespeak confused her.

On most days, Meenakshi stayed at home and gained knowledge of the outside world through television. She watched shows from all over the world on cable TV and found out that though Mumbai was so hugely different from her village, there were other places that were far away, and they were far more different. There were languages she could not make head or tail of, buildings she would not know where to enter from, foods she would not know how to pronounce the names of, and clothes that did not look like anything anyone could wear.

And there was a world of weathers out there. It wasn't hot and humid everywhere. In some places it snowed, and some places had huge mountains, both snow-covered and fire-spouting. Some had vast stretches of cold, cold oceans. All this put the fear of nature in her heart. Something deep within her told her that there was nothing more terrifying than the magnitude of nature. Man could not hold a candle to nature's whims and fancies.

That is where her thoughts usually stopped. The voice that came from deep within her put an end to her mental ramblings. That voice told her that she knew more than she knew. That this face she wore was just a face, a masquerade, and within it lay the real her. And the real her was different; it did not seek this knowledge, because she already had it. The real her did not want an aunt or a husband to take care of her. The real her was dangerous. She was buried deep within her, waiting to come out.

And sometimes, on those lonely nights when she lay on her bed in that now-familiar room, that real her clawed at her. It prodded her into wakefulness, telling her that there was more to come. That this was just a transitional period and it would soon pass.

✿

Days before her birthday, Meenakshi spent an afternoon rereading the letters that Harikumar had sent her. Those sweet-smelling aerogrammes always did something to her. They made her feel loved, and for a few minutes, she could be one with them.

But that voice would raise itself sometimes, and it would prick at her like a pin punctures a forefinger for a blood sample.

'*Looking forward to him, are we?*'

Meenakshi would then throw her hands over her ears, though she knew that she could not be shut up this way.

'*Well, suit yourself. I only hope he's nice to you.*'

'Dare you try anything on him, bitch!'

'*Why? Have you fallen in love with him?*'

Meenakshi opened the letters. The first letter was written soon after his parting. She reread a part of it.

> *I hear you are quite well-adjusted in Tara Aatya's house. That's a good thing. You be a good girl too, and don't trouble her much. I cannot tell you how much I miss you, how much I want to hold you and be with you. I love you. Please stay well till the time comes.*

There was another letter two weeks later.

> *So, I have finally received the call. I will relocate to New York in a week. It is a big city, bigger than Mumbai, and it is in this country called America. How I wish I could take you there and we could be together in that faraway land!*

I have heard there are beautiful girls in America, a lot of them, but I promise to stay away. Only for you. I want to give you all of me when the time comes.

There was another when she completed high school.

Congratulations! Do study further. You will probably have started your graduation course by the time we meet again. Tara Aatya and I have discussed some courses that you could attend from home via correspondence. She will guide you.

Don't worry about me. I am doing great here. The Americans love us Indians for our brains and hard work. I am impressing them all! Quite a few ladies too! But all of me is for my Meenu, and I think about you every night. Wink wink! You know what I mean!

Another letter was fairly recent, but it was the most creased. Meenakshi knew that word by word, and she directly went to the paragraph that she loved to read the most.

Wow! Is that how you look now? How will I finish the rest of the letter now? I want to stop everything right now and fly to you. This instant. Meenu, I am saving myself for you despite all the temptations I have all around me. Yet, that is not entirely true. The truth is, after seeing you, I just don't feel aroused by any other woman. It just does not work the same way it used to earlier.

If only there wasn't this restriction of your age, Meenu... When will these few months pass?

A smile dancing on her lips now, she came to the last one she had received at the beginning of the month. As she read it, the colour on her face began to change.

So, it is done! This is my last letter to you from here, Meenu. In four weeks, I will be with you, in your loving embrace, and there will be nothing to separate us. I will make love to you all night and feel your magic, for which I have been longing all this while. I am sure it will be worth the wait.

I have already packed my bags, and I have what you wanted, that lingerie you asked for. To be honest, I cannot even look at it, for then I imagine you in it.

Just a few days more! I cannot stop smiling. How will that day be when I finally take you to my house, which will now be truly our house. I hope Tara Aatya will understand my longing for you.

Meenakshi felt the rising pang in her chest now. She looked at the calendar, and particularly at the one date that she had circled in red ink about a hundred times.

16

Black Thread

She felt Harikumar's fingers on her waist, tapping on her skin lightly, stopping only for a moment to circle the slight bump of her navel, and then moving downward.

A sigh escaped her lips as his other hand moved to her back and cupped her rear. He pulled her closer, till skin met skin in a tingling union.

'Don't worry,' he breathed into her ear. 'We will go slow. We have our entire lives to do this.'

Meenakshi nodded, and felt him guiding her hand to the front of his groin. On his face was an assuring smile, coaxing her, encouraging her, telling her this was all right now, nothing would go wrong. With her hand still resisting, she pondered. Every pore of her body wanted to reach out to him, to touch him, to let him touch her. There was a dam inside that was waiting to burst, but there was also the fear.

She retreated, leaving him breathing hard. 'Sorry,' she said. 'I am sorry.'

'Don't, Meenu,' he said. 'I can't take it anymore.'

She was depriving him. Why didn't he get angry? Why didn't he yell out at her?

Maybe, just maybe, love would conquer everything. Maybe the creature inside her would not dig her evil claws into this man because this was not lust, this was love.

Maybe that creature did not even exist anymore?

But no…she felt the prickling in her fingertips. Oh, she was there all right! And she was seeing the naked flesh of Harikumar too, but with a totally different view. While Meenakshi wanted to treasure every cell of that body for eternal life, the creature wanted to ravage it with her talons and fangs, tear it to shreds, make a bloody pulp of it.

'*Isn't he just another sleazy bastard?*'

'Come, Meenu,' implored Harikumar. 'It is all right.'

Meenakshi held him. But the voice wouldn't shut up.

'*Just look at him. The only life in him right now is in his groin. Perverts, all of them.*'

'Come,' he said.

Her eyes were now focused only on him. He reached out and pulled her closer. Taking her to the bed, he tucked his fingers into her waistband and pulled the garment down.

She sighed. Never before had this happened to her; she had been told this was an experience to cherish. The man she loved was looking at her with love and respect, at every inch of her, and nothing would be wrong. Nothing.

'*Don't like it, you fool!*'

He gently pulled her legs apart and brought himself closer. 'Relax, Meenu. Nothing will happen,' he said.

She shut her eyes, trying to quell that scratchy feeling in her fingertips. She breathed hard, letting him guide her.

'*Oh, don't give in! The shame, the submission! I'll take care of this.*'

Her fingers erupted even as he made the first thrust. While he was blind to everything else right now, she could only see the fingers of her right hand, as the skin peeled off from the tips and retracted, and the bloody red maw inside was exposed. She saw her nails uprooting and falling on the bed, like many bloodied petals, and her fingers begin to swell to monstrous proportions.

'Isn't this heaven, Meenu?' Harikumar sighed, trying to thrust into her in a soft rhythm as though to some unheard music.

But she didn't respond. She couldn't respond. She was paralysed now. The thing inside her had taken over. Her hands flew up, those bloody red things, and they landed on his naked back.

'Wha—?' he said, and his eyes bulged out. Those thin red veins in them turned redder. The skin on his face contracted and fissures erupted on it like it were about to crack, and then it did crack.

He was hurtled away to the wall, howling like a madman, and as that happened, his skin ripped apart and came off in the fiendish talons that her hands had become.

She sat up, half-human-half-demon now, and she saw in disbelief the skinned man collapsing, making whatever sounds his ruptured larynx could make, and then flopping to the floor, twitching away to lifelessness.

She became aware of something dangling from her fingernails— the two halves of her husband's skin that she had pulled out.

'*That's it. He will bother you no more.*'

'NOOO!' she screamed, and everything went blank.

As she sat up in her single bed, which was now wet with her sweat and tears, Meenakshi realized that this wasn't new. The nightmare haunted her every night. Her gaze fell on the calendar up ahead, and she saw, to her immense relief, that this wasn't the day. There were still two days left.

But oh, what a nightmare! Or was it a premonition?

❦

The next morning, Meenakshi was awoken mid-sleep by a tapping on her arm. She rubbed her eyes open to see Tara standing by her side, her silver hair flying in the breeze like threads on a chewed-up ragdoll.

'Come outside,' she said. 'There's a surprise for you.'

'Hari?'

'No, silly. He's coming day after. Impatient?'

Tara went out, leaving her to guess. Meenakshi yawned her way to the bathroom to wash up before stepping out.

The moment she stepped out, though, she could not hold herself. Her eyes welled up and her throat choked up as she found her Aai-Baba seated on the couch by the window.

Renuka ran up to Meenakshi and hugged her, and there was that sweet village smell again, and Meenakshi knew what she had been missing. 'Aai...Aai...' she tore up as she hugged her back. 'How...all of a sudden?'

She could not remember the last time they had visited.

'Just a little something for you,' said Shantaram, getting up. He made as if to hug her but then made do with a faint peck on her cheek instead.

That 'little something' was three sacks lying close to bursting on the floor.

'Oh, my God, Bhau! What is all that?' said Tara as she came out with a tea tray.

'Fresh produce from Vatgaon,' Shantaram beamed. 'Just some jackfruit and raw mangoes and coconuts.'

'And some rice laddoos that I made myself,' Renuka chimed in. 'Do not refuse us, Tai.'

Tara was overwhelmed at the address of 'Tai'. Though loosely spoken, the word carried respect, for it meant 'older sister'. 'Okay, sure,' she said. 'All of it will go to Harikumar's house anyway.'

'No, this is for you. And that is why we have come here,' said Renuka, sitting down and pulling Meenakshi down beside her. 'Day after, our girl will go to her husband's house, and you know how awkward it will be to visit the son-in-law's house.'

'Ah, doesn't matter,' said Tara. 'Come here as many times as you please. Think of this as your house in Bombay.'

'Mumbai,' corrected Shantaram. 'It is Mumbai now.'

'Ah! Don't get me started,' Tara retorted. 'I was born in Bombay and will die in Bombay. Politics can go to hell.'

Tongues really loosened over lunch. Though the Patils had visited earlier, this turned out to be the longest visit. Despite the standing invitation for future visits, everyone knew there was a kind of finality to this one.

'So, how is everything back in the village?' Tara asked, warily guiding the conversation to deeper waters.

The undercurrent of that thinly-disguised question did not escape its listeners, especially Renuka. She plonked her spoon in her bowl of dal and said, 'Everything's fine, Tai. With four daughters married to wonderful husbands now, we are a happy household.'

'Good to hear,' said Tara. 'And the house? Village? All well? Neighbours and all?'

The last part of the question hung in the air.

'Yes, Tai,' said Renuka. 'Now, what to hide from you? You have been a mother to our daughter for five years now, so you know everything about the village.'

Renuka looked into her plate again, but her mind wandered. She saw glimpses of the villagers avoiding her, children throwing egg shells in her verandah, no one wanting to be their tenants anymore.

'We are happy Meenu is fine,' said Shantaram. 'You have brought her up with motherly love and made such a fine lady of her. We can never thank you enough.'

'Oh, drop that!' Tara brushed away the praise with a wave of her hand. 'Your daughter is intelligent. Why, now she wants to work! Be a model, no less!'

A moment of silence ensued as three pairs of elderly eyes bored into Meenakshi. She fidgeted with her plate.

'Anyway, that's for her husband and her to decide,' said Renuka, rising to wash her hands.

❦

Just before leaving, Renuka took Meenakshi into her room for a little private talk. Closing the door, she said, 'So, he's coming back on Sunday?'

Meenakshi nodded.

'Your married life truly begins now, Meenu,' said Renuka. 'Are you happy?'

'Aai, you know...'

'Yes, I know.' Renuka gently put Meenakshi's head on her bosom in a bid to give her comfort. 'You are worried that...some harm will come upon him...'

Meenakshi looked at her with fearful eyes.

'Like what happened with others?'

Meenakshi stayed silent.

'I anticipated your fear,' said Renuka, 'and that is the real reason why I came here today.'

As Meenakshi continued to look at her, Renuka thrust her hand into her purse and brought out something. It was a black thread.

'A Swami came to our village a few days ago,' she said. 'Without telling anyone, not even your father, I went to see him. Barefoot, as the condition was. At first, he brushed me aside like I were some ordinary visitor, but when I told him some specific things, I caught his interest. He spoke to me, and he said some things that you should know.'

'What?'

It was evident that Renuka was finding it difficult to produce words, though she had a lot to say. 'You have to steel yourself, Meenu. It is time you knew.'

'Say it, Aai.'

'He confirmed my fears, actually. He said you have signs of some kind of possession. Usually, possessions last for a short while. Like a few hours or, at the most, days. But whatever is inside you has been in you for very long. Since your birth itself.'

Meenakshi just stared.

'You don't know a few things, Meenu. After six daughters, your father wanted a son. So, when I got pregnant again, we performed an elaborate ritual in the seventh month to appease a spirit. The spirit of a Yakshini.'

Cold sweat began to grow on Meenakshi's back. 'What's a Yakshini?'

'Yakshinis are female deities, like demigods, with great wish-fulfilling powers. If a Yakshini blesses you, you get what your heart desires. But they are unpredictable. They can be good or bad.'

'So, why am I not a boy?'

'The ritual went wrong. There were things to be done

specifically, and the tantrik did not have the right knowledge. I was sitting next to him under the sal tree in our garden, which is where we performed the rite. At one point, through the corner of my eye, I saw something horrible coming at us from the skies. Then I felt this searing pain in my womb and immediately the tree caught fire. That was not a good omen, Meenu. The tantrik abandoned the ritual and ran away.'

'But the sal tree is—'

'I know. That was a miracle too. When you were a toddler, you touched it once, and new leaves sprouted on the charred tree the very next day. That was when I knew that there was something special about you.'

Meenakshi looked on, not understanding, not knowing what to say. 'Yakshini? What am I to do, Aai? You tell me this thing inside me, this voice that I cannot stop hearing, is a Yakshini? This one is definitely not wish-fulfilling, Aai. She is destroying my life.'

Renuka could only stare at her with benign eyes.

'What do Yakshinis do?'

'They do different things, Meenu. Not all of them are harmful. But the one that's inside you—the Swami told me—seems to be dangerous. He told me this Yakshini is one who feeds on amorous men. She is irresistible to men and when they are at the height of passion, she feeds on them.'

'Oh!' said Meenakshi. 'That explains. Tappu. Govind. But, but Hari? I don't want any harm—'

Renuka handed the black thread to Meenakshi. 'That's why I am here today. Tie this thread on your left upper arm, near the heart. As long as you have it, the Yakshini inside you will stay inside. When you…will be with your husband, it will protect you. And him.'

Renuka tied the thread on Meenakshi's arm.

'Think of it as protection,' she said. 'Not all women are lucky enough to be able to ward off unwanted men. You can!'

A faint smile broke on Meenakshi's lips. But then there was also the fear—the fear that her Hari would be the test.

17

Honeynoon

*O*n the morning that Harikumar was to arrive, Tara went to Meenakshi's room to find that she was already awake, sitting up in bed, and staring at nothing in particular.

'Ah, I can understand the impatience!' Tara said with a mischievous smile.

Meenakshi attempted a smile.

'Well, get up then,' Tara urged. 'Flight's on time. We'll take an hour to reach the airport.'

Meenakshi did not stir. She opened her mouth to say something, but then closed it again.

Tara came closer. 'What's it? Are you all right?'

'Just feeling uneasy.'

Tara's grin widened. 'I can understand that! Do you feel like your stomach is flying away? Like your mind wants to run ahead of you and your feet are too numb to carry you? Like your blood is hot and cold at the same time?'

Meenakshi smiled. It was a genuine smile this time.

'Well, I was young once too,' said Tara. 'Once when your Uncle was out of town for seven days, and that was soon after our marriage, I was in a similar condition on the day he was coming back. A bundle of nerves. Felt like I'd collapse.'

'Aunty,' said Meenakshi faintly, 'is it possible…that only you go and pick him up? I…I don't think I can…'

Tara ran her fingers through Meenakshi's long tresses. 'Hmm, okay. Will do that. Anyway, he's going to be all yours once he reaches here.'

'Thank you, Aunty.'

'Meanwhile, you use the time to dress up as well as you can,' said Tara. 'I know you are the most beautiful girl I have ever seen, but this is a special occasion. Not just for him but for yourself also. Don't think women dress up for men; they dress up for themselves. It makes them feel better; makes them feel special. There is not going to be another day like this in your life.'

Meenakshi shivered at the truth of those words. She kept sitting in her place for a few minutes after Tara left, and then slowly proceeded to the bathroom.

❧

Meenakshi dressed up in a saree. She draped the red and green one with the golden border, and she did it perfectly. The creases and folds hung on her like they were hugging her.

She said a silent 'thank you' to her Aai, who had taught her how to drape a saree.

But now, as she felt the caresses of the saree, it pained her. This was just a garment, and she could easily make it a part of her, but could she do that to a living, breathing person? What if she couldn't? There was the fear of losing someone she had come to love, but there was also the fear of being exposed for what she was hiding within—the rotten truth of her existence.

She had never been afraid for herself. On her first night, Tara had asked her if she'd be scared to sleep alone in that room, and Meenakshi had laughed. Sometimes while watching TV shows with Tara, there would be gory scenes and Tara would look away, but Meenakshi would be unaffected. Were there any fears she hadn't experienced yet?

Yes, there was the fear of losing a loved one. The fear of pillaging, ravaging, tearing to shreds the person she loved.

❧

She opened the door at the tenth ring.

Harikumar was at the door, standing like an eager child, covering his eyes with his hands. Beneath those hands, Meenakshi could see an almost-boyish smile. The same one he had left her with. It gladdened her heart.

After all those years, the first words she heard from him were: 'I am not going to open my eyes so easily.'

Tara came up behind him, huffing as she climbed the last of the stairs. 'Lift is not working,' she panted, 'and this boy didn't even wait for me.' She smacked him on the head, walked past him, went inside and realized he was still stuck at the door. 'Hari, what game is this?'

'You go inside, Aatya!' said Harikumar. 'You won't understand. I have heard that my wife has turned so beautiful that no one can take all her beauty in at one go.'

'Young romantic fools!' Tara shook her head and went past them.

Still standing at the door, Meenakshi blushed. 'Are you going to stand like that forever?' she asked coyly.

A radiant smile grew on his lips. 'Ah, that voice!'

'Well?'

'Wait, wait!' Harikumar protested. 'You know how you should not look at the sun directly? It burns your eyes. Just like that—'

'You don't look at eclipses directly too.'

'You break my heart, Meenu. Here I am, comparing you with the most beautiful, the most brilliant thing in all the universe, and you are doing yourself this disservice. Let me look at you slowly. I have won that right fair and square.'

Meenakshi rolled her eyes. 'I see America has done something to you.'

'That was the whole point of going there,' he said, and winked.

Meenakshi saw the wink through the gap between his fingers. So, he had been seeing her all along! Slowly, playfully, she began to back off, her silent feet leading to the bedroom.

'Oh, okay,' said Harikumar. 'Both of us can play childish games, of course!'

He took one step further as she took one back. Thus they

walked, matching step for step, one going back and the other going forward, till they were in the bedroom. She stood in the middle of the room, while he positioned himself at the door.

'Safe,' he said. 'Now let me see the dazzling beauty that everyone in the city is talking about.'

'Everyone?'

Slowly, he parted his fingers. As he opened his eyes, they grew wider, and he whistled. 'Oh my holy goodness! Do I deserve you? Everything is so perfect about you. And look at me, all skin and bones!'

'I am glad you are back.' Trying to steer the conversation away from her looks, she asked, 'Did you have a good time?'

'As good as one can have without their soul.'

There was the smile of a joyful reunion on his face. Meenakshi realized that she hadn't ever received that smile from anyone else. This was a smile of pure happiness. 'I have been waiting for you for so long!' she said.

Harikumar held her hand, and something warm coursed through her. 'Aatya talked only about you all the way here. Or maybe I asked only about you! Anyway, Meenu, after lunch I will take you to our house. Our house! Can you believe it?'

Meenakshi did not tell him that that was all she had been thinking about for the past few weeks.

'It's all set up there. All primed to receive its queen.'

'I cannot wait...' she said, her voice trailing off.

❧

All through the way to the new house, Meenakshi sat dazed, not daring to speak a word. Instead, she leaned as far back as her seat could go, and thought of the life that awaited her.

The face of Harikumar had never left her thoughts. Now that he was here, the man who had saved her life in a way, she was overwhelmed. And she could not stop fidgeting with the black thread on her arm, as if it were a rosary she was praying on.

Finally, Harikumar drove the car into a building gate.

He pointed somewhere high up and said, 'That's our home. Nineteenth floor. Just you and I.'

From that step on, everything was a new experience. The way the watchman stood up saluting her, the swanky lobby of the building lined with exquisite stone, the automated lift that opened by itself, and their door with its sophisticated locks. They overwhelmed her as he ushered her in, holding her hand all the way. One wall of the house was only made of glass from top to bottom, and she could see the furious sea in the distance, the waves constantly lashing at the sands and receding, their ferocity spent.

'Your house is like the five star hotel rooms I have seen on TV,' mused Meenakshi, absently running her fingertips on the walls of the house.

'*Our* house, dear!' Harikumar held her hands. 'One of the safest neighbourhoods in the city, and the safest house in the neighborhood. Meenu...' He made her sit on a chair and went down on his knees by her side. 'How can I let you live just about anywhere? This house which we shall now turn into a home was bought with everything I inherited. And, you know, even then, it is not the dearest thing to me. Can you guess what that is?'

An unfamiliar fear gripped Meenakshi's heart. Did she really deserve this man?

'Come in, my darling!' Harikumar got up and led her. 'With you by my side, I will buy fifty such houses. But now, you cannot tell me to stop myself any longer.'

Meenakshi knew what he meant and she proceeded with slow steps. She saw the room ahead of her, the one with the shut door, and she knew what was going to happen.

Harikumar pushed the door open, and all of a sudden, a strong whiff of jasmine and rose filled their nostrils.

He grabbed her arm playfully, and she looked. The bed was right in front of her, adorned with petals of blood-red roses, waiting to be lain on. Much beyond, she could see tiny ant-sized people playing in the tumultuous waves.

'This is our paradise,' said Harikumar, 'and this is our wedding night. Technically, afternoon! Not honeymoon but honeynoon!' He laughed.

Meenakshi worked a smile on her face. She moved towards Harikumar—her Harikumar—and placed her head on his chest. She could hear his heart thumping, and she knew that every thump bore no other thought but of her.

Harikumar stepped back. Delicately, he took the end of her saree and began to unroll it. He did it as one unwraps a delicate confectionary, taking care not to disturb the preciously crafted contents inside.

'You will have to forgive me if I do not do justice to your beauty,' said Harikumar. 'I am new at this, just as you are. Let's learn together.'

As he unhooked her blouse, Meenakshi's reflex was to throw her hands over her breasts, but he tenderly moved them away. Each movement of his, each caress, was filled with care. Painful memories flashed through Meenakshi's mind, of lecherous men, groping hands and lustful eyes, but there was none of that here. Lust and love are both four-letter words, and now Meenakshi was learning the difference between them.

Like a baby he lay his head between her breasts, and she welcomed him in her protective embrace, and they stayed like that for a long minute before moving over to the bed.

When Meenakshi opened her eyes, she found herself in the perfumed bed, and her man in the form that nature had made him, with a smile on his lips, tenderly bringing himself closer to her. She saw an assurance in that smile, and she knew it was okay to let go.

'I promise to be gentle,' he said, and took off the last piece of clothing that separated him from her.

And then she gave in and stilled. This time the stillness was not due to any memory or the hundred fears that were plaguing her. She was seeing her husband's male member for the first time.

As Harikumar eased, not taking his eyes off her, and lowered himself into her, Meenakshi kept her hands over her head. With concern writ large on his face, he said, 'Do not worry. This will be good.'

'Now tell me. Isn't he just one of them too?'

Meenakshi's breath stuck in her throat. Here she was. Coming now.

She held the black thread that was on her arm as tightly as she could, as if goading it into action.

'Hold me, Meenu,' said Harikumar. 'Keep your hands on my back.'

'Horny bastards. All of them.'

Slowly, reluctantly, she brought one hand out, and placed it on his back, fearful that it might turn into a clawed appendage during the journey from her head to his back. But it didn't. She moaned, and her fingers, still human and tender, made contact with the small of his back and then moved upward, as if guiding him to enter her.

❦

'I could write a poem about your breasts,' said Harikumar later, lying next to his wife, spent. He was now admiring her form like a painter does a muse that he's just about to immortalize in his art.

Meenakshi laughed. It was a nervous laugh, for she was still reeling from the aftereffects of what had happened and, more than that, what could have happened.

Harikumar turned to face her. He reached out and felt her hand and held it till it stopped quivering.

'Meenu,' he said, 'we have to spend a lifetime together. I don't want you to be afraid of anything. I don't want you to begin things with any doubt. All you have to do is trust me. Things will be all right.'

Meenakshi had a reply to that, but she kept it to herself.

'I trust you, Hari, but can I trust myself?'

'What are you worried about?' he asked.

'I worry that this happy moment might not last.'

'We will make it last.'

'How can you say that, Hari?' Meenakshi's voice gained confidence, now that the barrier of the first sentence was broken. 'How can we depend on ourselves to make it last?'

'Who else does it depend on if not on you and me?'

'I love you, Hari, but the truth is that I don't know you,' she said. 'I only have sketchy details of you, mostly fed to me through others.'

'What do you want to know?'

'That first day you came,' Meenakshi gulped. 'Wasn't it for my sister? You liked her. Then what happened all of a sudden?'

Harikumar smiled, 'I knew you'd ask me that.'

'Well, tell me.'

'You want to hear your own praises?'

'About time.'

'Your sister is beautiful. She is intelligent and mature and I am sure her husband is a very happy man. But you are something else. Your beauty is incomparable. If your sister is like a rainbow, you are like the sun peeking from the clouds that herald that rainbow. The moment I saw you, Meenu, everything else blurred. From then on, I had eyes only for you. I forgot all manners, all thoughts, all etiquette. I gained courage. Words came automatically to me. And never have I been surer of my decisions than of the one I took that day—that I wanted to make you my wife.'

'Which you did,' said Meenakshi after Harikumar fell silent. 'Despite hearing things about me.'

'How was any of that your fault, Meenu? What could you do if a boy went missing after breaking into your house? Of course, I heard that. How does that reflect on you?' Harikumar shifted and continued in a more sombre tone, 'Yes, there is more. I was in the village for a while. I heard things about you. I heard some very lewd talk going on back there. I wanted to break a few bones. But the talk did not deter me. It only convinced me that I had to take you away from there as soon as possible.'

'And here I am.'

'Here you are.'

'Thank you, Hari, for pouring your heart out to me,' said Meenakshi.

Harikumar waved away her thanks, and then he said like it was just a casual afterthought, 'So which Devi do you pray to?'

'Me? None.'

'Then what's that black thread?'

Meenakshi felt a sharp current run through her.

'What…'

'That black thread on your arm. Looks like it is representative of some Goddess.'

'It isn't.'

'Oh, don't tell me it is some black magic thing…'

'No!' said Meenakshi. 'It is just something to ward off the evil eye.'

'Ah, the evil eye! Well, keep wearing it then. You are liable to attract the evil eye!'

Laughing, he fell back on the bed, and slowly his hand went back on his new wife's velvet-soft abdomen.

Minutes later, he was asleep, his head nuzzling her side. But Meenakshi was wide awake, staring at the ceiling. Late-evening shadows were beginning to loom over her now, and she felt she would choke on the secrets she was keeping hidden within her.

18

Special Delivery

*W*eeks passed in bliss. The new couple spent every possible moment together, getting intimate with each other—both physically and mentally. Meenakshi laid bare her soul, bit by bit, frightened at first and then giving in, and she saw that her husband was a well-educated gentleman who did not like violence, loved home-cooked food, was courteous and respectful towards women, had few friends, and lived an uncomplicated life.

She had adjusted to living in a bubble, but she knew it would not last. She knew that she was a married woman now and soon the time would come when she would have to step out of her house, as her husband would want to introduce her to his friends. Or there might be parties he would want to take her to. Or he may just plan something out of the house—a dinner date, a movie outing, a trip to the mall—anything. And she feared how that would burst the bubble she was living in.

How could she tell him that his wife had brought along a dowry, a creature living inside her; and that creature was always a part of their communion, and would probably also be in part a mother to their future children?

These were her demons. She had to battle them herself. Every time she glanced at her husband, when he came out of the bath or when he was dressing up, she saw the frailty of his body. It wouldn't take a moment to snap it in two.

That very thought of her husband being killed by herself during a night of steamy passion would not let her live in peace.

'Let me out. Let me have a go at him. It will be a feast.'

That voice inside her constantly haunted her. But no. Not this time. 'I won't allow you to have your way,' she would say. 'You will die in there, in my body that you have invaded. But you will not lay a finger on him.'

Her black thread had been her rescuer so far, but for how long? Every morning when she went for her bath, she saw the thread wearing away, fibre after fibre of it coming loose. She felt the tingling under her skin getting more intense every night. It was as if the thing inside her was winning. How long would it be before the thread came off?

Maybe it would come off when he was making love to her, when his guileless face was looking at her, and nothing else. And then the Yakshini would emerge, and dance on the body of her loving husband till a mangled bloodied heap would be all that would be left of him.

🌷

One morning, she received a call from her mother.

There was silence after the initial hellos, and then Renuka said, 'You okay, Meenu? Is everything all right?'

Meenakshi said meekly, 'Yes, Aai.'

'Good. I am glad you are keeping your husband happy.'

'How are things back in the village?'

'Great! We got a proposal for Rutuja. Decent guy. Lives in Delhi. Kayastha family. Everything matches. Your Baba says we should go for it. All our girls are scattered in different cities as it is.'

'That's good, Aai. I am happy. Then you will be left with only Kumud.'

'Ah, she is getting her fair share of attention too,' said Renuka. 'I did not believe in God much once, but now I do. It is only because of the blessings of Amba Mata that things worked out for all of us and we came out of that black hole.'

Meenakshi cleared her throat and said, 'Things…aren't quite out of the black hole, Aai.'

'What do you mean, child?'

'Aai, the black thread is coming off.'

'What black thread?'

'You don't remember? It's on its last tethers now. I don't know what will happen. Aai, my life is literally hanging by a thread here.'

After a pause, Renuka said, 'Meenu, do you really think the black thread saved your marriage?'

'What else then? I can feel the…the thing inside me trying to come out. I can feel it, Aai. There's that tingling in my fingers.'

'Oh!' Another moment of silence ensued. 'There is no way to get another thread, Meenu. That Swami was a wandering hermit. Who knows what part of the world he is in now?'

Meenakshi stayed silent.

'But don't worry, child. Pray to Amba Mata. Visit her temple. Ask Hari to take you. Things will be all right.'

'Okay, Aai. Give my regards to Baba.'

⚘

Five mornings later, she almost lost the thread in the bath. She didn't realize it right away, but when she looked in the mirror, she saw not her face but the horrific face of the Yakshini staring back at her with blazing red eyes and an obscene hunger in them. And then she saw that the black thread wasn't there. Shaking all over, she turned off the faucet and splashed the pooled water all around, kicking and beating the soap suds away. Her heartbeat returned only when she saw a slender line of black making its way to the drain. She lurched and caught the last centimetre of the thread, pulling it out before it disappeared down the drain, cutting her finger from a chipped tile in the process. She held it on her arm and stood up. The entity in the mirror was gone; she was herself again.

It was a challenge to tie the thread back on her arm. She tried tying it with the help of another thread, but the tingling wouldn't go. She wrapped the thread in plastic, rolled it into a tube, and then tried to glue it together, but it didn't work.

Sniffling back her frustration, she managed to stretch the

much-beaten thread as much as possible and tied a small knot to secure it. It was on her wrist now, and she hoped it would work. The thread had shrunk; it barely went around her wrist once. Somehow she had managed to bring the ends together and work up a weak knot.

That evening, Harikumar seemed super-charged when he returned from work. He had won a small victory by signing a deal with a new service provider, and he expected to be rewarded. He dropped amorous hints all through dinner, and Meenakshi responded with nervous giggles, and then he suggested they go to bed early.

'You don't seem to be in it, Meenu,' he said, after he pulled off the last fabric that was on her.

Meenakshi shook her head. Her hands were on top of her head now. One hand clasped the other wrist, doing its best to keep the thread in place.

He lowered himself and kissed her on the chest. 'Come on, put your hands on my back. You know I like that.'

Praying, Meenakshi put her hands on his back. She moved them slowly in an arc, her eyes minutely observing the thread, and then placed her fingers on his naked spine.

'I like this! Squeeze harder! Hold me tight.'

Meenakshi's fingers trembled on his back. She moved them in faint lines along his ribs.

He laughed. 'You are tickling me! Is it some new game?'

She held him tighter. And then she felt him sliding into her, and in that moment, she lost all other senses. Her eyes closed, she let out a deep moan of ecstasy and quivered along with him.

'Now! Your fingers on his helpless back. One jab and it'll do it. Let me come out! Lose that black thread.'

'Damn you!' said Meenakshi.

She did not stop praying now. The voice was back, louder now, persistent. She hoped he'd come soon, while the thread still stayed. Somehow, it seemed, this night too would pass.

But fate had other plans.

'Your fingers...' said Harikumar, 'they feel wonderful on my back now, Meenu.'

'Hee Hee! You thought you could stop me?'

That was when she opened her eyes, her pupils dilated. Those words made her alarmingly conscious; it was a sick, scratchy consciousness that started at the tips of her fingers.

Yes, the demoness was winning. She felt her fingers hardening, matting up as they used to. She could not see them now, but she could visualize the rough-as-sandpaper scabs that must have grown on their bulbous tips, and then they would move upward, upward to her palms, and then her arms and then the whole of her.

The thread was broken. Lost. She knew it.

'Let's take this bastard out, shall we?'

'SHUT UP! SHUT UP!' Meenakshi screamed and immediately threw her hands over her ears. With all the strength that she had, she struggled and threw him off her.

Harikumar landed by her side, puzzled, his face like she had never seen before.

'Meenu...what the hell?'

Just then, the doorbell rang so loudly that it made her scream.

'Now who?' said Harikumar.

The doorbell continued to ring persistently.

'Go look,' said Meenakshi, gently pushing him away.

Harikumar pulled on his boxers and went out, grumbling. The moment he was out of sight, Meenakshi got up and began to look. She pulled away the rumpled sheets and the pillows and looked in the crevices of the bed. She looked in their clothes that were randomly strewn on the floor. The thread was nowhere.

She heard voices outside. He was talking to someone. Slowly, she peeped out of the bedroom to look.

Someone in a delivery boy's uniform was at the door. The smell of slightly burnt Chinese food wafted into her nostrils. Harikumar was explaining an address to him.

'Did you get that now?' he asked the man in a vexed tone.

The delivery guy looked beyond Harikumar's shoulder, and under that overlarge uniform cap he wore, Meenakshi could see his eyes boring right into her. She pulled her gown tighter on her cleavage.

'What is it, Hari?'

'He came to the wrong address,' said Harikumar and proceeded to slam the door on the delivery guy.

Just then, the guy said, 'Madam...'

Meenakshi stiffened.

'What is it?' asked Harikumar with greater annoyance.

'There is something on the floor.'

'Where?' Meenakshi looked.

'There,' said the man, pointing.

Then Meenakshi saw it. It was the thread. Lying on the floor tile in front of her; an impossibility, of course. How could it have come here? But this talisman was different. Whole. Not frayed. It was a new thread!

She quickly stooped and picked it up and mumbled, more out of reflex than out of intention, 'Thanks.'

The man tipped his cap. That was when Meenakshi recognized him.

This was no delivery man.

It was him again. Krita—the naked man from the grove.

19

The Party

*H*arikumar planned to usher in Meenakshi's nineteenth year by creating new memories with family and friends. 'It also marks one year that we have lived together as husband and wife,' he told her while setting things up. 'So, actually, our first wedding anniversary too!'

Since morning, the couple had been pottering around the house, setting things right. Among the few guests they had invited were Meenakshi's parents, and Meenakshi could not bear the thought of her mother scrutinizing the home that she had built, as she was wont to do. She had arranged the dinner plates six times so far, and each time she had found another speck on one of the plates, which meant they had to all go back to the wash.

'Why do you fret so much?' Harikumar quipped, comfortably parked on the couch.

'Fret?'

'Of course! Your mother is the warmest person I have met. And Tara Aatya. Both of them are going to be busy gossiping. You think they'll have time to look at your plates?'

'You really don't know women, do you?'

But a part of Meenakshi knew that she was not worried about her mother's peculiarities. What she was really worried about was that her mother was meeting her husband for the first time since all those events years ago.

Her chain of thought was broken when Harikumar said aloud, almost as if it was an announcement, 'So, Nishikant is on his way.'

Meenakshi turned sharply.

'But you told me…he's not coming?'

'Now he is,' Harikumar laughed. 'He's really so impulsive; I wonder why we are business partners. He must have decided at the last minute that he has nothing to do at home.'

'I'll have to set an extra dinner plate.'

'Yes,' said Harikumar. 'He doesn't eat much, but—'

Meenakshi did not hear the rest of the sentence. When Harikumar had been suggesting people for the party, she had tactfully thumbed down most of the males. In fact, all of them. But she hadn't been able to keep away Nishikant Rajan, with whom Harikumar shared a childhood friendship and now a business too.

The only problem was that Nishikant was a single young man, and single young men spelled trouble in her book.

❦

The birthday cake was a dark brown chocolatey affair. Meenakshi's name was written in red jelly diagonally across the cake, looking as if it was a blood wound slashed right across that hunk of brown.

A small crowd had gathered in the house. Her parents were there, and so was Tara. Meenakshi had invited some of the ladies in the building she had made friends with, and they had brought their kids, who made it a very noisy house at the moment.

'You have to make a wish and blow the candles first!' Tara urged.

Meenakshi had celebrated a birthday long ago, back in Vatgaon, and that one did not have cake. Her four birthdays with Tara Aatya had been simple dinners at the local Red Hut Chinese Restaurant.

'What do I wish for?'

'Oh, you should be flattered!' Tara patted Harikumar's back. 'A wife who doesn't know what to wish for is a true compliment for a husband.'

Harikumar crossed his heart.

Meenakshi mumbled something and then blew off the candles. The kids, who had stopped their games for a moment, sang the birthday song, screeching out the part that went *'MEENAKSHI AUNTY'*, and then looked expectantly at the tempting slices of cake that were passed around from one elderly hand to the other.

And just when the kids thought they'd finally get the sinfully saccharine cake, they had to wait longer. For, after sucking the cream off his fingers, Harikumar cleared his throat for attention and then thrust his hand into his pocket.

'Ooh, expensive gift alert!' someone squealed.

Harikumar smiled sheepishly and said, 'I wish you a happy birthday, Meenu!' As he said that, he handed over a shiny box to Meenakshi.

'Oh my God, Hari…' Meenakshi said as she opened the box. Multicoloured slivers of light reflected from a solitaire ring into her dazzled eyes. 'How did you know my size?'

'What kind of a husband would I be if I did not know that?' Harikumar winked.

Meenakshi beat Harikumar playfully on his chest and then hugged him. Suddenly conscious of her parents, she moved back. 'You should not have—'

Her sentence was interrupted by another voice from behind the circle of people around the cake. 'Oh no, am I late again?'

That male baritone, hitherto unheard in that house, made all the ladies do a double take. Hands helping themselves with cake froze midair.

'Ah, Nishi, well, come on in,' said Harikumar.

In walked Nishikant Rajan, cutting right through the guests, walking past the table on which the cake was placed, bringing a box wrapped in glittering red paper to the birthday girl.

'Oh…' Meenakshi stammered. 'Is this…'

'Yes,' Harikumar nodded. 'Nishikant. My buddy and business partner.'

'Happy birthday to my best friend's wife!' said Nishikant with a smile and a stare.

He was tall, a full head and a half taller than Meenakshi, and he had to stoop to come down to the level of his hostess. He held that pose, proffering his present, and holding a smile on his face that was partly hidden by a well-mowed moustache and a beard.

Meenakshi took the present, and the man made a show of heaving a sigh of relief. 'Thanks!' he exclaimed. 'If I had to stoop for a second more, I'd have gotten a slipped disk.'

'You don't get a slipped disk by stooping,' said Harikumar. 'Now come…let's begin our *real* party!' He led Nishikant away to the corner table where bottles of sparkling fluid were already arranged. Halfway, he turned. 'Baba, you come too!' he told Shantaram.

Shantaram looked at Renuka, who nodded.

'Go, go!' said Renuka. 'An occasional drink is good for you.'

In another corner of the house, where the women had assembled, Renuka held fort. Meenakshi heard her as she updated everyone on the husbands of her daughters, counting off names on her fingers and listing their professions. Meenakshi smiled at how no one got bored even though all her mother was rattling off was a list. Childhood memories of how good her mother was at telling stories came back to her.

Across the hall, her father, now on his second peg, was talking loosely with the men. She wondered if she should intervene and stop him from going too far, but she decided not to. Maybe this, this moment, was a new memory being etched right in her mind. She'd be a fool to abort it.

It hit her hard then—how her world had both drastically changed and not changed at all. These were the people she had grown up with, and they still had the same foibles. Her father had grown frailer and her mother had grown plumper, but even so, his coughing and her tittering were unchanged. She thought of the house, which was now silent and empty. With only Kumud left behind, it was probably just a shell of what it had been.

'How's my sal tree?' she asked her mother.

Renuka replied with a shake of her head, 'Still there. But it is ageing too. Its leaves are falling faster now. Your Baba says it is perhaps nearing its time—'

Meenakshi did not hear the rest of that sentence, for at that point she caught sight of Nishikant. The look on his face made her frown. Shantaram was sharing a particularly juicy anecdote with his son-in-law, but this new man was sitting upright with a twinkle in his eye, which was directed at her. Gaze met gaze, and Meenakshi realized only a moment too late that she should have lowered her eyes.

❦

Twenty minutes after dinner, only the closest people were still in the house. The neighbours and their kids had bid their goodbyes, and Meenakshi busied herself in the kitchen, arranging the dishes in the sink for the next day's washing. Meenakshi heard the flush being pulled in the bathroom that opened up in the corridor outside.

She turned to see who it was and was unnerved for a moment to see Nishikant. Just like that, with that tall man looming in the corridor that separated the rest of the house from the kitchen, she felt trapped. To add to it, he turned to look at her with an inscrutable expression on his bearded face. She could not quite see his eyes now; the light of the kitchen fell the other way.

'Do you want something?' she asked in a faint voice.

He smiled a refusal. But he held his gaze. He just stood and looked at her, as if he wanted to say something, but the words would not come out.

'Here's another sleazepot!'

Meenakshi touched the thread on her wrist.

'What is it?' she asked again.

He broke into a goofy laugh. From the other end, Harikumar walked in just then, and Nishikant said, 'How did this idiot manage to get you as his wife, Bhabi ji?' Then he went away, laughing.

When the moment passed, Meenakshi thought about it again and smiled at the word 'Bhabi ji'. No one had called her 'sister-in-law' before.

20

Red Shining Present

'That wasn't bad, was it?' Harikumar said above the din of the windows that Meenakshi was slamming shut. 'Few people, small gathering. Even weddings should be like this. Why invite the entire town to burp and fart and complain?'

'Our wedding *was* like that,' Meenakshi quipped.

'Ah, yes!' Harikumar laughed. 'Leave those windows now. Hop in.'

Meenakshi turned to look at him. He was in his boxers now, sitting up on the bed, looking at her expectantly.

She laughed. 'All right. Wait a moment.'

'What else have you got to do?'

'I have to make sure everything is latched properly.'

'It is. No one can break through these locks. Come to me!'

Meenakshi turned around, making sure that her talisman was in place. It had now become a ritual, just like one checked the temperature of a pool before diving in.

'I don't know how you can become more beautiful night after night. Look at me; I have got my first wrinkle.'

'You are way too young for that, Hari.'

'I envy you sometimes. It is like you have this well of youth inside of you and it just keeps springing,' he said, gasping as he pulled her closer.

'Perhaps I have grown into a woman? The first time you saw me, I was a child.'

Harikumar laughed.

'Paedophile!' Meenakshi laughed back.

Harikumar's face suddenly lost colour. Pushing her aside, he withdrew and rolled on his back.

Meenakshi knew she had crossed a line.

'I am sorry, Hari,' she said. 'Please, I did not mean that. You are one of the finest men I know.'

'Never even as a joke, Meenu,' said Harikumar in a hurt voice.

'I am sorry.'

'When you were that age, Meenu,' said Harikumar, turning to face her and propping his head on her arm, '*even* when you were that age, you were different. I did not see a child in you. I saw a grown woman. It was instant love. People only talk of love at first sight; I felt it. I still remember that jolt today, like electricity had coursed through my entire being. When you looked at me, you weren't a child to me either. You showed such understanding...'

'I know. I am so sorry...'

Meenakshi placed her hand on his chest. With her finger, she tapped on his chest lightly and then drew small circles on it.

'Can't even stay cross with you, can I?' Harikumar smiled warmly. Meenakshi smiled back.

Then suddenly, Hari, out of nowhere, asked, 'Don't you think it's time we had a child?'

A child? Now he wants a child?

Meenakshi flinched.

'Why the flushed face?'

'Hari,' she said, 'I don't know.'

Harikumar planted a soft kiss on her cheek. 'Why, Meenu? You will make a good mother.'

'Will I?'

'Why do you doubt it?'

A sudden flash crossed her mind. She saw, in her mind's eye, herself in the form of the naked hideous Yakshini sitting cross-legged on the floor with a helpless mewling child in her lap.

'No!' she said. 'Not now. Let's wait, Hari...'

'Well, all right. If you say so! Let's wait.'

☙

Early next morning, when Harikumar began to leave for work, Meenakshi stirred. She quickly sprang off the bed, realizing that she had overslept, and ran up to the door to find him fully dressed, stepping into his shoes.

'Thought I'd just sneak away, let you sleep,' he said.

'It's all right. I am awake now. Do you want something?'

'Nope!' He stood up and straightened the crease of his trousers. 'It's a new business. Needs my constant attention. Have to leave...'

'All right. Do eat something though.'

'Don't worry. I'll have a bite with Nishi as soon as I reach.' Then he turned. 'Yeah, speaking of Nishi, you seem to have forgotten the present he gave you.'

She looked at where his finger pointed. The shining red package was still on the coffee table, waiting to be opened.

After her bath, Meenakshi left her hair loose, to dry it. Shuffling to a relaxed position on the couch, she took the red box in her hands.

It had lain there for half the day, escaping her attention. Or, she was probably subtly telling herself ('herself' being her inner monster) that the giver of the present meant nothing to her. She could do without seeing it.

Now she held the box in her hands, one placed below it for support and the other toying with the butterfly ribbon knot on the top.

She undid that frilly knot. The red shining wrapper came loose and fell apart. Inside was a box with some electronic device.

Its picture was on the box. It was what many people were using those days. A cellphone.

She opened the box with the excitement of a child. The device tumbled out. It was nothing like anything she had seen before, but she knew what it was. She knew that people could make calls with it, and she turned it over and over to look where the cord was, and when she did not find one, she was flummoxed.

She held the small device with the many numbers and signs

on it. It felt surprisingly heavy for its size. She lightly touched the numbers with her fingers and let out a slight gasp when they pressed down.

A light went on, a blazing blue light that lit up her face.

Written in a strange arrangement of dots, she could see words now. Instinctively, she pressed the arrow buttons and the light toggled from one of the words to the other. She laughed at her smartness.

When she came to Contacts, she paused.

So, this was much like Tara Aunty's phonebook. She had an electronic one, which opened like a tiny briefcase and had a keypad with which you could enter names of people.

Meenakshi pressed on Contacts.

There were only three names. One of those was Nishi. It did not surprise her.

Playfully, and filled with curiosity, she pressed the green button and held the phone to her ear.

And it rang! It really rang!

Terrified, she fumbled with the phone and pressed the red button, and there was silence.

Why would a stranger gift her a phone?

Then something happened that made her jump out of her skin. The phone began to ring.

For long moments, she did not touch it. The contraption kept ringing on the table, vibrating and ringing, making the whole thing shake in frightful harmony. She did not touch it till it died out. The light faded. Then it came on and began to ring again.

With a trembling hand, Meenakshi pressed the green button and held the phone to her ear.

'I see you opened my present, Bhabi ji!' came a cheerful voice from the other end.

'Why…why this?' she said.

'Logical, no?'

'Why such an expensive gift?'

Nishikant laughed. 'Expensive? Bhabi ji, this is the cheapest gift. Do you know what business Hari and I have?'

'No...he hasn't told me yet...'

'Phones! Cellphones! New technology. Gen Next and all that. We are getting these phones cheap from Taiwan and selling them in India. We will bring the cellphone revolution in India soon.'

'Good,' she said. 'It's a good way for me to talk to Hari at work now. Is he in yet?'

'Oh yes, he came in twenty minutes ago and has already left for his meeting with—'

The sentence flowed out of him like a gush, but it stopped at the last word like it had hit a barricade.

'With?' Meenakshi asked, cheerfully.

'With his secretary.'

'He has a secretary? What's his name?'

There was another moment of silence.

Meenakshi laughed. 'You must think I am being the curious wife! Who's he?'

'It's a she.'

Meenakshi laughed all the more. 'My husband with a female secretary! That very picture makes me laugh.'

Nishikant laughed too. 'Roopali is our shared secretary,' he said. 'She accompanies us when we go out to meet clients. Takes down notes and all. Good, efficient girl. And...quite beautiful too!'

'Oh...okay.'

There was a slight pause between the words that didn't go unnoticed.

'Oh, you are worrying! I should not have told you that!' Nishikant said quickly. 'Roopali is just efficient, that's all. Your husband is a meditating saint.'

Meenakshi laughed. 'I know.'

'You cannot say the same about me, though.' Nishikant laughed. 'Don't want to keep you long now...'

'Oh, wait,' said Meenakshi. 'Since we are talking, tell me, how was the party last night? I mean this is the first time we hosted a party and I don't even know if I did half the things right.'

'It was fun, Bhabi ji! Sitting with friends, drinking, relaxing—what could be better! Your father is a hoot too!'

'He really takes off when he drinks.' Meenakshi's mind drifted to the pleasant memories of her father from a long time ago.

'Well, all right,' he said, 'now I need to go.'

'Sure!'

'Thank you for liking the present, Bhabi ji.'

'Thanks.'

'And, oh, before you go, may I request something?'

'What?'

'I mean…I don't know how to put this delicately but…it might not be a good idea to tell Hari about this present. The cellphone, I mean. I don't know what I was thinking yesterday when I brought one of the stock pieces I had with me as a gift. The SIM card is in my name, so don't worry about the bills. But Hari might think I'm flirting with his wife!' he chuckled.

Meenakshi rolled her eyes but was also amused at his candidness.

'You won't tell him, will you? It's nothing big.'

'No, I won't tell him,' said Meenakshi. 'And I will call you on and off. Will be a good way to keep tabs on my Hari to see if that secretary is digging her claws into him.'

'Ah, rest assured on that front. If any woman has claws to dig into something, I will offer them my back and protect your husband!'

Meenakshi sat cradling the phone for a long time after the call ended. Of all the experiences she had had with men so far, she just could not get over this one. It put a whole new spin on things. She had just spoken to a man on a phone. The Yakshini could not lay her hands on him. No worries.

And there would be nothing more. Just pure, plain conversation.

Yes, technology was good. She kissed the phone and left a

wet lip mark on the dial, and then felt embarrassed with herself for doing that.

❧

When Harikumar came back home, Meenakshi led him to the kitchen and opened one of the pots. A thick aroma of lentils and vegetables wafted into his nose and he proceeded to dip a finger into the sambhar, his mouth drooling.

'Hey, patience!' said Meenakshi. 'No grimy fingers in the food. Go wash and come.'

'I never knew you could prepare this.'

'Give a lady time, the groceries she needs, and a free hand in the kitchen. You will be surprised every time.'

'But, idli sambhar?' Harikumar opened the other vessel that still had the piping hot idlis. 'And the idlis are so soft!'

'You don't know the talents your wife has. Except for the one in the bedroom. What kind of a husband are you?'

'The idiot kind!' laughed Harikumar. 'Okay, let me take a quick shower before I settle down.'

He returned in a T-shirt that read LONG NIGHT COMING, with his hair dripping wet. He plonked on the dining table, where Meenakshi had already laid out the goodies.

For a few minutes, nothing was said. The only sounds were of chewing and chomping, and of him smacking his fingers in delight.

'Hari,' Meenakshi opened the conversation when they were two idlis down each, 'you never told me exactly what work you do.'

Harikumar laughed. 'You never asked.'

'Okay, tell me.'

'You really want to know? Well, my dad left me with various businesses, but I sold most of them before going to America. Now I have invested in a new venture with Nishikant. We are into telecom now.'

'Telecom? What's that?'

'Telecommunication. Our business is with phones. Mobile

phones. They are quite hot these days. Going to be really big in India. We are bringing them to the country.'

'What's the name of your new company?'

'Conyo Telecom,' said Harikumar. 'The name is Nishi's choice. Still haven't gotten used to saying it out loud.'

'Well, it's good.'

'Like this sambhar.' He took another helping of it.

'So, there are many people in your company?'

'We have enough.'

'I'd like to visit someday,' she said, pondering.

There was the briefest of pauses, and then he said, 'Why do you want to visit?'

Meenakshi looked up at Harikumar, her eyes all lit up. 'You know, Hari, I've been thinking. I am alone at home all day, with nothing to do. If I could do something...'

She let that sentence hang in the air and observed her husband's face. It looked as if a shadow had passed over it.

'Like that modelling thing?'

'No. I am past that. What if...you give me some job in your firm?'

Harikumar kept the idli back in the plate, threw his head back, and laughed. He laughed aloud for several seconds.

Meenakshi did not say anything. She observed him laughing and waited for him to stop.

'Sorry, sorry,' he said. 'Not that I doubt you. You will do a great job. But the thought of you and I working at the same place amuses me! Just think of the whispers whenever you enter my cabin!'

'Why will they whisper? I am the boss's wife...'

'Yeah, the category that's bitched about the most. Plus, an employee. You will get no work done at all.'

'Then let me officially be in your room. Let me be your... secretary.'

She hoped it sounded like an afterthought.

'Secretary? Really? Do you know what a secretary does?'

'I'll learn.'

'Well, okay then! Let's see.'

He moved to wash his hands, and Meenakshi was left there, hanging, not knowing where she was headed.

21

The Real Problem

*I*t is difficult to keep a sapling from growing once the seed is sown. Once a thumb presses the seed into pliable soil, fertile with desires and ready to be impregnated, there is no way to stop it from bursting forth and sending its tiny shoot skyward. More than that, it is not naturally possible to prevent the roots from sprouting. And as the roots go deeper inside, they hold on to the soil with greater tenacity, getting nourished by it till the plant becomes a force in itself.

In Meenakshi's mind, this seed was sown the day she opened the red shiny present. And every day that her husband returned from work, reluctant to share what transpired at work and what meetings he went to, the roots went in deeper and deeper.

Over the weeks, Meenakshi alluded to a job several times, even emphasizing how she could be a good secretary to him. But the reply was either a laugh or a scoff. As the days passed, he stopped even that; he either changed the topic or ignored it.

Why was it so?

She spoke to Nishikant a couple of times after the first time, making it sound as casual as possible. Harikumar would never be in the office. His secretary Roopali wouldn't be in either.

❦

Meenakshi visited her husband's office for the first time on an afternoon post lunch hour. Dressed in drab clothes to avoid needless attention, she walked in without ceremony and stopped at the receptionist's desk. She immediately saw Nishikant hopping from one cabin to another.

'Oh, come, Bhabi ji,' he said. 'Hari didn't mention you'd be visiting.'

Meenakshi felt foolish now. 'He doesn't know—'

'It's perfectly all right,' Nishikant opened a cabin door. 'You can visit anytime. In fact, I wonder why you haven't visited before. This is Hari's cabin. Best place for you to wait.'

'Wait?'

'Ah, Hari is not in right now,' he said apologetically. 'He has just stepped out for a meeting.'

'You didn't go?'

'No...' Nishikant switched on the air conditioner. 'I don't usually go. Three is a crowd for client meetings.'

She did not turn to see the door close behind her, but the moment he left, she felt alone. The walls were a shade of cream, and save for a clock high up on one wall and a heavily-marked calendar flapping away on another, there was nothing on them. She saw his chair—the boss's chair. With some trepidation in her heart, she went to the seat and sank herself into it. The chair was unexpectedly soft, and it swivelled as soon as she sat.

From that vantage point, the seat of the boss, she saw the room in a new perspective. She had come with apprehension, but now, seated in her husband's office, she felt a hint of pride. The door swung open and a boy came in with tea, and she said 'thank you' gracefully.

She thought of calling her husband on the phone that was on this desk, but then decided against it.

Slowly, she laid her head on the desk and shut her eyes. The faint hum of the air conditioner and the buzzing voices of people outside, everyone engaged in some task; it exhilarated her.

Then the words spoke out to her. Loud and clear.

'What do you think your husband is doing right now?'

She sat up straight.

The door opened and Nishikant walked in.

'Sorry to keep you waiting, Bhabi ji. I had something urgent to do.'

'Where has Hari gone?'

'He's in Hotel Matador.'

'Hotel?'

'Yes. They are meeting the client at the restaurant on the ground floor.'

'They?'

Nishikant mumbled something, and then said, 'Oh, Bhabi ji, your tea has gone cold. Should I call for another?'

'It's okay.' Meenakshi stood up. 'I think I should have called...'

'Oh, please sit down!' Nishikant stood up. 'Please don't leave. Hari will be mad if he knows you went back.'

'Yes, sit down. I am loving this. This one is juicy too.'

'He's a decent man,' Meenakshi breathed.

She looked at Nishikant's bearded face, the friendly smile, the perfect teeth and shining eyes. And then a vision—him lying broken on the floor, blood seeping through the shreds of his white shirt.

She rushed out of the office as soon as she could.

❧

Meenakshi flung her handbag on the couch as soon as she reached home and sat with her head buried in her hands till it became dark outside. Her mind was flooded with a deluge of thoughts. She tried to shut those images out, but they would not leave her. In all of those, she saw her husband naked and in the throes of passion, and the woman whose skin he was licking was not her.

'Screw him. That adulterous bastard. Take that thread off. Let me come out. I'll rip him apart tonight.'

Meenakshi slapped her ears, trying to shut out the voice, but it hit her so hard that tears ran out of her eyes.

Darkness consumed the hall now. The glow of the vehicle lights far below was the only ambient light in the room. Her hand moved to switch on the light, but then it retracted. Something told her she wanted the darkness. Yes, it was good. Darkness was good.

In that darkness of the house, she walked alone. Her own mind became a stranger to her as it buzzed with so many rational and irrational thoughts that she didn't know which was which. When she went in front of a mirror, she looked at herself. It started as an absent-minded glance, but when she became aware of her reflection in the mirror, a little scream escaped her mouth.

Was this her? The hag in the mirror with the unkempt hair and reddened eyes and lipstick marks smeared all over her cheeks? When did she become this hag?

'He is having the time of his life right now in a hotel room.'

She stiffened. No, nothing was wrong. She did not know anything for sure, did she? He was always good to her. There was no reason to suspect him. He loved her, and it was pure, unmitigated, undiluted love. She could see it, of course.

Still staring at her reflection, she vowed to put things back on track. Her mind was idle. Devil's workshop and all that. She'd talk again about a job. Yes, a job or at least some semblance of a life that was not confined to those four walls, would put things on track. He would probably refuse, but could he be faulted? He was only protecting her from the outside world. Why was she not seeing the good in him?

She shrugged. It was time for him to come home. She had to get ready. Dress up.

A defiant smile broke on her lips. She wouldn't listen to the bitch inside her. She was instigating her, leading her on to her doom.

She took a step towards the bathroom.

But then she froze, and very slowly, she turned.

Back to the mirror.

Just as she had stepped away, she had seen something in that mirror. Something that was not her. And as she turned back to look, she saw it still standing there.

A large creature staring at her like a predator might look at its prey.

'Don't fool yourself. You cannot control me forever.'

The Yakshini was speaking to her now, directly, in that painfully scratchy voice. No, she was not in her right mind anymore. Here at long last was the demon—looking at her!

And Meenakshi screamed. It was a scream that came from the back of her throat and made her sides ache for hours.

⚘

That night, Meenakshi was scared to even touch her husband as he lay on her. She kept her head firmly turned to one side. On the other side there was the mirror, and she had no courage to look at it.

Even as his lips nuzzled the softness of her cheeks, they did not arouse her. She did not feel his caresses anymore.

Harikumar winced. His hold on her arms tightened, his chest muscles went taut, his neck craned backwards, and Meenakshi felt him shuddering over her.

After a moment of relapse, he got off her and walked to the bathroom. She saw him as he washed up.

'Something is different about you these days,' he said.

Meenakshi looked away.

Harikumar came back and sat by her side of the bed. He placed his hand on her forehead and said, 'Are you okay?'

'I am fine.'

'What is it then?'

'Hari,' she said, 'I went to the office today.'

He sat up straight. 'Now, did you?'

'You weren't there, so I waited a bit. I loved every bit of being there. It was like I belonged.'

'I see.'

'No, you don't. You don't live in the house all day. You don't see these four walls like I do. When everything is silent, they talk, you know? They fill your mind with things.'

'Don't get agitated, Meenu. I will look for suitable jobs for you. There are companies that will be glad to have you.'

'But not yours?'

'Why are you hell-bent on working with me, Meenu? I have told you a million times—a husband and wife working at the same place is not a good idea. Our personal and professional lives will be in conflict.' Then he softened. 'The next time you visit, let me know beforehand. I will be there.'

'Perhaps you can take me to your meetings?'

Harikumar laughed throatily. 'Meetings? Do you know what they are?'

'Yes. You were at one today when I had come.'

'These are not fun outings, Meenu!' His voice had turned explanatory, but to her it sounded condescending. 'You need to know stuff to talk to clients and convince them.'

'Is that why you take your secretary along? Does she convince people well?'

'Ah, so you have heard about the famous Roopali!'

'Famous? Why is she famous?'

'Oh, that's just an idiom, Meenu. What's wrong with you? Roopali has worked in many companies. She knows a lot of things.'

'Are most of your clients men?'

'Most of them are.'

'Then I can understand why you need a good-looking lady to explain things to them.'

Harikumar frowned, as if he were trying to make sense of things. Then he spoke. 'What exactly is the problem here, Meenu? I don't understand. Is it that you want to work, or you don't want to be alone in the house, or is it that you think there's something going on between my secretary and me?' He scoffed at the last one, and then frowned again.

Meenakshi had no words now. She realized she had spread the conversation in so many directions that she did not know which thread she should pick up. He was right, though. What was her real problem?

Your real problem is him. HIM.

'Let's just sleep, Hari,' she said loudly. 'I need to clear my head.' But she knew there'd be no sleep, and her mind would definitely not be any clearer either.

22

The Struggle

*M*eenakshi dialled her mother's number the next afternoon and waited. She pictured her mother in the large empty house walking all the way from her room to the landline phone next to the kitchen, negotiating the entire corridor. Hardly could anyone in that house pick up the phone before eight rings.

'Hello, Aai,' she said.

'Ah, Meenu! Oh my God, is everything all right?'

'Yes, Aai. Don't worry.'

'Whenever any of you girls call, I get worried that something might be wrong.'

'We should call more often then.'

'Ah, no. Once a week is enough. Difficult to walk all the way to the phone now.'

'Aai, you must get a cellphone now. Then you can carry it with you wherever you go.'

'No way! Technology is good only for youngsters like you. Forget that. Why did you call?'

'Just like that. To chat.'

'Okay, then let me sit down.'

Meenakshi heard the sound of a stool being pulled up.

Then Renuka spoke. 'Hari went to work?'

'He's always at work.'

'Nice. And you? Ate?'

'Yes. Cooked and ate. What else will I do?'

'What's it, Meenu?'

'Nothing, Aai.'

'Meenu, let me tell you something. I know the city has changed you and all that, but there are some things we older women were doing right too. Why do you think we women did not go out of the houses and work in those days? Do you think we could not? Of course we could. Your grandmother and I, we could have wrapped our husbands around our fingers if we wanted to. We could have multiplied this property ten times more than your father and grandfather did. But we chose to stay at home and look after the house and the children. Do you know why? Because that is way more difficult than going out and working. And the big secret it that we do not trust our men with that difficult job.'

Renuka let out a short conspiratorial laugh after that revelation, and Meenakshi laughed along. But then she again took on her gloomy voice and said, 'Aai, I get bored sitting at home all day.'

'Then you know what is to be done.'

'What?'

'Do you know Manda is expecting her second baby?'

'Ah, Aai! Not that again.'

'Of course, that. You have to bring new life into this world. Only women have the ability to do that, and why will you not use that gift? Is everything all right between Hari and you? In the bedroom, I mean?'

'Yes.'

'You know why I ask,' said Renuka. 'I would rather not pry into the private lives of my daughters, but you know... Are you really all right, Meenu?'

'I don't know, Aai. Everything is quite all right on the surface, but I feel something bubbling within. That thing wants to come out of me. I hear voices. I saw something the other day, Aai.'

'Saw what?'

'I saw my face. Only, it was not my face. It was her. The... Yakshini. I saw her, Aai.'

Renuka stayed silent.

'Aai?'

'I have been thinking about that too, Meenu. I don't tell you, but I am doing some special prayers for you in the temple here.

I cannot tell anyone, of course. That Tappu's mother still doesn't talk to us, and we cannot go to Jamblekar's clinic for anything. We have to hire a cab and go all the way to the next village if anyone falls sick.'

'What will happen to me, Aai?'

'Don't worry. Everything has gone all right for so long now.'

Meenakshi laughed. 'Aai, but there are so many things I cannot control.'

'Like?'

'Hari is different now. He looks at other women, which he did not do earlier. He laughs at my simple rustic ways. He does not take my requests seriously.'

'Don't talk nonsense, Meenu.'

'The new black thread is losing its power too. I can feel it. The tingling is back. Any morning...I might just...'

'Meenu! What's wrong with you? Are you talking to yourself?'

And indeed, she was. She had quite forgotten that there was someone at the other end. Halfway through those words, she had taken the phone off her ear and was now speaking to the wind.

At the other end, Renuka gently kept the receiver down.

❧

Meenakshi was still sitting on a couch in her living room, her mind filled with meaningless thoughts, when the door clicked open. She looked up to see Harikumar walking in with a smile on his face. But the next moment, his smile vanished.

'Meenu, is something wrong?'

Indeed, there were dark circles under her eyes as if she had not slept for days. Her hair was a mess, each individual strand jutting out in a different direction.

'Everything's fine,' she mumbled. 'You sit. I will lay out dinner.' She walked two steps and then stopped abruptly. 'Oh, I didn't make any dinner. Can we order from that Chinese place?'

Harikumar walked up to her and took her in his arms.

Meenakshi's heart wasn't just beating; it was pacing.

'What's wrong, Meenu?'

'I'm good...I'm good...'

Suddenly, she became aware of his touch. For some reason that she could not fathom, she did not like that touch. It was the same touch that she had enjoyed for so long, but right now, she felt uncomfortable, like there were maggots beneath her skin and they were biting away the inner wall with their horrible white mouths and soon they would burst forth from her.

She shoved him back and looked at him, horrified.

'Meenu, are you sick?' he asked.

He placed his hand over her forehead but she slapped it away.

'All right,' he said. 'I think you need to go rest.'

She nodded. But the look in her eyes was that of frightened submission.

⚘

Meenakshi did not sleep that night, but pretended to be in deep slumber. When Harikumar entered the sheets and pressed his body against hers, she kept her eyes tightly shut. She thought her heavy breathing would be a giveaway, but then she heard him turning away and pleasuring himself, and slowly a tear rolled off her eye.

She was still in the same stance in the morning when he woke up, went for his bath, and dressed for work. Before leaving, he went into the bedroom again and placed a hand on her forehead.

'Doesn't seem like you have a temperature,' he said.

She didn't stir even when he announced from the door that he was leaving for work. It did not matter. But an hour later, when she could not resist it, she called up Nishikant. And just as she had expected, Harikumar was away at a meeting. Angrily, she slammed the phone down.

She spent all morning walking around the house, zombie-like, thinking of the various things happening behind her back.

Oh God, America! Was that a lie too? How could a man who

could not keep his thing down for even a night have spent five years without sex? That too in the land of temptation? She had seen those bikini-clad women in dance shows such as *The Grind* on MTV, and surely all of America was filled with such half-naked bimbos dancing on the streets? TV and magazines had told her that in America, people weren't coy about sex. They spoke about it openly, did it openly. They even spoke with their parents about their sex lives over dinner.

He surely had had it there. He had lied. The lying bastard! He had probably had a new whore in his bed every night.

And now...he was in his secretary's arms. Client meeting, her ass! What client? Maybe the client was also a woman and they were all together inside a hotel room. Why hotel anyway? Official meetings were supposed to be conducted in offices.

Why did it throw him off when she told him about her visit to his office?

'*I have been telling you all along...*'

Meenakshi twitched as that hoarse voice came again from within her.

The mirror was right in front, and she did not want to look there, but how could she avoid it? That voice...it wasn't a hollow, disembodied whisper anymore. It was a full-throated voice; it was her own voice.

She lifted her head and looked. Sure as death, there she was—smiling, with her red eyes, and awful white strings of slime flowing out of their corners.

'Who are you?'

Meenakshi's lips moved, but the lips of the reflection in the mirror, that horrid monstrous pair, did not.

'*You know who I am.*'

'Why are you in me?'

The Yakshini laughed an evil derisive laugh.

'*Why is anyone anywhere?*'

Meenakshi stood still for a moment, looking at the chest of

the creature in the mirror, which heaved like a pair of blacksmith's bellows.

'I…don't want you. I want to be free.'

'Stupid girl! Do you think I am here of my own free will? You think I like this form? I am trapped too. Our destinies are entwined. We have to live like this, whatever happens.'

'But…but you are a murderess.'

'You should be thanking me. If it weren't for me, you'd be used and thrown away already. I protect you.'

'But why? Why do you need to protect me?'

'Stupid human! Your body is my body too. Why won't I save it from these lecherous men?'

'No! Please go away. Let me live peacefully with my husband.'

'Your husband? You mean the one who is fucking someone else right now?'

'You don't know that.'

'Do you?'

Rage swelled in Meenakshi like a many-headed beast. Without another thought, she picked up a snow globe that was on the table and flung it at the mirror.

As it smashed and fell, shard by shard, the Yakshini broke into a laugh. Then the laughing stopped and all that remained was Meenakshi and a deathly silent room.

❧

That night, she suddenly woke and found Harikumar next to her in bed, snoring. She did not know when she had fallen asleep, or when he had come next to her and fallen asleep.

Something had startled her in her sleep; now she felt that presence. From the corner of her eye, she saw something that alarmed her and she gulped.

There was a faint yellow glow in the hall outside.

It appeared as if someone had lit a candle there, and when she tried to look through the gaps in her fingers, she saw a shadow moving in the glow.

Forgetting the state she was in, she tried to wake Harikumar. But then she stopped. The glow turned softer, benign. She felt it calling out to her.

Without making a noise, she got to her feet. The cold floor stung her feet and she drew in a sharp breath. She walked out, step by step.

It was him. Krita.

'Krita!' she rushed forth like she were meeting a long-lost friend. 'How did you get in?'

'Don't be daft,' he scolded. 'Doors cannot hold me.'

Meenakshi felt a sudden warmth growing inside her. All of a sudden, it was the very antithesis of the pain she had been feeling all these days. The only thing she wanted right now was to hold Krita's hand and sob on his shoulder, tell him what was going on with her.

'Don't say a word,' he said, and placed an arm on her shoulder. It relaxed her. It was a healing touch.

'Help me...' she said.

'I cannot. There are limitations to what I can do. I cannot fight your fate, or I would have done that long ago when you were a child.'

'What are you, Krita?'

'I am the song to your sorrows, the balm to your pain. I am your one true companion, here to take care of you. And you, Yakshini, you are mine.'

'Oh! Who are you here for then, me or the Yakshini?'

'For both,' said Krita, coming closer to Meenakshi, comforting her like a parent comforts a child. 'You are her human vessel, but I try not to let the Yakshini have her way either, for she is angry, and anger makes us do things.'

'Is her anger directed at me?'

'No.'

'Then why am I being punished with her?'

'The ways of the Gods are mysterious,' said Krita. 'Who can argue with them? At times they do things that we see as irrational, but it is later, sometimes millennia later, that we know they were right.'

'Stay with me, Krita,' Meenakshi implored. 'Don't go. Be with me. I am alone.'

'I am always with you. Always. Even when you are in bed with your husband, I am with you.'

The mention of the word 'husband' stiffened her.

'Here is some advice,' offered Krita, 'and that is what I have come to give you. Don't stop loving your husband.'

'How?' Meenakshi cried. 'How is that possible? Knowing that his lips, his hands, his manhood have been elsewhere? Knowing that he has been sharing himself with another woman, and probably still is?'

'You don't know that.'

'But you do. Tell me. Is my husband cheating on me?'

'I don't know either. I am not omniscient.'

'But the Yakshini...'

'If you let her come out, she will kill him.'

'I know,' mused Meenakshi. 'That is why this black thread is so important to me...'

At that, Krita laughed. It was a free laugh, full of mirth, and he looked so handsome when he laughed that her heart missed several beats. 'You think that flimsy black thread has been stopping the Yakshini so far?'

Meenakshi looked up at him, bewildered.

'That thread is of no consequence, girl! It is just something that aids your mind. The only thing that has stopped the Yakshini from coming out of you and digging her talons into your husband is the purest emotion of all.'

Meenakshi was stunned, like some transfixing magic had been cast on her.

'LOVE...the most powerful thing there is. The thing that can give life. That can preserve life. In your case, quite literally. The Yakshini can do nothing to the person you truly love. Your love is her cage. That is why it is difficult for her to come out of you; your love suppresses her, smothers her. But the day it dies—'

Meenakshi, now terrified, backed away from the still-smiling man.

'Don't let your love die if you wish to keep your husband alive!' he said, and then, after gracing her with an enigmatic smile, he disappeared.

23

Showdown

*L*ong after Krita had left, his words began to make sense to her. So far she had thought that she had to protect Harikumar from the Yakshini; but now she knew she had to protect him from herself. That was infinitely more difficult.

All day she thought about it. She had to work up the courage if she wanted Harikumar to live. She'd have to agree to live in the adulterous hell he was pushing her into, if she cared for his life. She saw no way out. None.

Did she value his life more than the hurt he was giving her? Even if his adultery was real, did he deserve to be brutally torn to pieces? A man who had saved her once?

If she had to keep the flame of love burning, she had to know more. She had to be an active doer, not a passive victim. She had stayed aloof for too long; the time had come for her to take stock of the situation.

It was simple, really. She would ask him directly. If it was a 'no', everything would continue as before. But if there was the remotest sign of a 'yes', then heaven save him. She had to take the chance.

'*You cannot let him decide his own crime.*'

The Yakshini's voice was now also the voice of her conscience, pricking her till it bled.

She ignored it. Preparations had to be made.

That night of judgement, Harikumar came home punctually, his face creased with worry and nervousness. He had called her thrice that day to ask about her health. Every time Meenakshi had told herself that he still cared for her. Voices in the head be damned!

The moment he entered, he touched her forehead. 'No fever,' he said cheerily. 'Why, you actually look better!'

His gaze was now on her physical form. The fact that he took note of it made her lips tremble into a smile.

She had taken care to prepare herself for the evening's showdown, which she feared might be the last happy evening with her husband. Scouring through her wardrobe, after much contemplation she had decided on a pure freshly-bathed look, the hair still dripping wet and the hypnotic bath scents still wafting off her body. Harikumar had a thing for white, hence she had chosen a white saree with tiny cerise flowers on it. She had left her wet hair loose, held together only by a loose hairclip.

'What's the occasion?' he asked.

'No occasion,' she smiled.

Bemused, Harikumar walked in. 'Even the house looks different.'

She took his bag from his hands. 'You go freshen up. I'll get dinner.'

She walked to the kitchen, completely conscious of her husband's eyes on her retreating form.

When he returned ten minutes later, she had set the table—a table for two—by a wall of the house. The plates and dishes were laid out. Two tall red candles stood unlit on the table.

'Turn off the light when you come in,' said Meenakshi.

A smile formed on his lips.

The moment darkness fell, a match was lit with a hiss, and a flame lit up the room. Another flame followed, and Meenakshi's face was lit up by the red glow.

'Come, sit,' she said. 'Everything is set here.'

Harikumar walked in, wiping his hands, and neatly placing the towel on the armrest of his chair. 'Sure I'm not forgetting anything?'

'Why? Don't you like this?'

'What's not to like? It's as romantic as it gets. But sometimes romance gets too close to horror.'

Meenakshi laughed. The gust from her mouth made the flames quiver. Red shadows danced on her face. 'Relax. Let me serve you.'

She opened the casseroles and the aromas rushed forth.

The meal started in silence. For the next few minutes, as they sampled the food, the silence continued. Meenakshi nibbled at her food, hardly eating anything, while Harikumar dug into it right away.

When they were halfway through, Meenakshi said, 'How was your day?'

'Oh, good,' Harikumar said with his mouth full. He swallowed and continued, 'We will probably be striking a deal with another retail chain soon. Cellphones are here to stay. By the way, you should have a cellphone too. In fact, I will give you one. We are getting these couple handsets soon, a his-and-her kind of thing. We could have one each.'

'More kofta?' she asked. 'There's phirni too, for later.'

'Ah, dinner and dessert! What's going on, lady?'

Meenakshi giggled.

'No, really, I am curious,' said Harikumar. 'In a movie that I saw once, a man prepares a special meal for his wife. But—spoiler alert—he was plotting to kill her all along. It was the poor woman's last meal!' He winked. 'Do we have similar plans?'

Meenakshi smiled. 'That depends,' she said.

'Depends on what?'

'How this evening turns out.'

Meenakshi walked to the refrigerator and brought out the dessert.

Everything was planned down to the finest detail. The food and the ambience; it was no less than intoxication for a man like Harikumar, who would soon begin to expect the next best thing.

Moments later, the lights were put out, the doorbell was silenced and the phone taken off the hook. Even the black thread was in place despite what Krita had said, just in case. There would be no disturbances tonight.

He lay on the bed first, pulling off his clothes as per habit, and drawing the sheet over himself. Meenakshi saw him and threw him a tentative smile, but took her own time to do her tasks before retiring.

Harikumar stayed wide awake for several minutes, and when she finally went in, he said, 'Well, finally!'

Meenakshi let it pass. Slowly, she slid into the sheets.

Harikumar lost no time in turning to face her and place his leg on hers.

Meenakshi did not stir. Instead, she said, 'Did you have a good time today?'

'So far, yes. But the best is yet to come.'

Meenakshi kissed him on the neck. Her lips wanted to form some words, but she wouldn't say it.

'Go on, say it,' said Harikumar. 'I know you want to say something.'

'I was just wondering how you can have such boundless energy in you all the time.'

'Boundless energy, you say?' Harikumar laughed. 'I guess there's a little kid living inside me somew—'

Meenakshi's hand flew to his mouth at that and clamped it shut.

'Do not say that! Never say that,' she said in agitation. 'You don't know what might actually come to pass.'

'What do you mean?'

'You don't know how it feels if someone is actually living inside you…' she mumbled.

Giving her a strange look and letting it pass, he slowly began to pummel his leg onto her, the knee beginning to dig into her thigh.

Meenakshi felt the unmistakable hardness of his organ. This was the moment when all his humour would recede, and he would enter the throes of passion. The iron had to be struck now.

'Tell me one thing, Hari…'

'What?' he said. It came out as a broken groan.

Meenakshi felt the pounding inside her chest now. This was the moment; she had to ask. Words were fighting inside her, forming themselves into questions, racing against each other to tumble out.

Those words were her ally in her quest for the truth. Soon they would force themselves out of her mouth and seek the answer she was looking for.

'What, Meenu?' he asked.

'Have you...have you ever been unfaithful to me?'

There it was. The stakes had been laid, waiting to be picked up.

He had been caressing the smooth skin on her belly. At this question, his hand froze, and he retreated. He took his leg off of her and said, 'Why...why do you ask?'

Meenakshi did not flinch now. 'Tell me, Hari, are you sleeping with someone else?'

His mouth fell open.

'I don't care what you did before we got married. Heck, I don't even care what you did in America. I am talking about now. These days.' She grabbed his penis, now limp. 'Has anyone else seen or touched you these days?'

He winced. 'Meenu...no...'

Then it began to happen, the thing that she was afraid of. But when it did, instead of alarming her, it made her sad. Just sad. She heard the voice inside her.

'You know he's lying. Shit-faced two-timing liar.'

Her fingers, still clasped around her husband's organ, began to change. She felt the throbbing, the matting of the ends, the thickening of the skin, the growing of the nails. All of that, every bit of that, was back.

Harikumar was only looking into her eyes. 'What's going on, Meenu?' He became aware of something happening down south. 'Meenu...' he groaned. 'You...you are pressing too hard.'

But she would not release him now. She could not release him. Instead, in a voice that came from the depths of her throat, she rasped, *'Have you ever cheated on me?'*

'Meenu, what nonsense is this? Of course not!'

'Not even a bit?'

'I have been tempted, Meenu, but I have never...aah!'

'Is that the truth?'

'Meenu, your voice…your eyes…what's wrong?'

'What about that slut?'

'Who?'

She brought her face closer to his even as he winced, and then said in his ear, 'Roopali.'

'Oh, God…aah…I haven't even touched her…ever!'

'Why not? Have you never lusted after her?'

'What the hell, Meenu! What is this? I never think of anyone but you.'

For a second, Harikumar did not realize that she had released him. When he did, he backed off. He hopped right off the bed and hit the wall on the other side, and looked at himself with terrified eyes.

'What did you do? Oh fuck…I am bleeding.'

Under the sheets, Meenakshi felt her hands go back to what they were. She rubbed one against the other and her nails retracted… the smooth skin was back. She saw her husband crouched like a foetus on the floor by the wall.

'Oh no, oh no!' she yelled, throwing the sheets aside and running to him. The anger, the suspicion, the hurt was gone. Realization was back, realization of a sense of loss, that she had done something irreparable.

'Stay away from me!' Harikumar yelled.

'No, no, Hari…I am sorry…I don't know what came over me. Let me look…oh! That needs care. You need first aid, Hari. Oh, I am such a vamp…'

'What are you doing?'

'I am dialling Dr Gaitonde…'

She ran up to the landline phone in the hall. She held it against her ear, panic swirling within her now. All she could think of was her husband with his bleeding groin, and she didn't want it like this. What had that one moment of hate done! Damn, she did love him!

The phone was pressed against her ear, but all she could hear was silence.

'The phone is dead...'

She heard her husband's groans, and saw the blood staining the floor. Had she killed the man inside him forever? Oh, what would she do!

The cellphone. Yes, that was it.

She went to the wardrobe and flung the door open.

'What are you looking for?' Harikumar asked, his words slurring with the pain.

Meenakshi threw her clothes haphazardly on the bed and took out her jewellery box. Throwing it open, she pulled out the cellphone from inside it.

'That phone? It's from our company. How did you—'

She dialled the number she was looking for, and then she said, 'Just listen...there's been an accident in the house...no, I am fine, but Hari...cannot tell you...please, please, get Doctor Gaitonde... thanks...'

'Whom did you call?' Harikumar asked.

Tears fell on the screen and she realized she was crying.

She banged the wardrobe shut and it slammed hard. Then she saw herself in the mirror again.

'Why are you saving him? Don't you see? That man is a cheat. A liar. So what if he is your husband? You have to set yourself—'

The voice shattered midway. Meenakshi flung the phone at the mirror with all her strength.

'SHUT UP, BITCH!' Meenakshi screamed at the mirror in accompaniment to her action.

'Who...' Harikumar gasped.

The phone rang. It was on the floor now, and on the smashed screen, Harikumar saw the name of the caller.

'Nishikant!' he said in astonishment that defied his state. 'You have been talking to Nishi? He gave you this phone?'

Meenakshi sat on the bed, her shameful head buried in her hands.

'Meenu? Have you been...oh no! Then what was all that about me cheating on you? Will I not be right to suspect—'

'Shut up, you stupid man!' Meenakshi yelled. 'Shut up! Shut up! All of you! Don't you see...how everything is so, so fucked up?'

The doorbell rang.

Meenakshi wiped her tears and ran to the door.

It was Nishikant in his nightclothes. 'I came as soon as I could. How is Hari? Everything okay?'

He ran into the house, to the bedroom, and saw his friend groaning in agony, clutching his groin.

'Gosh! What happened here?'

'Where's the doctor?' Meenakshi asked.

'He's coming...I ran up ahead.'

'Hey, Nishi,' Harikumar said through gritted teeth.

'You be quiet, Hari...' Nishikant went down next to him trying to make sense of his condition. 'How did this...how did this even... what were you trying...'

'I am all right,' Harikumar wheezed. 'You don't need to worry about me. So, since how long have you been talking to my wife behind my back?'

'What are you saying, Hari?'

'Did it start on the day of the party or when I first showed you her picture?'

Meenakshi opened her mouth to say something, but then she saw Nishikant's face. There was a look on it, a look that told her she mustn't say anything. Words froze in her mouth.

'How long have you been talking, Meenu?' Harikumar went on. 'What have you been doing behind my back?'

Aghast at how the tables had turned, Meenakshi now spoke, 'Hari, there is nothing. Nothing at all. You have to—'

There was a rustling at the door just then as a huffing Doctor Gaitonde rushed in, and then froze mid-step. 'Oh, my stars! What dangerous sex game were you two playing?'

24

The Parting

*H*arikumar passed out the moment he was injected with the sedative. Meenakshi saw his eyes droop through the glass till she could not bear to look at him any longer.

There would be stitches, she was told. The delicateness of the region made the procedure complex. The scrotum had been torn, but thankfully there was no damage to the tubes or the testicles. There would be some inconvenience in urinating for a few days. Sex was off the table for now, but Mr Harikumar Deshmukh would be fine after the ordeal was over.

Meenakshi was quizzed by the surgeon. Dr Gaitonde chipped in and informed him with a sly wink that it was a sex game gone wrong. The surgeon, an old man, looked at Meenakshi and smirked. Then Nishikant took over.

When Meenakshi returned home, back to those bleak walls, the reality of the situation truly hit her. The monster had begun to wail now, and Meenakshi was sure that the wail was only meant for her. Shutting her ears did not help. She beat herself up and put fingers down her throat, but the wailing did not stop. The malevolence was inside her; how could she remove it?

'Why do you torment yourself like this, girl? Why do you weep over a man's plight?'

The mirror showed her the monster again; there was no escaping her.

Meenakshi stood firm and faced the Yakshini, this time filled more with anger than fear. The wizened skin, now in its full glory, did not appall her. It caked on her skin like hardened flour and she could feel the tightness, and as it squeezed and scrunched, she feared that her skin would just rupture within and bleed. But she did not look away.

She was still in that white saree with cerise flowers, now draped tightly around her. She did not want to see herself naked. The warts would be on her skin, everywhere.

Then she felt her lips stretching. They stretched to such an extent that someone would have taken it for a smile, but it was another of the ways in which the Yakshini was tormenting her. In the mirror, the Yakshini smiled.

'Don't weep over a man. Go out into the world. You are free.'

'I AM NOT FREE!' Meenakshi screamed, and her lips felt fit to burst. 'You are in me. A fiend. A monster. A freak. I will…I will kill you.'

'You think so? You really think you can kill me? You think you are the one trapped?'

'What would you have me do then?'

'Get away from here. Get away into solitude. Let's live together like the conjoined sisters we are.'

❧

Meenakshi stood outside the hospital ward, unmindful of the nurses and ward boys milling around her. No one noticed her as she stood there in her white saree, now stained and soiled with the rigours of the day. Victims of injuries walked into the hospital and left after first aid. She looked like a patient herself.

She didn't stop to look at anyone. Her eyes were only fixed on her husband lying inside the emergency room, whom she could see through the glass window. He was now bandaged around his midsection, his eyes closed. In any case, she would not have gone up to talk to him. There were no words anymore.

His eyes opened and she hid behind a pillar. She saw the other door of the room opening and Tara walking in with a lunchbox in her hands.

Harikumar tried to sit up, but the lady gently pushed him back onto the bed. Sitting on the lone chair in the room, she opened the lunchbox on a hospital tray and the warm steam of home-cooked food rose up in the air.

Meenakshi had a tear in her eye. She should have been there in that room, tending to her husband, looking after his needs. But no…what was she thinking? If it hadn't been for her, he wouldn't have been in this condition at all.

She had been kidding herself for too long. She had been blind to the evil that she was. Who was she deluding? The evil inside her wasn't a different entity. She herself was evil.

The only way to come out of this and seek some semblance of happiness was to face the reality of her self. That she was not made for anyone. She was a curse. A man-eating curse.

The bitch was right. She did not belong here anymore.

Meenakshi wiped her tears and bid a silent farewell to her husband.

⚘

'I saw her just now. She was right here.'

Harikumar was staring into the space beyond the steam of the various foods, right through the glass window.

'Relax, Hari. It is not her,' said Tara.

'Where is she? Why didn't she come to visit?'

'You ask that still, my poor boy? Look at what condition she has put you in. Forget her.'

'How can I forget her, Aatya? She is my life. If she goes, my life goes with her.'

'They say love is foolish. I am seeing it now.'

Harikumar turned his head to the other side and wept into the pillow.

25

Woman of Nature

She didn't want food or drink or rest anymore. She did not consciously look for it. That was the first sign of her beginning to lose her human nature.

After days of wandering in lonely places and traversing on unpeopled roads, Meenakshi began to lose sense of who she was. She had left the city behind a few days ago, and now she ambled along on the desolate stretches of the highway where only vehicles zoomed by busily. But this was good. She did not want people around her. She was done with people.

Hunger and thirst were satiated from whatever she could forage from the trees and shrubs along the forested boundaries of the highway. At times, she would chance upon some small eating establishment along the roadside, and deftly nick the food when the vendor's attention was elsewhere. It was easy to steal in these unguarded shops; they did not have much to protect anyway.

Once she got nothing but a raw chicken breast, ready with spices on it, waiting to be put into a tandoor. She waited in the bushes for the person to prepare it, but he wouldn't. Finally, she showed herself to him, emerging from those bushes, and he was drawn to her as if in a trance. When he returned to his shop minutes later, disappointed, he found the chicken breast gone.

It was difficult to bite into raw meat for the first time, but she learned it. She had done worse; she no longer had any reservations about the kind of food she put into her mouth.

She never stopped in one place for long. After stealing from one spot, she would move on to another, making sure to stay away from human eyes. It came to a point where hiding became a matter of instinct.

The woods made her both more beautiful and more hideous. After a few days on the run, most of the unnatural artifices on her skin had worn away. The makeup withered and dried away and the kohl faded. Her hair lost its shampooed smoothness, and the oil in it dried up and vanished somewhere into the forest air. Her nails and toes outgrew the paint she once used to put on them, and her ornaments fell off one by one and became part of the earth.

But this made her more real, more natural, more earthy. Without those trappings, her true form emerged. As she traversed the forest paths, she still looked human. She still had that whiff of natural beauty with a lost-doe look in her eyes.

What made Meenakshi hideous though was the being inside her. There was no provocation for her to come out now, but she was right there, bubbling under the surface of her skin. At times, the Yakshini would threaten to rip that human skin and emerge, and Meenakshi would scream in agony. But the agony would be lost somewhere in the canopy of the tall trees and die away, unheard and uncared for.

Only a few things still remained on her body. The white saree, now muddied and soiled, still remained. As she walked among those dense trees of the jungle, sometimes the white of her saree would shimmer from between the tree trunks and even the animals would stop and wonder what new creature had entered their domain.

The other thing that persisted was a single anklet, the one on her left foot. Everything else had fallen off, but this one stayed like an obstinate lover refusing to part ways. It was a slender silver affair with tiny round bells attached to it, and it made a faint tinkling sound as she walked. As the days passed, Meenakshi came to love the sound it made; its melody helped to kill the rasping voice inside her.

&

This particular night was a strange one. There was no sleep. Nightmares played out constantly, and they were so real that they did not seem like they were figments of her mind, but that they were playing out for real behind the curtains of her shut eyes. And all of those nightmares were of the Yakshini coming out and going forth, towering like a giant on the lonely roads of the cities, picking up lone men and ripping them apart like wrapping paper from a birthday present.

By the middle of the night, the bubbling under Meenakshi's skin increased. She woke up in a sweat. She had come down with a fever, and saw, to her great horror, actual bubbles rising on her skin as though there were some trapped liquid in there trying to boil and burst out. She screamed at the sight, a scream that deadened the howling of some faraway wolves.

It was the Yakshini. She wanted to come out now. She wanted to feed. And she told her, wordlessly:

'I smell a man.'

The moment had come. The Yakshini had fallen off the deep end. She was savage now, a predator, and Meenakshi was her vehicle.

The torment was like a hundred ulcers burning under the skin. It would not let her sit. The bubbles emerged under her thighs and her buttocks, and she sprung up. She felt her steps being directed, and with great helplessness she realized they were moving to find a victim for the Yakshini.

She cried. She sobbed. She screamed. If it were at all possible, she'd have cut away her own flesh and fed the brute, but the Yakshini had no taste for female flesh. It was a man she wanted, and she was growing hungrier and angrier.

'Take me to him. Take me. NOW.'

The woman in white stood still. She did not know where she was. Everywhere there was the forest, and every direction looked the same as the other. She stopped at a point and peered. There was a faint sound of a faraway vehicle.

She sighed.

❧

Balram Singh had been driving the truck on the highway for twenty years. He had learnt to drive it when he was thirteen, a mere boy in shorts, and he had taken to it right away. When his father died, the truck became his livelihood.

On this night, he was transporting several bales of cloth. He had headed out from Surat in the late evening and now he was on the highway going southward. He was passing by Mumbai now, and it would be a long time before he reached his destination.

The night was catching on. It was one of those forest nights that were always cold, irrespective of the season. The roads were mostly unlit, but Balram Singh had had his dippers checked before setting out on this journey.

He lived for such long chilly night drives. He drove for quite a while and then he stiffened.

There was something on the road ahead.

He instantly decelerated like the pro he was, but a cold fear gripped him that he would not make it.

The truck slowed down though, and as it ground to a halt, Balram Singh saw that this was no animal. This was a lady!

Dressed in a white saree, she was walking by in a mindless daze. A drifter from the nearby village? A pang of apprehension hit his heart first, and he wanted to follow his brain and move on, but then he made one mistake he would repent for the rest of his life.

As he began to accelerate again, he turned just once to look at the woman in white, and he saw her face.

That was that. The next instant, the accelerator sputtered and died, and he hopped off the truck.

The woman looked at him and smiled.

26

Ratisundari

'*I*s this what you are reduced to now?'

It was a kind manly voice that had called out to her. *Who had dared to come upon her?* Drawing a blood-soaked finger out of her mouth, Meenakshi looked up and saw him.

Instantly, her comportment changed. She felt humiliated, squatting thus on the ground, picking up pieces of meat from her recent man-prey's viscera, and finding the best chunks to suck the blood out of. She was also embarrassed that she was not the beautiful woman he had seen before. She was now an uncouth, unkempt monstrosity who had developed a taste for human blood, or more specifically, man blood.

She attempted to say something, but words failed her. She had been out in the wilderness for too long, devoid of even the remotest form of human communication. Language was slowly becoming alien to her.

As Krita stood in her presence, all that came out of her were guttural sounds.

'*Your screeching is proof of your deterioration. It pains my heart.*'

She groaned, making an exaggerated apish gesture.

'Do you forget who I am? Look at me. I am Krita.'

It was him, she knew, but she could not speak. He stood there in his magnificent glory, his bare body beaming, but she was speechless.

He came closer. He stood by the corpse of the recently slain truck driver, blood still oozing out of it, and shook his head. 'Middle-aged man. Late thirties at the most.'

She willed her head to move. It was a nod that went ever so

slightly up and down, and she knew it wasn't her who was doing the nodding. It was the Yakshini.

Krita laughed. 'It is funny how a person's punishment is never really confined to the person. When a murderer is hanged, it is not just the murderer who suffers; it is his entire family, for they have to face the shame, and the loneliness. When a man is exiled, his family has to do without him or go with him. When a king is punished, that sentence is borne by all his subjects, at times for generations to come. So has been your punishment. It has caused nothing but suffering to everyone around you.'

'What punishment? Why?' she wanted to ask, but she could only make a gurgling sound.

Krita moved closer to her and placed a hand on her shoulder. 'My heart weeps for you,' he said.

She stiffened. As his fingers fell tenderly on her skin, something warm coursed through her. Something flashed through whatever remained of her mind. But it was still away—still a shapeless haze.

The Yakshini moved her head to look at him, directly into his eyes now. His glow made her eyes burn.

'It's about time that I tell you your story then, my dear Ratisundari,' said Krita with a compassionate smile.

Part Three

- - - - - - - - - - - -

The Seed

Year 1981

27

The World Between Worlds

That realm, hidden by clouds, is situated between the Deva Loka, which looms over it, and the Bhoomi Loka, which sprawls under it. It lies on a flattened peak somewhere in the highest Himalayas, blanketed by never-moving clouds. For those who think that the Everest is the loftiest peak on Earth, it would be a matter of great disgrace if they ever discovered this kingdom. For though the mountain peak was sliced into half to create the flat land of the realm, it can still tower over seven Everests stacked end on end.

Impenetrable as this kingdom is, it stays away from the human eye, and will remain so even if the entire Kalpa passes and another arrives. But the unattainability of this world is not due to any design of nature; it is because the creator of this world himself does not wish it to be found by mortal eyes. And so, it stays that way.

This enchanted kingdom goes by various names, but the most preferred name, given to it by its denizens, is Alaka or Alakapuri—the land of the demigods.

When the divinities created the earth, they bestowed upon it every beauty that they could conjure. But, of course, their greatest act—and undoubtedly the most challenging—was to make this beauty sustain itself. That they managed, or purported to manage, by granting what is known as 'life' to some of their creations. Life was not an ordinary gift. Those who received life were able to produce more like themselves, and thus keep going. That was the actual marvel of the world-creators, a fact that was mostly lost on the world in times to come.

But it is not so in Alakapuri. The beauty they have created is their own. They have great riches, the greatest the world has ever known, and they flaunt those in every inch of their space. There is not a single spot you could look at without some glittering gold or a sparkling diamond offering a feast to your eyes. The floors are of uncured diamond, and the pillars are of the most expensive stone that earthlings can dream of. Here, even the reptiles carry emeralds on their heads. The poorest here are richer than the entire human population put together, and, by some accounts, even richer than all the Gods put together.

※

Around twenty years ago, this kingdom saw a momentous celebration. The occasion was the five-thousandth anniversary of their victory over the Snake People, the Nagas, a grand historical moment when the Naga wealth was added to the coffers of the demigods. The Naga Vijaya, as the festival is known, was to be celebrated in the sprawling garden of Chaitrarath, high on the slopes of Mount Mandara, and the king of Alakapuri himself was to make an appearance.

The palace of the king, which overlooked this garden, was lit up with lights encased in glittering jewels, and the demigods—Yakshas, Kinnaras, the very elusive Guhyakas, and even the Gandharvas—thronged the garden in countless numbers.

Males, females, and offspring—all creatures milled around. They wore scant clothes, mostly nothing at all, but their bodies were covered by the heavy gold ornaments that they wore. The ornaments were so huge that from Deva Loka it looked like a river of gold was in motion, and the clanging noise they made was so loud that it disturbed the sages meditating in the Bhoomi Loka below.

But the ornaments had another important purpose, a purpose that no denizen of this realm would openly admit. The yellow metal hid their deformities.

Now this was a sordid fact but bitterly true—the Yakshas who were born in Alakapuri were born deformed. The deformities manifested themselves in the form of an unnatural number of appendages, or incongruently placed eyes, or broken teeth, or a misshapen skull. A few of the lucky ones could hide those deformities, but for most, they were right out in the open.

Over time, however, as the city gained wealth, and as they became more isolated from the rest of the world, the people stopped caring about their deformities.

On this particular day, their natural condition was the least of their concerns.

The able-bodied (to whatever extent they were so) males rushed forth. They had gotten the whiff of a particular scent that had put their extremities on end. Quite literally, for they could not hide their arousal as they rushed to the garden.

'Do you smell the Yakshinis?' said a male Yaksha.

'Run faster! I don't want to miss even one glimpse of them!' said another.

It turned to a stampede as the males rushed forth, even stepping on each other and grabbing and throwing whoever dared to obstruct their progress. When they finally reached the garden, they stood awed, their mouths open, unable to take in the beauty all at once.

※

The Yakshinis were thirty-six in number. They were the inhabitants of this land too, but they were not cursed. While almost everyone else was born deformed, the Yakshinis were the epitomes of beauty. In every way, they were celestially perfect. There could not be an aphrodisiac better than these immortal and ever-young beauties; if they wanted, they could put even an old celibate sage in heat and make him commit a sin he would repent for all his remaining births.

On this occasion, the Yakshinis stood in a neat row, displaying their unimaginable beauty. They were guarded by some of the demonic Yakshas, who formed a protective fence around them with their large bodies. And yet, as each moment passed, it was becoming increasingly difficult to control the audience.

Then there was a loud flapping noise from the skies above and everything went silent.

From the sky descended the Pushpak Vimana, the special chariot of their king. The assembled creatures bowed their heads as their royal leader stepped off his steed and placed the first of his three feet on the ground.

This was their king, the fearsome demigod monarch who had defeated the Snake People five millennia ago. He was the one who had appeased Lord Shiva himself and had attained from him the status of overlord of all semi-divine beings. He was the master of all the wealth of the world and the treasurer of the Gods themselves.

And also—he was born an asura, a demon, having come from the seed of the same father who had given birth to Ravana, the once-dreaded king of Lanka. He was the one whom even the gods feared.

He was the Yaksha king, Kubera.

☙

For all his wealth and might, however, there was one thing missing in Kubera. Good looks. The curse was upon him too, and probably because he was the monarch of the land, it had hit him the hardest.

Lord Kubera stood only five feet tall, shorter than most of his subjects. Even the Yakshinis were a full head taller than he was. He looked almost comical when he moved, for he carried an excessive paunch that wobbled ahead of him, like a true embodiment of his curse. One consolation, however, was that his paunch fell over his groin and hid his modesty. And to cover whatever his belly did not, he bedecked himself with rich ornaments from head to toe.

His third leg was the most symbolic embodiment of the curse. Merely a hindrance, that extra appendage dragged behind him as he walked, arising incongruously from the left of his hip.

His short arms could not go around his belly even if he tried, and they were not helped by his stubby fingers on which fingernails never grew.

His face wasn't spared either. Warts and spots covered most

of it, leaving only the eyes and the mouth out. To speak of the eyes—he had only one that was natural, the other having been lost early on. A topaz now shone in that eyeless socket. His overlarge lips enclosed eight teeth that were separated from each other. When he broke into one of his rare grins, they resembled nails holding his lips together.

He walked on now, with a bowl of gold coins in his hand, and went up to the centre of the podium. He took a handful of the coins and threw them on his subjects. No one stooped to pick them up though, for no one really needed the wealth. This was merely an auspicious start to the celebrations, and it was followed by hoots and cheers that pervaded the atmosphere.

'Dear people of Alakapuri,' King Kubera began, 'welcome to Naga Vijaya. We have been waiting a long time for this day, and we will make the most of it. There will be no talk of governance today. We shall only be entertained. For that purpose, we have the Yakshinis here, and also the Gandharvas who have come to be in our midst.'

Abruptly falling silent, Kubera went and occupied his throne, a sparkling seat that miraculously arose from the middle of the stage.

This was a cue for the festivities to begin.

The denizens receded to make space for the performers on the stage. A hush fell all around, and then there was a heavy shuffling of feet.

The crowd turned to look.

Four Gandharvas, dressed in dhotis that went down to their knees, came up holding sticks and took centre stage. Their well-sculpted bodies, which were on scintillating display now, drew gasps from the audience, and even the Yakshinis turned to look at these perfect specimens of celestial masculinity. The Gandharvas arranged themselves in a formation, and then, in perfect synchronization, began tapping the ends of the sticks on the stage floor. It took the audience a moment to understand that this was not any random tapping; it had a rhythm of its own. It was a song.

And then the dance began. The two Gandharvas in the front leaped over the two at the back and then they moved their lithe bodies to the beat. They tossed themselves in the air, and bounced on the balls of their feet, and pirouetted like they were spinning tops.

Music filled the air from an unknown source, a tune that was not just notes but had an intoxicating undercurrent that hypnotized the listeners and held them in a trance.

Then, at once, the attention of the assembly was consumed by another entrance. The sound came first—a low hum that grew to a louder, more persistent sound—and everyone hooted again, for they realized what the sound was.

It was hissing.

These were the Nagas!

Or, technically, young Yakshas dressed up as Nagas. The performance would now be a grand spectacle, for it was now evident what it was going to be. This was a reenacting of their victory over the Nagas.

The poor beings who were dressed up as Nagas came slithering upon the floor. Their bellies rubbed against the ground as they moved, and they held their hands over their heads to depict hoods.

The Gandharva dancers paused in synchronized choreography when the Nagas slunk up to their feet. A hush fell over the audience again, an anticipative hush that gripped their hearts. Then, just as the Yaksha boys poised their fake Naga hoods to strike, the Gandharvas raised their sticks and brought them crashing upon their skulls.

The act turned only too real. For, indeed, it was real. The sticks had come down with resounding crashes on the heads of the poor Yaksha younglings, and though it was a performance, that part of it was truly done. They lay now, dead on the dance floor, their skulls bleeding where they had caved in.

The petrified audience could not close their agape mouths for a long time, even as they watched the gore in terror, not knowing if this was meant to happen.

Then there was a loud laugh that broke the silence. It was Kubera himself, standing up now, hopping in glee, and then, like an unruly child, he broke into applause and a cackling laughter.

A ripple ran through the crowd then, and they laughed too—at first only nervous giggles, which then turned to a huge uproar. The music started again, and the Gandharvas completed the rest of their dance over the dead bodies.

But Kubera was least bothered about the 'deaths'. For he had the power to restore life, and he would do so in time, which would be after the show reached the spectacular heights he meant to take it to.

❧

When the dance ended, Kubera was the loudest in his applause.

'You see,' he began, 'dear people of Alakapuri, we do not spare effort in anything that we undertake. Be they our battles in unknown lands or entertainment in this land of our own.'

People cheered in unison, and then broke into shouts of 'Digpala! Digpala!' Digpala meant world ruler, the honorific that the subjects had bestowed upon Kubera.

'Now we pause,' Kubera frowned. 'Something has come to my notice. And I need to take care of it now.'

Silence spread over the audience again. Jaws clenched, lips pursed, and muscles stiffened at the ominous words.

Kubera looked at the Gandharva dancers. Their bodies were now glistening with sweat, and as soon as the king's eyes fell on them, their chests began to heave in nervous trepidation.

'You!' Kubera pointed at one of them.

The hapless Gandharva looked at his other three companions, and said, 'Yes, Digpala!'

'Come forth, you.'

He took two steps forward, while the other three backed away slowly.

'Kneel.'

He knelt.

'You danced well,' said Kubera, stepping forward, his belly oscillating as he took each step. 'It was a delight to sore eyes, and though you are male, you did something to me.' He laughed in a maniacal, obscene manner at his own joke.

The Gandharva kept his head bowed.

'But...'

The hush over the audience became more intense.

'...I think you were a wee bit distracted.'

'Digpala?' said the Gandharva fearfully.

'Don't you know what I am talking about?'

'No, Digpala.'

'Well, it is written all over your face, you poor thing!' Kubera picked up the stick lying on the ground and with it, lifted the Gandharva's chin up. 'Even right now you are looking for her, aren't you?'

'Her, sir? Who?'

'Oh, the innocent act! People, can't you see the love on this Gandharva's face?'

Kubera pointed to a random old Yaksha in the audience, and his words rushed out in panic, 'I do, Digpala, I do.'

'We all do!' Kubera laughed. 'Who is she you were looking at during your dance? Come on, you have to tell us. And, remember,' Kubera raised his chin even higher, 'I know much more than you think I do.'

The Gandharva fearfully turned and looked at the Yakshinis. His eyes rested on one, distinctly the most beautiful of the lot.

'As I thought!' Kubera bellowed. 'Come forth, Yakshini.'

The Yakshini, scared to bits, looked at her friends. But they all stood stone-faced, as if they had suddenly decided they wanted nothing to do with her.

'Do you know this Gandharva?' Kubera asked.

She stayed silent.

'I don't like to repeat my questions, Yakshini.'

'Yes, Digpala,' she said. 'We are in love.'

'Oh, that common disease that blights the Gods and demons alike!' Kubera guffawed. 'Well, tell us your name, Yakshini.'

The Yakshini cast one fearful look at her kneeling lover, and then, with her face paler than the whites of her eyes, said, 'Ratisundari.'

28

The Banishment

'*My*, my, my...aren't you the loveliest of them all!'

Kubera went forth and stood next to the Yakshini Ratisundari, not at all minding that he was a dwarf in her presence. Yet, he tried to place his arm over her shoulders as if posing for a portrait. With his eyes firmly fixed on her jewellery-adorned breasts, he said, 'Aren't you every male's wet dream?'

Ratisundari looked at him sharply. She tried to release herself, but didn't make the effort too obvious.

'Now, now, little one...' said Kubera, and the irony was painfully obvious, '...don't you try to squirm away from me. I know everything about your little misdemeanour.'

'I have done nothing, Digpala.'

'Oh, the sweetness of your voice! No, not just a voice. A trap for all males.'

'I apologize for what you think I have done, Digpala.'

'I THINK?' There was an edge to his voice all of a sudden. He took his arm away from her so abruptly that she almost keeled over. 'You think I am a fool? I don't know what I am saying?'

'I didn't mean that, Digpala.'

'Oh, the insolence! What makes you so proud?'

Ratisundari quivered like the last fibre holding a torn cloth together.

'You have flouted the rules of this land,' said Kubera, mincing no words, 'with the assistance of your lover here.'

'What...I...'

'Don't mumble! Fall at my feet.'

Ratisundari looked around. There was not a single compassionate eye for her in that crowd of hundreds now. Meekly, she obeyed, and joined the Gandharva in the middle of the stage.

'Accept your folly,' said Kubera. 'Tell everyone what you did and your punishment will be light.'

There was silence all around, only broken by the heavy breathing of the Yakshini and her Gandharva. She looked sideways at him and he nodded.

Then she spoke, 'Sire, I…I went to Deva Loka. This… Gandharva here…he took me there.'

'And what did you do in Deva Loka?'

'I roamed around, fascinated, looking at the marvels—'

'SHUT UP!' Kubera roared. 'No one wants to hear about the marvels of Deva Loka. There is nothing in Deva Loka to surpass what we have here in Alakapuri. Tell us of your crime.'

'I…I entered Indra's durbar in disguise.'

'Ah, Indra! Now why doesn't that surprise me? And what disguise was it?'

'Of an apsara.'

'Apsara? A heavenly dancer?' Kubera snorted. 'Could you not be more inventive?'

'And then I went into Indra's hall and danced with the other apsaras.'

Kubera seethed. His lips, those lumpen mounds of flesh, flattened as much as they could. But his words were calculated and slow as he said, 'Why did you do that?'

'I just wanted to see the Gods' world.'

'QUIET!' the Digpala roared. 'You fool no one. We know what a lust-laden whore you are. You went there to seduce the Gods. You have tried your wiles on all these males here and now you want their attention.'

'No…no…'

'Did no one find out?' said Kubera, returning to his calm voice.

Ratisundari bowed her head. 'No…'

'Did nothing happen to the Gods? Did they even get aroused?' Kubera laughed. 'Ha! But what am I saying!'

Ratisundari kept her head bowed.

'You have committed a grievous folly, as you say,' Kubera pronounced.

'I...I... This will never happen again.'

'No, it will,' said Kubera firmly. 'The only reason we are able to sustain ourselves is because we don't condone mistakes. You see how precarious our position is? Neither are we humans, whose very nature is to commit mistakes, nor are we Gods, whose mistakes are mistaken for divine deeds. We are in the middle, and we have to preserve that position. Such a huge slight cannot be ignored. I am sure Indra found out. And Indra of all beings? Don't you know of his reputation with the ladies? He knows all his apsaras intimately.' Kubera winked at the audience as he said that. 'No one touched by Indra goes unpunished; you know better than that. Haven't you heard of that human woman who was cursed and turned to stone just because Indra touched her?'

'Forgive us, Digpala,' said the Gandharva. 'We will never do anything of this sort again.'

'No. There will be punishment.'

Kubera's offenders then kept their heads bowed, knowing that their entreaties would fall on deaf ears.

'You, Yakshini, are the bigger offender here. You are a seductress, and it is not the poor Gandharva's fault that he did your bidding. You made him dance on your fingertips. Hence, your share of the suffering will be heavier.'

'Please...'

'Deprivation of something you yearn for is the biggest punishment,' Kubera proclaimed. 'Henceforth, you are deprived of what you cherish so much—your beauty. You will no longer be beautiful but will turn into a creature so hideous that even Shiva will blanch to look at you.'

'No...!'

'And you are forthwith banished from Alakapuri. You shall

stay banished till you begin to value this land of ours. Go unleash your hideousness somewhere else.'

Ratisundari looked at him, stunned.

Kubera continued, 'You have been lusting after the male race for long. But now you shall be a scourge for these very men. You will look upon all men as your enemies and will never be able to find love.'

Then the Yakshini broke out, 'Mercy, Digpala, mercy!'

Kubera raised a hand. 'Yes, I am merciful, and hence let me make it easier for you. I shall give you a home during your exile. If my brother Ravana were alive, I would have sent you to Lanka to work in his Ashok Vatika. Anyway, there is a man down there in Bhoomi Loka whose wife is pregnant with their seventh child. He has had only daughters so far, and he is praying for a Yakshini to come and bestow him with a son.'

Kubera came closer to Ratisundari. 'This is good for us. Through his rituals, he has opened up the pathway between his Bhoomi Loka and our kingdom. You will be going down that pathway and be born in the body of his seventh child.'

'What? A human life?'

'Yes. An entire human birth. And it is poetic irony. The child in this woman's body is already a boy, but their foolhardy yajna will now make it a girl—you. So much for foolishly praying for a boy child! I will never understand the human race or their hankering for male children. You shall be born in the body of this couple's daughter and will live in her body till she dies.'

'Won't this be a punishment to that poor girl too?' the Gandharva cried. 'What is her mistake?'

'The girl is already cursed. The moment the father started these rituals, he played with the child's life.' Kubera turned back to Ratisundari. 'But I will transfer your beauty to her. It will be some compensation to her. She will be the most beautiful girl humankind has ever seen.'

'But...'

'Silence, Yakshini! Don't you see how light this punishment is? Human life is short, and the girl will die. And whenever she is fated to die as per Yama's decree, you will be released.'

'But…but I won't know how to lead a human life.'

'You will learn!'

The Gandharva stammered, 'And…what about me?'

'I don't care about you. Go anywhere. Never show your face in Alakapuri again till your lover is released.'

At that moment, a hole appeared in the floor of the land, right in front of where Kubera stood.

'The pathway is now open. The man's ritual is coming to an end. You cannot be here a moment longer.'

The duo stood. With trembling feet, they proceeded. The Yakshini stepped up first, and with one look at the crowd, she prepared to jump into the hole.

'Go now!' said Kubera. 'From this moment on, you shall forget every shred of your life in Alakapuri.'

Ratisundari took one last look at the Gandharva, who was now standing as resolutely as ever. Then she told him, 'Farewell, dear Krita, till we meet again.'

Krita nodded. 'Go. I shall never leave you alone, dear Ratisundari. Go in peace.'

Part Four

The Withering

Year 2010

39

White Witch of the Forest

*H*ow do you kill something that's inside you like an incurable disease, a cancer? A thing that has a life of its own? You know it lives within you; it thrives within you. It breathes your share of air; it eats your portion of food. Why, even when you have sex, it robs you of some of that pleasure. You cannot give yourself anything without giving that parasite some of it too.

You know that thing is your archenemy, your nemesis; and yet, getting rid of it is not in your hands. The only way is by putting an end to yourself. But would you be so vengeance-filled or angst-ridden that you would do that? Ending yourself to end your problem can never be a solution.

You will spend every waking moment thinking of ways to get rid of the affliction, and when you cannot do that, a huge ball of despair will engulf you. You will let it engulf you, because you have no choice. You will sink into that ball, bit by bit, till what is inside comes out and taunts you, derides you, and gloats over its victory over you.

That's how evil disease is, an invention of the Gods to keep humanity in check.

Living inside this girl was a being that had been transformed into hideousness. It was a creature that infested not just every physical cell of her body, but also her abstract conscience.

The Yakshini was her disease.

❦

At that moment, she wasn't herself any longer.

Out on the road that ran through this forest that the city had grown around, she could hear a vehicle zip by. The night was nigh, and the road was desolate. It was probably another late-hour straggler trying to make his way home via the direct route that passed through the forest.

She started walking in a hurry, leaving the remains of her previous victim, hoping to catch sight of this one before he zipped away.

A row of shrubbery parted the forest from the road outside. By now she had come to know the layout well. She stood still, listening to the sound of the approaching vehicle, drew in a deep breath, and emerged from the bushes.

It was an autorickshaw, sputtering its way to the end of the long road that led outside to the highway. Within, the rickshaw had blazing lights on, and one of those godawful songs that only rickshaw drivers seem to play on full blast. With those blinding lights and cacophonous sounds, the black-and-yellow vehicle looked like a three-wheeled gremlin, one that was formed out of some unholy amalgamation of man and machine.

The Yakshini peered. The driver was alone. A healthy young man. She smacked her lips.

Coming out in the middle of the road, she stopped, and put out her bosom as seductively as she could.

❧

Vijay Jaiswal drove his three-wheeled steed on the forested road, with Altaf Raja's latest superhit blaring. He was singing along too, egged on by the two beers that were inside him, and the sole thought in his sozzled brain was of his little bride Neha preparing the bed at home.

Over drinks, his friends had advised him against taking this route. They had spoken about 'incidents' that had occurred on this road, the infamous Aarey Road that cut through the Aarey Forest like an interminable python. But Jaiswal had just laughed them off. Then he had chugged the beer and gone on his way.

He needed to take a piss break now. He stopped his rickshaw

by the side of the road—on this road any spot was a toilet—and he stood facing the dense shrubbery. He undid his zipper, took aim and let out a long and deep sigh of relief.

Then he saw something.

About twenty feet away from him, there was something white in the middle of the path.

Quickly, he turned to finish. He looked again. There it was—a feminine shape, draped in white, standing in the middle of the path. Suddenly, he grew cold. The beer was out of him now. He stood there, frozen, not knowing what to do. 'Who are you?' he said with a whimper.

The thing did not move. Apart from the slight swaying of the white saree in the cold forest breeze, he saw no other movement.

'Oh my God!' Jaiswal murmured to himself and promptly got into the rickshaw. Without another look in that unholy direction, he bent to start the vehicle. But he had sweat and urine on his hands. His hand slipped.

'Bhench*d! Start!' he yelled at his rickshaw as if it were his saviour dragon, on whose back he would fly out of this infernal place.

He held the shaft again, and this time it purred, and he was just about to pull, when he suddenly stopped.

A smell of jasmine permeated the air around him. In fact, somewhere right next to him.

Terrified now, he looked into his rear-view mirror.

There she was, sitting in the back seat—the most beautiful woman he had ever seen. With something in her eyes. Something that was now drawing him in. Suddenly, his hands went limp, and he let go of the shaft gently.

'Where...do you want to go?' he asked, his throat dry.

The woman smiled. The smile came out as one of those cutesy pouts that he had seen on the mouths of those sleazy actresses in the B-grade movies in those curtain-partitioned one-room 'theatres'.

Without another logical thought, he turned and unashamedly looked at her bosom, for the palloo of that white saree had now fallen.

'Do you...' he said. 'Do you want to go somewhere?'

In response, she scooched slightly in her seat and patted on the empty space next to her.

'Oh, f**k!' he smiled, not really believing his luck now. 'You want me to sit next to you?'

She nodded.

'But I don't have any money...' he said that just like that, from the experience of his unmarried days.

She laughed, a tittering taunting laugh.

He went and sat next to her. He became aware of something now, a rock-like hardness in his nether regions.

With unceasing breaths now, he put his arm around her shoulders, his eyes refusing to leave her bust. Unable to hold himself, he leaned to place his lips on her lean waist.

Almost right then, unseen by him, the woman's fingers began to change. His eyes were shut, and his lips and tongue worked frenziedly, but even if he were in a conscious state of mind, he would not have been aware of the transformation that was happening behind his back.

Those rosy lips had vanished too. Cracks had appeared there, and if he would now have stopped paying attention to her bosom and gone and kissed her, he'd have a bleeding mouth to begin with.

The hand, now with claws at its ends, raised itself, poised to strike the man in his heat.

But just then, something happened.

Jaiswal tried to reach out to the other breast. In doing so, he opened his eyes just momentarily, and in that one moment, his glance fell on the front of his autorickshaw. That was where the small plastic effigy of the orange Hanuman dangled.

That was all it took.

He looked at his little Hanuman who was now dangling

furiously, his mace upraised in his hand, as if about to strike, and he recoiled.

He had seen her face in the rear view mirror.

It was the face of a witch. Or demon. Monster. Whatthef**kever!

Coming back to himself in the nick of time, he pushed the creature with all he had, throwing her clear out of the other side of the rickshaw. He hurried to the front and started the vehicle.

Hanuman blessed him; the vehicle started.

Without sparing another thought for anything, he zoomed by, refusing to even look in his side mirrors.

It was only after he had driven on for about five miles that he realized how narrowly he had missed death.

❧

When Vijay Jaiswal sat with his friends again, he narrated to them the story of what had happened to him, without any embellishment, because they were finding it hard to believe it as it were. And his narration was punctuated with multiple thanks to the Monkey God for his protection.

Those friends told the story to other friends, and they told it to yet more friends, and then more stories emerged and still more, until 'Aarey Jungle ki Safed Chudail' or 'White Witch of the Aarey Forest' became a legend, preying on lonely libidinous young men.

30

A Courageous Act for Cowards

The beast lives inside all of us. It takes on various names—envy, anger, hatred, vengeance—but it is there, boiling under the surface, making us do things that we wouldn't do if we were only human. What keeps this beast in check is the fact that we live in this world with other humans, following a spoken or unspoken, written or unwritten code of ethics. This preserves our humanness and suppresses the beast, so that it stays within and does not rear its ugly head.

But if we are taken out of this world and kept in isolation, our humanness starts diminishing. We turn from creatures of thought to creatures of instinct. In isolation, our inner beast comes alive. When no one is looking, it takes us over. In time, it erodes our human aspect and we become the beast we have been suppressing for so long.

With Meenakshi, the beast was literal.

The day she entered the forest, she had no reason to hide who she was.

Over a period of time, there were only faint shreds left of the girl she once was. Her outward appearance stayed human, but that was all that was human about her.

In all other aspects, the Yakshini took over.

This transformation happened bit by bit, bone by bone, drop by drop of male blood, and took a period of ten years.

❦

If she had still been in her previous world, people would have been celebrating her thirtieth birthday. She would have been surrounded by her family, all of who now looked like hazy figures in a stifling mist, and they would have sung the birthday song for her. Ha! The birthday song! She did not even remember the tune of that anymore.

The jungle was her abode now. Over the decade, she had made friends with every bird and beast of the forest. She had become intimate with the trees (though they woefully reminded her of the sal tree from a bygone age) and she had trodden on every path with her naked feet with just the one anklet on it. The grains of mud, the splinters of wood, the pollen in the wind, all these elements entered her every day and every night, and she took them all in.

She was thirty now.

What could she have been? A mother? A daughter looking after her ailing parents? A wife accompanying her husband in the journey of life?

But no. Here she was. Torn and forlorn, a beast of the jungle.

'*You are done, Meenakshi. Finished. Only your kernel remains; the flesh inside is me. It is I now. Only I.*'

She was thirty. And unclean. It didn't matter anymore.

❦

But darkness is never absolute. No eclipse is total; a sliver of light is always left behind. For this savage woman in the cave, that sliver of light was one man, the one she had left behind.

Harikumar.

On those lonely nights when she fed herself well and lay on the floor of her bloodied den, there was this little glimpse that she would have. Just a flash, no more, but it was enough to take away her sleep for the night. For some reason, she would always see this vision of him—bare-chested, his hands on her, looking right into her eyes, preparing himself to make love to her. It would be so real that she would forget her present state for a moment and shuffle herself, so that he could position himself on her, and then place his lips on hers. But the next moment, she would see it was just the wind.

Harikumar wasn't there with her.

Of what use was this existence if it was bereft of everything that she had held dear? An existence that had snatched away the most basic right of a human—the right to love and be loved?

When she was in such a mental tussle once, a line stood out in her mind:

'Human life is short, and the girl will die.'

It seemed tempting. She had been struggling for so long, but the solution was right there in front of her. Beckoning her temptingly. She had been blind not to see it.

The Yakshini had indeed taken over now, and that tipped the balance in favour of the decision. The Yakshini could now see the life she had left behind in Alakapuri and had begun to yearn for it. Release was what she wanted at any cost.

One snap of the finger, and she could end this girl's life. And then be free; free to go back.

The question now was: how would it be? You are in a prison, confined behind bars; you can do your best to break the bars, turn them and twist them so that they provide a gap big enough for you to pass through. But what do you do when the prison is your own body? How can you break your own body?

Killing oneself—a courageous act for cowards.

So, how would it be? What would be a painless surefire way that would lead her out of this imprisonment?

In the distance, she heard the honking of an approaching vehicle.

Yes! That could be it. She hoped and prayed that that vehicle was a truck. It sounded big enough. She could just throw herself under its giant unforgiving tires. It would be over in a flash, and she would be back to where she belonged.

Without wasting another moment (more so because she did not want her courage to falter), she glided through the jungle towards the sound of the speeding vehicle. As she swiftly moved past, the boughs of the trees caressed her body, as if making a vain plea for her to stop and rethink, but she was not alive to the touches of those companions anymore.

'*Everything will be over now, Meenakshi. I'm setting you free!*'

With a smile on her face that belied all reason, she went to the middle of the road, and with a bosom that was heaving with both thrill and trepidation, she stood, waiting, as the roar of the vehicle drew closer.

She hoped the driver wouldn't see her too soon and step on the brakes.

'Okay, here it comes. Yes!'

The vehicle turned the bend, which was about a quarter of a mile away, and as it grew larger, she saw it.

It wasn't a truck. It was a bus.

A red BEST bus, to be precise, one that ferried passengers from one edge of the city to the other, cutting through this forest road.

A sigh left her mouth.

'*Fasten your seatbelt, Meenakshi. We are going for a ride.*'

This was it. This was the moment that would finish all of it and take her to the place that she never should have had to leave.

❧

The BEST bus driver was humming a song as he drove on this desolate untrafficked road. At this evening hour, there was nothing on this forest patch, and, if he could ignore the fear and stories that were widely circulated, this was actually the most thrilling part of his day. Cutting through the forest. What pleasure! He felt the cold wind hitting his face as he zipped by on this monstrous vehicle. He lived for this!

Every evening on this trip, when the forest path would start, he would tune off from the chattering sounds of the passengers behind him, ignore the conductor, draw in a deep breath, feel the wind on his chest, and just drive. The depot was just outside the forest path where the city resumed, and that would be the end of his workday too.

That day, it was quieter. It was a Sunday and there weren't many middle class employees returning home on his bus. In fact, apart from a young couple seated in the front and a group of young friends at the back, there was no one else in the bus.

The driver thought of his brother's wedding that was to happen next month in his hometown, Satara. Christmas holidays would begin soon, and perhaps he could put in a leave for a week's holiday and go plan the wedding? There were invites to be distributed, the hall contractors had to be shouted at, the lousy caterers had to be cussed and made to do well...

'Oh, f**k, no!' he screamed all of a sudden and swerved sharply to the right.

The conductor came up running. 'What happened?'

A volley of abuses left the driver's mouth in the ten seconds that it took for the bus to come to a screeching halt in the middle of the road.

'What? What?' the conductor went on.

'F**k! There was a woman on the road.'

'What?'

'Standing right in the middle of the road.'

The conductor looked back at the passengers. They had been jolted and were still gathering their bearings.

'Mangya, what are you saying?'

'Arre, a**hole. There was a woman standing in the middle of the road.' He took a moment to make himself calm down. 'I was just about to hit her when she turned turned sharply and left.'

'Where is she now?'

'She ran away into the forest.'

'What?'

The driver looked out of the window and vented. 'You motherf**king bitch! Couldn't you find another vehicle to kill yourself?'

'Mangya, Mangya...'

'What?'

The conductor placed his hand on the driver's arm. 'Get out of here. Quickly.'

'What?'

'Get out quickly. I am telling you.'

The driver looked at the conductor. It was that look.

'Oh, damn.'

The conductor smacked his lips. 'The stories are true. Just get out of here, please!'

'You think it's the White Lady of Aarey Forest? Did I just see the damned White Lady?'

The conductor opened a bottle of water and sprinkled some on his face.

The driver, his palms sweating now, held the steering wheel and stomped his foot on the accelerator. The bus sprang to life and started to move again.

When the bus had moved barely ten yards, the male passenger sitting in front went up to the driver and asked, 'What just happened here?'

'Go and sit!' the driver ordered. 'Let me do my work.'

The conductor gently pushed the man back. 'You sit, sir. Don't worry. Everything is fine.'

'But, tell me...'

'There was someone in the path.'

The man, realizing he'd get no information now, slowly went and sat next to his woman.

'What happened?' she asked.

'Nothing.' He held her arm. 'You relax.'

But he was disturbed. He had reason to be. It was just a flash, but he was sitting on the front seat, and he had seen the woman on the road.

There was no mistaking it, unless his mind was playing tricks. It was her.

'You are breathing hard,' said the woman, placing her hand on his chest.

'Don't worry, Roopali,' said Harikumar. 'It's nothing.'

❦

The scream that left Meenakshi shook the very trees, making their fruits fall, and sending the birds flying away to the belly of the jungle. Why did fate have to deal this cruel hand?

Couldn't it just have killed her and rid her of this misery?

No!

Fate was a one-legged bastard grinning through its miserable one-toothed face.

Just when she thought it'd all be over, it had to show him again. Him, of all people! And he looked younger than ever. Just as she had left him. Just as gentle, just as handsome.

No, no, no! She had thought the Yakshini had taken over completely, but she was still Meenakshi; and she could fight back. Looking at him—Harikumar—was what had made that happen. It brought her back to her senses.

And she knew then—she did not want to kill herself!

Gone was the desperation to end herself. Instead, it was replaced with hope to live for an eternity.

But he was with a woman.

The funny thing was, she was almost sure who that bitch was.

That secretary!

A painful image of her bare-chested bespectacled Harikumar thrusting himself into that secretary danced in front of her eyes and she roared again.

Deceit! Men were full of deceit.

For once, the Yakshini did not talk back. Maybe she was pissed off too.

31

A Visit Long Overdue

*M*aybe you cannot rip people apart at the middle. Maybe you can. Who knows? Who has tried?

But if you could rip humans into two through the middle, perhaps it would feel just like this—just like how Meenakshi felt in those moments following the accidental sighting of the one man she never wanted to see again.

Meenakshi was torn. One half of her wanted to rush to the man whom the evil quirks of destiny had put into her path again. But there was also this other part of her which wanted to give up everything and exit this world of misery and hopelessness.

Two halves of her, wanting to sprint in two different directions. If that would not rip someone apart, what would?

No, this could not go on. The turmoil had to stop. This wasn't an existence—living a solitary life, cursed to live only by killing.

But maybe—just maybe—here was a gleam of hope. Maybe that sighting of Harikumar was not just a mere coincidence, but part of a divine plan. Maybe it was a sign. For she knew now there still was love left in her, and rekindling it might be the answer to all her problems. Love could erect monuments; it could bring the dead to life. What was yet another miracle for love?

When a whole day had passed with her sitting on a rock in front of her den, staring unflinchingly at a touch-me-not plant whose leaves didn't droop even once, she stirred.

These thoughts wouldn't lead anywhere. It was time to stop this. If only they would let her...

'Ratisundari...'

The voice came from somewhere in the brush. She turned so sharply that she tore a ligament.

There he was, radiant like a glowing lamp in the forest, his body exuding handsomeness till it overflowed, with a benign smile that started on his lips and permeated through the jungle.

'Krita...' the being within her wept.

'Ratisundari...'

'Where have you been all this time?'

'Watching you.'

'Why didn't you come and talk to me?'

'I am not allowed to talk to you much, Ratisundari.'

The Yakshini ran to him. Smoke hissed from the spots where her fingertips touched his skin. 'I don't care,' she sobbed. 'End this for me, Krita. Stop this torture.'

'It is not in my hands.'

'Oh, it is. Kill me. Just stab me. Drive something through my heart. As you said...when the body of this ill-fated girl is no more, I will be free.'

Krita wiped her tears. 'You look lovelier each day.' He kissed her on the eyelid, an eyelid that she willingly closed for him to kiss. 'But, my Ratisundari, everyone who is born has to go through the cycle of life and death. This girl you are in, her time is not up yet.'

'When will it be?'

'I don't know, but I can sense it is near.'

The Yakshini hugged him then, and he, after a moment's hesitation, brought his arms around her.

'Oh, that makes me so glad!' she said. 'I will be free...I will be back again in that beautiful celestial world that I have been longing for since I heard of it from you.'

Krita took a step back and released her from his hug. 'But there is one problem.'

The Yakshini looked at him sharply. 'What?'

'It's the same thing that has caused most of your problems. Love. You will be confined to Earth as long as you have that other love in your heart.'

'Harikumar?'

Krita nodded.

'But—'

'The choice is yours. You and the human girl have blended with each other so much that no one can tell where Ratisundari ends and Meenakshi begins. And what of Harikumar? Is he Meenakshi's love, or have you developed feelings for him too? You cannot straddle two boats. You have to end your love for Harikumar, and then when the girl's life ends, you shall be back in Alakapuri. With me.'

'How do I end her love for Harikumar?'

'You have to figure that out yourself,' Krita sighed. 'Ten years is a long time. He has changed. Go see him.'

'Should I go?'

'Yes,' said Krita. 'It has to end where it started.'

❦

This place was as good as new. The soft floor under her naked feet, the perfumed smell in the air—things she knew but had forgotten. Sights, sounds and smells, all seemed to betray her. They were hers once, but now they were alien.

She was standing in front of Harikumar's office.

It was a late hour, and she stood in the shadows lurking in the compound in front of the office, from where she could see directly into his room through his window.

He was there.

It warmed the cockles of her heart to see him working. In that form, her old Harikumar was back, the one whose mind would be full of only two thoughts—his work and his Meenakshi. Oh, how she longed to be the Meenakshi in his thoughts once again!

With slow steps, and looking furtively in all directions, she stepped out of the ferns that were her hiding place and inched closer to his office.

❦

Harikumar looked up sharply. That familiar pang was back. He had smelled the whiff of a scent that he had tried hard to forget for all these years, but it wouldn't leave him; it was as though its molecules had tiny little pincers and had clamped themselves on the walls of his nostrils. But this time the pang was sharper. Like it had come from somewhere close.

Just like that night in the bus three days ago when he thought he had seen her face.

Would she never stop haunting him? Why was she everywhere—in all the mirrors that he looked in, in all the empty rooms of his house before he switched on the lights, even by his side of the bed? His psychiatrist had told him that he was still grieving and in shock, and that these were symptoms of a long-prevailing form of Post Traumatic Stress (PTS), but those were just words. No one could really label what he felt.

But wait, what was that?

The sound of an anklet!

He let go of his papers and stood up. The chair protested with a creak as he left it, and he tried to shush it with a gesture, and then realized how idiotic that was. When silence prevailed again, he turned his ear to the spot where he had heard the sound—outside the window. Yes, it was there, faint, but distinct. He pressed his ear against the glass of the window.

And then there was a tap, right into his ear.

He let out a short scream and recoiled and fell back on his still swivelling chair.

He gasped when he saw her figure at the window, still dressed in the white saree with cerise flowers that he had last seen her in.

❦

Meenakshi, wearing that beauty like a curse, pushed the floor-length sliding window aside and walked into his office.

'How...'

Harikumar was glued to his seat now, too numb to move.

'It is I, Hari,' she said, her words coming back to her again with the rest of her memories.

'You are not real. You...you are a ghost.'

'I am not a ghost. I am standing here in front of you, as real as anything else in this room.'

'But...you are...you were...'

'Not dead.'

'Where? Where were you then?'

'Away. Not far from the spot you saw me that night.'

Harikumar shot up. 'I saw you, didn't I? I saw you! I really saw you! I am not mad.'

'No. Who says you are?'

'All of them do...they talk behind my back and think I don't hear, but I do. But, Meenu, how are you here?'

She moved closer to him. She had grown taller. Or so it appeared to the crouching Harikumar. Suddenly her form filled up the cabin.

'I had just gone away. After all the trouble I caused.'

'Oh, Meenu!' Harikumar wept. Painful memories came back to him. But then they had never left.

She stepped forth, her hands rising in a bid to hold him, hug him, but they fell back again.

'I came to see you.'

'Why?' he asked.

And that word broke her. A tear rolled out. 'You didn't want me to?'

Harikumar sobbed. 'I loved you with all my heart,' he said. 'Was anything amiss? I lost everything. I gave it my all to build it up again. Even Tara Aatya—'

'What happened to her?'

'She has left. She found a sixty-year-old widower and married him. They are in the States.'

'What about you, Hari? How are you?'

'Surviving each day with a smile.'

'And love?'

Harikumar shot a look at her. 'Go away, Meenu. Go away to where you came from. Don't stir passions in my heart again.'

She looked down at his crotch. 'Is…it all right?'

'It is! It took me three surgeries. Now I am building my life again, and there cannot be place for both of us in it.'

'You know why he is saying that, don't you? Look around. You will see their wedding photo. Him and the secretary.'

She went closer to him; he pulled his chair back.

'Is there someone else then?'

'Oh, damn you, Meenu! Just go away, please.' Another fat tear rolled down.

'Is it that secretary? The one for whom—'

Harikumar stood up with such force that the chair was thrown back. It hit the wall with a bang and some files on a nearby rack toppled over.

He strode up to her and held her by the shoulders.

'What do you think, Meenu? That you will walk in and out of my life whenever you choose and I will be the same as you want me to be?'

A wail grew somewhere in her throat and she parted her lips to let it out.

Harikumar went on, 'You had a chance. A beautiful life. But you did not care for it. You left, changing me from a man filled with goodness to this—a self-loathing, vengeful swine. What did you expect I'd do for you, Meenu? Isn't it enough that you haunt me every waking moment of my day and even while I am sleeping? Why are you back?'

'You will never see me again,' she said, choking up now. 'Just tell me once. Is she with you?'

'Don't, Meenakshi. This has to end. Why do you want to know?' he asked.

'I don't want to know. I need to know.'

'Why?'

An intense fire grew in her eyes.

'Do it now. Do it. What are you waiting for, you pathetic bitch?'

Her fingers quivered. She felt it coming, and she could battle it no longer. All she could see now was the exposed region of his neck above his collar, the region where she had once planted soft kisses.

'Go away, Meenu, and have a great life.'

'Just tell me...is that Roopali...'

'NO!' Harikumar yelled out so loud that her eardrums popped. 'NO! She is not. She never was. I only hired her because she was Nishikant's girlfriend. And now...they are married and—'

'Nishikant's girlfriend?'

'Well, didn't you know? Didn't you talk to each other on that secret phone, Meenakshi?'

It hurt her. It hurt her that he called her 'Meenakshi' and not 'Meenu'.

'Didn't you see through it at all?' said Harikumar, uncharacteristically excited now. 'Nishikant has been a flirt. Right from his school days. But just having a girl did not satisfy him. He had to win her over. That's what he was doing to you too, Meenakshi. Bhabi ji! Damn! He wanted to sleep with you, and that's why he poisoned you against me.'

'How...how do you know?'

'Do you know he played with Roopali too? Pretended he hated her, and when she—she, mind you—fell for me, he began to trick her and win her back. Poison her against me. That is what he does. He has ruined many lives. His previous fiancée, Roopali, you, me. That's a snake in a man's clothing. Don't you see?'

'But...you were together again. In the bus...'

'So what, Meenu? So what? We are compatible with each other. You weren't here for ten years. What if we are finding comfort in each other now? After all these years...'

The fire came back in Meenakshi's eyes. Her red glowing orbs shone in Harikumar's eyes, but he was too choked up to see or notice.

'What will you do?' he asked. 'Will you hurt me again?'

Those words calmed her. This was defeat. Sadness. A plea, even. She stepped back.

'No! You are bound to him. You still love him. As long as you love him, I cannot go back to my land. I am killing him. Now.'

'YOU ARE NOT DOING ANYTHING OF THE SORT!' Meenakshi yelled. 'I FORBID YOU!'

If those words frightened anyone, it was Harikumar. So, this was it. Those things Dr Gaitonde had said back then about her—all that talk about split personalities and schizophrenia—it was real.

'You cannot stop me now.'

Clouded with tears, and gasping for breath, Meenakshi slid up to Harikumar. With swollen eyes filled with tears, she said, 'I...I am sorry, Hari...'

'F-for what?'

'For...for what this thing inside me is going to do...'

Her fingertips burned now, so bad that she had to scream. She tried to hold them with the other hand, but they seared her skin. Every cell of her wanted to stop this, but how? The Yakshini was fighting to get out, to assume that gargantuan form, and to smite the one man who had ever really cared for her.

Harikumar looked at her face, stunned, standing like a trembling leaf in his own office, his eyes and cheeks coloured with the fear of death.

And then, there was a noisy ring. A cellphone danced on his desk.

Her claws withdrew; the focus was lost.

'Take the call,' she said, staring at the phone.

Harikumar, his eyes still on her, ran up to the phone.

'Hello...'

His expression turned to shock and then profound grief.

Ending the call, he stared at her without blinking. 'Strange... strange are the things that happen. This call...'

'What was it?'

'It was from Vatgaon.'

'My parents?'

Harikumar nodded. 'It was your father.'

Pictures of her house sprang in her mind and danced in front of her eyes till she could take it no more.

'What did he say?'

Harikumar placed a hand on her quivering shoulder. 'Be brave, Meenu. It's not good news. Your Aai is no more.'

32

The One Pending Thing

*W*here would she go now? How would she end this? Was there any place that still called out to her?

All that echoed back to her was refusal.

When that happens, there is only one logical thing to do. Finish the things you have to do. Your duties, your responsibilities. Then, leave.

Meenakshi knew her duties lay towards her mother's corpse in her hometown. She had to go and pay obeisance. She had to see that face one more time, lifeless though it was now, and thank her for everything. Bid her farewell on her onward journey.

But before that, there was just one more thing that had to be done. A chapter that had to be closed.

'Yes! I know what you are thinking, Meenakshi. That is the right thing to do. Go on! Take me there.'

Meenakshi turned her steps in the direction of Nishikant's house.

❦

There she was, standing outside Nishikant's beachside house for the first time. There he was, in the bedroom. He was not alone. In his arms was some woman. She did not recognize the woman.

Meenakshi could not hold it any more. She walked up to the door and pressed the doorbell as hard as she could.

The door opened. Nishikant, with just a towel around his waist, yelled, 'Who the…' and when he saw who it was, almost collapsed. 'Gosh! Is that…is that…'

'It is me. Your Meenakshi Bhabi.'

'Bhabi ji, oh my God, sorry, sorry…but how?'

From within, there was a voice, 'Who is it, Nishi?' He ignored it and went out, locking the door behind him.

'I always thought you would come back one day,' he said, 'but I never expected—'

'I am getting bored, Meenakshi. Let me take over.'

And Meenakshi said, 'Fine. He's all yours.'

'What did you say?' Nishikant asked.

But there was no Meenakshi now. In the same form stood a different being, a different creature, and that creature took a step forward.

'I came back for you.'

'For me! What do you...are you...'

'Come on,' she said. 'Haven't you always longed for me? Look into my eyes.'

'What is going on, Bhabi ji?'

'Meenu. Call me Meenu.'

'Oh...what...what are you looking for?'

Her fingers dug into the rim of his towel. 'The same thing that you had been looking for all those years ago.'

And he transformed. Like countless men had done in her presence, he came forward in a rush, a grin breaking on his face. He held her in a tight embrace. 'Finally...yes...I have always wanted you.'

'Did you want me so bad that you had to play all those games, Nishi?'

Nishikant flinched momentarily, but then he gave in and squeezed her harder. With one hand, he pulled at the end of her saree. 'But wasn't it unfair, Meenu? That wimp Harikumar with you every night? How unbearable! You need me, a real man! Come inside...let me show you...'

'But what of Hari?'

'Screw him. Now that you are mine, there are ways...'

With a dazed smile on his face, he began to pull her into the house. But she wouldn't budge.

'What happened, Meenu? Come inside...'

He planted his lips on hers, but she had now gone as firm as a stone statue.

He recoiled. 'What is this?'

She raised her head, and in her eyes were blood-red sparks. Words—terrifying rasping words—issued from her. *'You have played your last game, Nishikant.'*

❦

Her fingers were transforming now, in front of Nishikant's terrified eyes, and the blight went up to the phalanges. The skin dried up and cracked to form ridges over the bulbs of the fingers. She felt them burn within. She went up to him. Even as he stood, shocked, she pressed her breasts against his chest and he moaned. She wrapped her arms around him and brought her fingers over his back, just hovering, not touching him yet.

'Relax,' she said. 'I will give you such pleasures that you will forget every woman on Earth.'

She brought those fingernails, sharp as razor edges now, on his naked back. A faint line of blood emerged from his back where the nails pierced into his skin, but the cut was so fine and masterful that he didn't feel it immediately. Then he did.

'Ouch,' he said. 'What's that?' Reflexively, his hand went to feel the spot on his back that had now begun to burn. He fumbled at the spot and then withdrew his hand to see the blood.

'What is...'

But it was too late.

She laughed. In that moment, he realized this was not the woman he knew.

He came out of her embrace and then saw what she was, even as she finished the last vestiges of transformation.

As he stuttered and stumbled against the wall of the house, her body began to grow. Gone was the milk white creamy skin that he had been so besotted with just a moment ago. Instead, what stood now was a creature in cracked and blistered skin, pus and blood flowing out of its orifices. Wherever the skin remained, it was as thick as crocodile hide. Warts botched the face—it had no beauty any longer, or even any symmetry. The lips were no longer the petal-smooth things he had just kissed; instead, they were shapeless dangling blobs of flesh, moving with a life of their own.

And her breasts, against which his chest had just rested, were no longer soft like a sweet ripe fruit. Instead, they were like chunks of dried leather, tipped with hairy nipples hanging out disgustingly. The navel was a dark hole, surrounded by hair, and something was creeping inside it.

And then, he saw the vagina. It was a bleeding pair of lips, hairy and clamped shut, like the tentacles of an insectivorous plant. Then, even as he kept staring at the monstrosity of it all, that tentacle opened and out of it emerged a bleeding white worm.

'What the f**k...' he could only whisper as he stood, naked, shivering.

Stumbling, he tried to move. The beach was up ahead. If he could only unshackle himself from his stupor... He shut his eyes, and then made a running dash, his towel falling off as he did.

He streaked like a maniac on the beach, yelling, not minding the sharp pebble-ridden sand jabbing into his soles.

Behind him, the Yakshini broke out into a smile. It was the smile of a huntress who was happy because her prey had given her good sport. Games. Didn't he like to play games?

Then, when he had run a fourth of a mile, she made her move. It was a twitch of her neck, which creaked, sounding like a tree stump being cracked by some giant hand.

She stepped out onto the beach, her large feet falling on the sand now.

There was the puny man, a speck now, naked as nature had made him, running away to the rocks. He could never outrun her there. He could never outrun her anywhere.

Howling like the wind that was blowing in her face, her gait now changed. The calculated steps were done. It was now a gliding motion, accompanied by a wailing sound.

The next instant, she was ahead of the running man, and he, in his terror-stricken blindness, could not stop till he ran right into her.

The impact made him stop, and he beheld her humongous size, as large as a tree now, and cried, 'This cannot be real!'

The Yakshini made an accursed, unforgiving grunt.

'Forgive me! Forgive me, whatever you are!'

The Yakshini sat down on her haunches, like a frog. He could see her groin up close now, and that wormlike thing in it, and he covered his eyes. 'Let me go,' he wept and sobbed.

Slowly, she stretched her arm. She brought it to his shuddering leg and then clamped her hand around it.

'No, no, no…' Nishikant yelled.

But she did not care for his squeals. She lifted the man by his leg, hoisted him high and then brought him down with resounding force against the rock.

To someone looking from afar, the scene would have appeared no different than a washerwoman dashing a heavy wet cloth against the rocks in the dead of that night.

One dash was all it took.

Nishikant was now slumped in a bloody mess on the rocks.

When nothing identifiable was left of him, she walked back to the shack.

As she neared it, her feet began to hurt, and now she felt the sand. The pain hit her hard, and she began to run, realizing that she was turning back into a human.

On the beach, dogs drew out from various corners. They had no clue what had just happened. They had been too fearful to even bark at that colossal creature. But now they came, in ones and twos and then in packs, right up to the delectable heap of flesh left behind.

The first dog, a black-and-white mongrel, was the bravest. He moved ahead, clambered onto the rocks, and tore off the juiciest bit of the meat he could find. Following his lead, the other dogs moved ahead too, and began to pillage the rest. Then they took the bones and went into the water, playing and romping on the most sumptuous meal they had ever had.

Slowly, bit by bit, the waves lashed in, and took away with them the fragments of the man who had once been Nishikant Rajan.

33

The Funeral

*H*er face covered with her palloo, Meenakshi walked with slow steps on the mud path. All she could see was the way ahead of her. The overnight ride in the State Transport bus had been bumpy, but her mind was filled with worries that overrode all physical discomfort.

As she neared her childhood home, she felt the soil under her feet. Her feet crushed the particles of the soil, and the whiff of organic humus rose, wafting into her nostrils. She took it all in. If nostalgia could have a smell, this was it.

But now, she had to steel herself. She was walking to the most difficult sight she would ever see.

There it was—a gathering of people in the compound, all dressed in funeral white.

In this village devoid of entertainment, even a funeral was an event. She could see only the backs of the mourners; they were facing something ahead of them, something that she had to embolden herself to see.

She pushed through the crowd and they parted without looking at her. She made her way forward, passing one person after another, at times turning to see their faces—all silent, all bearing expressions of gravity and grief. Befitting a person's last repose.

She came to the clearing and stopped.

Her mother lay on the ground on a frame of bamboo sticks, handles jutting out from all four ends, to be lifted by able-bodied men and carried to the crematorium. The shroud covering her was spotlessly white and bedecked with garlands, their sickly-sweet fragrance spreading all over.

Her face was uncovered. Cotton buds were stuffed in her

nostrils and ears. A half-smile was dead on her lips.

Glimpses from her erratic memory flashed across Meenakshi's mind. She saw her mother standing in the middle of the verandah, her eyes blazing, angry words flying out of her mouth, directed at that Jamblekar woman. Really—had all of that happened in this life?

She saw her father in front of that crumbling house, weeping inconsolably.

He was there, by her side on the ground, beating his head with his palms, held back by Manda (she looked so motherly now!) and another of his daughters (was that really Kumud?).

'Why, why!' Shantaram wailed at the heavens. 'Why did you have to take her away? Never was a thing wrong with her. Never even a fever. I am the sick one. Why not I?'

His daughters patted his back, but he wouldn't stop.

'Who will be my backbone now? Who will fight for me? Who will save me from everyone's barbs and taunts?'

Meenakshi sniffled at that, so hard that a woman turned back to look at her. But her face was veiled.

Four men came up and placed their arms consolingly on Shantaram's back. One of them signalled at Manda and she helped her father to his feet. Shantaram broke into a louder wail now, and screamed, 'Take me with you! Take me! Don't leave me behind! Of what use am I alone?'

A young lad, shaved bald, whom Meenakshi had never seen before (perhaps Manda's son), went up, holding a small earthen pot dangling by ropes. There was incense in it that gave out smoke, and the smoke billowed forth as he walked.

The moment had come.

The men positioned themselves at the four ends of the corpse, and with a collective heave, hoisted the body on their arms. At that very moment, a chant broke out. The boy walked with the pot in his hand, and the corpse bearers followed. All the men joined in, leaving the women and Shantaram behind, too distraught to move.

❧

Later that afternoon, the courtyard was empty once again. Meenakshi had lingered, unseen, and now walked up to her favourite corner of the garden.

'Companion! How have you been?'

Her gentle caresses fell on the ageing bark of the sal tree, which had withered away considerably in her absence, but had still stood bravely.

There was movement in the tree, or so she thought. She looked up. There were hardly any leaves left on it to rustle. Only brown boughs that failed to provide any shade.

Another part of her nostalgia. Dying.

She wept.

'Sorry I did not come back to see you. Sorry I turned away from everything. I have been the most disloyal person ever. A disloyal daughter, a disloyal sister, a disloyal friend, a disloyal wife. Will there be any forgiveness for me?'

The tree stood stiff. Perhaps it did not remember her any more, just like everyone else there.

'Even you won't talk to me, Companion?'

She had come here to gain courage, but now she felt more helpless than ever. In the withered branches of the tree, she saw her hope withering away. She hesitated for a moment, and then turned to leave. She took one step.

And then a smile formed on her lips.

She felt the coldness beneath her foot.

With atypical quickness, she bent and picked up the gold coin that she had stepped on.

'O Companion! You always know how to cheer me up!' she said.

Meenakshi lurked in the courtyard for thirteen days and thirteen nights, the period of mourning. She did not know about the rites and rituals, but she knew that the bereaved did not perform major tasks in this period, for this was the time when the soul of the deceased made its transition. Anything done in this time could tempt the soul and disrupt its journey.

It was easy to stay hidden in the many shadows and corners of the garden. Whenever any of the sisters would come out, she would quickly duck behind something. Once Suparna's toddler crawled up to the garden when she was not looking. It was only when he tugged at her saree that she became aware of his presence. She was barely able to pull her saree away from him and rush into the bushes behind the compost pit when Suparna arrived, yelling at her baby.

In the nights, she saw the shadows of her family in the house. She also saw the dilapidated walls, the peeling paint, the old rotting furniture. She saw the imminent ruin. She knew that these people wouldn't be in the house for long. All her sisters would go back after the mourning to their respective houses and would forget that they had an ailing and lonely father back here. He would be left behind to cry through the lonely nights, and what could she do about it?

Another man in her life would be left to wilt and die.

Her heart broke again. It was the last piece that broke this time.

❦

'*You bleed too much, don't you?*'

Meenakshi did not want to hear the voice, not now. But it came. On the twelfth night of the mourning period, when she was sitting on a rock near the compost pit, it came.

'*The moment has arrived. You are withering. You cannot silence me now. Especially not when I am saying the right thing.*'

'You are never right. Nothing about you was ever right.'

'*What does this family mean to you now? You cannot even face them. Your mother is dead. Your father is dying. Your sisters hate you. Why do you linger?*'

'Just leave me. Please!'

'*Ha! You don't realize it even now, do you? I am not inside you.*

I am you! You are two people in one, my dear Meenakshi!'

'Then why can't I shut you up?'

'*Haven't I tried to shut up too? I did not say anything at your mother's funeral. Now, she was a strong lady! She would have done the right thing in a heartbeat. Wonder how none of her courage has rubbed off on you.*'

'You don't know anything about my mother.'

'*I know her just as much as you do. Do you know, on some of those lonely nights when she used to tell you stories, you would sleep but I would continue to listen? Your mother would think she was caressing your cheek, but it was mine she was caressing. So don't tell me I don't know her. That is why I allowed you to come here at this time.*'

'All right, I give up. I shall fight you no more. What do you want me to do?'

'*That's not for me to say. But I will tell you this—the world on the other side is bliss.*'

'You claim to know a lot about it—just because that naked man told you a story?'

'*Not just him. Krita was the narrator; but as he told the tale, I actually walked in those lawns of Alakapuri. I saw the ugliness of Kubera's Yakshas and the beauty of his gardens. Yes, I was there. I know. I am meant to be there again.*'

'Wait until tomorrow.'

'*What will you do?*'

'You shall see.'

❧

On the thirteenth day, Meenakshi sat in the last row of the mourners around her mother's garlanded picture. In her white saree, she blended well. Shantaram sat at the head of the mourners, and it was painfully visible how his body had become emaciated over the last two weeks.

A pundit chanted some Sanskrit verses for the eternal peace of the deceased. Most people there could not understand the words, but they knew they spoke of how everything that exists must come to an end. The chanting went on for an hour, and by then, the courtyard was so thick with the white fumes of incense that it looked like an untimely fog had descended.

One by one, the people stood up and went to the garlanded photograph. With joined hands, they touched it reverently, offered their prayers, and then, wishing a listless Shantaram their goodbyes, they took their leave. Manda's son stood at the gate with a bowl of prasad, of which every guest partook a handful as they walked out.

Meenakshi stayed put in her place, though. She did not notice when the last of them left, such was the daze she was in. Then that daze was abruptly lifted when a familiar voice spoke to her.

'MEENU?'

Stunned, Meenakshi looked up.

It was her father, standing upright now, looking at her as if she were a spectre.

Her sisters stopped their various tasks and grabbed their children as if trying to protect them from some infection that had walked into their midst.

'Meenakshi? Is that you, Meenu?'

She threw aside her veil and her sisters gasped.

Shantaram took two steps forward, but then halted. 'But how?'

Meenakshi spoke softly, 'I had to see Aai one last time.' No thought went into those words; they just came out of her.

'But didn't you leave us all? Abandon all of us?' This was Suparna, now holding her toddler, who was itching to run away and explore something.

Meenakshi cast her eyes to the floor. 'Trust me, Tai, if it were in my hands, I'd never have left.'

'Why have you come now?' Manda asked. 'Where's your husband? We hear he has gone mad in your absence.'

Meenakshi could not tell them that she had seen his madness already, and there was nothing she could do to take away that pain.

'I won't be here for long,' she said.

There was silence. No one asked why, no one cared.

'I have just one thing to do.'

'What?' Suparna asked.

'I need to go into the house.'

'Why?'

'Please let me...'

The single anklet on her left foot clinked as she walked, barefoot. Step after step fell on that verandah floor, leaving dirt prints behind. She passed by her mother's picture and her father, and stepped into the house.

The moment she stepped on the floor inside, a wave of comfort ran through her entire being. The floor was of red stone, hard as the scraggy surface of a cliff, but for her it was like treading on a cloud.

Suparna stepped forward, but Meenakshi gestured at her firmly. 'No, Tai,' she said. 'Let me go alone.' She looked at her father and beseeched, 'Please.'

Shantaram nodded.

Meenakshi went into the house and took a sharp left in the corridor. The years hadn't dulled her memory of the house. She saw her father's room and his chappals outside it, broken and thinned to a membrane. She recalled his proud leather Kolhapuri chappals from long ago and sobbed.

She went up to the staircase at the end of the corridor. Taking in the mustiness of the air, she stepped in it.

'What are you up to?'

'Shut up!' Meenu admonished the voice. 'You have no say in this.'

'Don't I? I know what you are going to do, but you cannot. This is not your decision.'

'I will do what I want.'

Meenakshi walked to the corner of the attic. The hanging cobwebs gave evidence that no one had come here for years. She lifted an old dusty tarpaulin, the only addition. When the dust flew away, she saw the storage chest, just like she had left it years ago.

With a squeal of excitement, she undid the clasps of the chest and threw open the lid.

All at once, the room was bathed in golden yellow.

The glimmer of a thousand gold coins shone in her face. Her lips parted and gave way to a smile.

'No! This is not your wealth. It is Kubera's, and I am its protector.'

Meenakshi saw the fat man engraved on those coins, and he looked severe. Now she knew who that man was.

'He means nothing to me!' she said. 'Think of this as my revenge against him for including me in your curse.'

'It won't bode well. Giving away Kubera's wealth is never good. Fool! This is part of his vast wealth that's hidden all over Bhoomi Loka.'

'Then he should not mind this at all.'

Meenakshi scooped two handfuls of the coins and held them against her bosom.

'But I am a Yakshini! I am supposed to guard Kubera's wealth.'

Meenakshi only smiled. She held the coins closer to her chest and walked slowly, retracing every step of the way, and went back to the courtyard.

Shantaram's mouth fell open as she put the coins on the table near her mother's photograph.

'What is this?'

'Don't ask, Baba,' Meenakshi cried. 'All I have caused you is pain and suffering. Please consider this as reparation for some of it.'

'But these are gold coins! Where did they come from?'

'Don't ask. Repair this house. Return to your glory. Get your respect back, which you lost because of me.'

Suparna went up to her now, with unmasked fascination in her eyes. 'Is this another of those magic things of yours?'

Meenakshi laughed. 'What is magic? Simply a name for things we don't know. Don't think about it. Just have a good life, all of you. Baba, there's a lot more of these coins in the attic. You will find them easily.'

Just then, the moment was interrupted by loud clapping.

Meenakshi turned swiftly to look, and despite herself, she was confounded to see what she saw.

It was Tappu, standing inside their gate. He had not grown much. He stood like some kind of hobgoblin with a hunchback and a twisted smile on his face, and he clapped with some ecstasy that only he understood. A well of emotions rose up in Meenakshi's heart as she looked at his pitiful state, and she said to her inner voice, 'Look at him. Does he deserve to be like that?'

'No. I should have killed him. Why didn't I?'

Meenakshi walked up to Tappu and held his hand. He jumped in joy, and said in a singsong voice, 'Meenu! Meenu! Meenu, hold my hand.'

That brought his mother into the compound, and the moment her sight fell on Meenakshi, she almost collapsed.

'YOU! YOU WITCH!'

Immediately, she ran out, screaming, 'Hey, listen, people! People! She is here! Come, come quickly. The witch is back!'

'Will you do one thing for me?' Meenakshi asked the voice in her head.

'What?'

'Be good for once. Heal him.'

'Really?'

'Do it. Do it for me.'

Shantaram went up to Meenakshi. 'You…you must go now. Before she brings Jamblekar and the others…' he said and went to the table to hide the coins.

'Yes,' said Meenakshi. 'The time has come anyway.'

She walked on, not seeing that Tappu was now beginning to stand erect, astonished with the change that was coming over him.

❧

Meenakshi walked to her mother's photograph, and with joined hands, paid her tribute. Her eyes were compassionate even in that picture, as if she understood what her daughter was going through. She had always known.

Then Meenakshi touched her father's feet and bade farewell to her sisters. Nothing about her was fathomable anymore; she was a mystic, gliding by in a trance.

Lastly, she went up to the sal, and just like she used to do in her childhood, she hugged it. No one could hear the words that left her lips at that point, but she whispered something to the tree.

And then she sat down. Cross-legged, in a meditative stance, her back reposed against the bark, and her eyes looking straight ahead.

She didn't see or hear her earthly family any more. All she heard was the voice within.

'So, you are doing it! You are!'

'I am freeing you from my body, dear Yakshini,' she said. 'However it was, we had a life together.'

Meenakshi saw something appear to her left, some kind of apparition, away from everyone else's line of vision, as if it was meant only for her. She smiled.

'Look, there he is,' she said. 'He has come for you.'

She turned. It was Krita, standing by the same compost pit, his face bearing the expression of one whose love was to be united with him soon.

'Oh! So he is! But what about you, Meenakshi? What will you do?'

'Who can take me away? This is my home.'

But none of those words could be heard above the din. For, while she was still in the middle of that sentence, a shout arose from the gate as Dr Jamblekar stormed in with a mob.

'WHERE IS SHE? THE WITCH! WE WILL BURN HER TODAY. RIGHT HERE!'

Shantaram ran up to them, waving his hands, trying to stop them from entering the premises, and then the girls went forth and even their children, but the mob wouldn't listen. They entered the courtyard and pulled out everything they could. Even the table on which Renuka's photograph was installed was smashed to the ground, and the courtyard was pillaged.

Then Tappu shouted, the voice of a grown man now. 'STOP! SHE IS NOT A WITCH!'

Everyone froze in that instant. They turned to look in the direction the strange man was pointing. It took them a moment to realize it was Tappu. But before they could rejoice over his return to health, their eyes turned to where he was pointing.

It was the sal tree.

Shantaram kept his eyes shut even as he turned. But when he opened them, he was consumed with utter shock.

The spot where his favourite daughter had been sitting was now vacant.

And he caught a flash, only a tiny flicker, of a piece of white fabric entering the bark of the withered sal tree.

Was it... No, it couldn't be!

The next moment, right in front of all the villagers, the dead sal tree once again burst with tender green leaves, sprouting from every node on every bough. Even as they looked, the leaves grew and appeared in their full bloom, and the flowers appeared too, those bright yellow-red flowers with their petals shaped as hoods, and they raised themselves as if in salute to the people beholding them.

And then...

There grew an aura of gold around the sal tree, and everyone held their hearts, which threatened to fly right out of their chests.

Epilogue

The sal tree stands in the Patil garden in Vatgaon to this day. It is no longer an ordinary tree; it is one of the most sacred spots known to humankind and is now one of the shalbhanjikas.

It took the villagers a while to understand everything. When the wandering ascetic (who had once given Renuka the black thread) visited the village again and told the people about the Yakshini, everyone bowed in reverence. It fit the lore perfectly, as sal trees have been associated with Yakshinis since time immemorial.

Shantaram Patil moved to another house to get away from the memories, and lived there until he died. It was after his death that his old house was converted by the villagers into a shrine for the Yakshini. Today, people come to this shalbhanjika from far and wide to experience the magic of the sal and the surrounding life, which has defied death over the ages. It is said that the Yakshini still visits the sal from her abode in Alakapuri at times and fulfils the wishes of those who devotedly pray to it. A few lucky ones find unearthly gold coins under their naked feet.

People of the village started respecting the Patils again. Busts of Shantaram and Renuka were erected next to the sal. Dr Jamblekar inaugurated them for the villagers.

Meenakshi's body was never found. The girl is believed to still reside somewhere in the garden. Some people claim to have seen her on lonely nights, and those who see her are blessed.

❀

Harikumar married Roopali six months after Meenakshi left. They visited the shalbhanjika a year after it was built and prayed for a better life and a child. The entire village gathered to see him at the tree, and as they watched, a cluster of flowers fell into his lap, as if offering him a special blessing.

But it was more than the flowers. As he circled the tree, his naked foot fell on something in the soil. His eyes clouded with tears when he recognized it. It was the lone anklet that he had seen on Meenakshi's foot the last time he saw her. Touching it reverently to his eyes, he slipped it into his pocket.

❧

The grand reunion happened in Alakapuri moments after the girl's becoming one with the sal tree. Krita was waiting for Ratisundari at the gates, now celestially adorned. He was decked up like a groom for her.

Ratisundari's celestial beauty was now restored, and Krita, handsome as ever, took her into his arms amidst much applause and cheer.

The applause and cheer stopped only for a moment when a loud bellow issued from behind the crowd, sounding not unlike an angry elephant's trumpeting. The assembled crowd turned to look, and there he stood, the demigod, King Kubera himself, his arms akimbo, a gold-spitting mongoose playing at his feet. Then he hollered too, and cheered, 'Welcome back, children of my land! Make this land your own once again.'

Thirty-one years mean nothing in Alakapuri. It was like nothing had ever changed.

Acknowledgements

The journey of Yakshini from a mere idea in my mind to the present form that is now in your hands has been quite checkered, and I wouldn't have been able to achieve this feat without the help of the people I mention hereunder.

ANITA, the woman of my life, who gives me the space to spread my wings and embark on my flights of fancy, and also keeps me grounded.

GILMORE and FELICIA, my shining beacons, for feeling proud of their Papa despite not being allowed to read a word of his works.

EVERYONE at Rupa Publications who made this book turn out to be so tantalizingly beautiful.

PALAK JAIN of Virtuoso Artsy, for designing the beautiful sketches that appear inside the book at short notice, which have vastly enhanced the aesthetic value of the book.

SUHAIL MATHUR of The Book Bakers, who relentlessly worked at getting my labour of love the best publisher I could dream of, and who continues to guide me on my literary journey.

BHUVANESH SHRIVASTAVA and VIKRAM RAI of Lotus Talkies Productions, who placed their immense faith in the story of Yakshini the moment they heard it and signed it up for a visual adaptation.

VISHAL FURIA, noted filmmaker and a friend, who enthusiastically provided his valuable feedback on a previous version of the story and helped me make it better.

ROHAN BHAT, the chairman of my alma mater, the Children's Academy Group of Schools, for his unstinted faith in my writing and always being ready to guide me and help me out with his infinite generosity.

KAVITA SINGH of Kaffeinated Konversations and The Book

Fairies Indore, who continues to bring this tale to more readers through her selfless efforts.

And those initial readers, fellow authors, and people from the media world who read Yakshini without prejudice and told me that this is a story worthy of publication.

I shall forever be in your debt.